Praise for Guillaume Musso's

THE REUNION

"This immensely satisfying thriller about a prep school scandal and three friends' buried secrets had me turning the pages well into the night. *The Reunion* has everything a masterful thriller should: gut-wrenching suspense, a twisting story with blindsiding surprises, and a narrator with a mysterious past. It's no wonder that Guillaume Musso is one of France's most loved, bestselling authors."

—Harlan Coben

"A fast-paced thriller, set on the Côte d'Azur, packed with a glamorous missing girl, a dead body, and enough references to *Twin Peaks* and raves and Belle and Sebastian to tickle anybody who came of age in the 1990s...Musso is not just a popular author but *the* number one bestselling novelist in France. So you're bound to emerge more *branché* than those people you see on the beach reading home-grown potboilers."

—Lauren Mechling, *Vanity Fair*

"The French call it a *coup de foudre:* a strike of lightning. That's how *The Reunion* zapped me, electrified me. For almost a decade, Guillaume Musso has reigned supreme as France's most popular author, and with this, his American debut, he's instantly poised to join the ranks of Stieg Larsson and Jo Nesbø. *The Reunion* zigzags so nimbly—between past and present, from intrigue to terror, amid possible suspects and potential victims—that you're at very real risk of whiplash. Witty, elegant, and peopled with complex characters, it's one of the most sheerly suspenseful novels I've read in years—and among the most enjoyable, too."

—A. J. Finn, bestselling author of *The Woman in the Window*

"Generations and eras intertwine against the backdrop of a murderous school campus...The perfect summer book to devour while lounging by a swimming pool."

—*Elle*

"Gripping...In Musso's masterful plotting, novelist Thomas faces fresh dangers at every turn. The atmospheric finale—which unfolds at Villa Fitzgerald and along Smugglers' Way, the coastal path near some of the most lavish properties on the Côte d'Azur—brings shocking revelations."

—Jane Ciabattari, BBC.com, "The 10 Smartest Beach Reads of the Year"

"What's better than a prep school scandal? A prep school scandal that takes place in France, obviously. Twenty-five years ago, nineteen-year-old Vinca Rockwell left the South of France during a snowstorm and was never seen again. Now, as three friends prepare to meet up for their reunion, a body is discovered in the campus walls."

—Mackenzie Dawson, *New York Post,* "Best Books of the Week"

"A vastly satisfying mystery...Written with fluency and charm, this is breathtakingly good. Do not miss it."

—Geoffrey Wansell, *Daily Mail* (UK)

"A disappeared prep school girl; her lover, the philosophy teacher; a corpse in the walls of the gym. Long-buried secrets will give way to the truth in this tragic, riveting story set on the French Riviera."

—Becky Toyne, *Globe and Mail*

"A high school reunion threatens to reveal long-held secrets in this thriller from one of France's bestselling authors... A multilayered mystery that's fueled by urgency and drama, and Guillaume Musso adds a menacing quality to the glamorous Côte d'Azur. With plot twists unleashed at a furious pace, *The Reunion* is a nightmare set in privileged utopia."
                                   —Frank Brasile, *Shelf Awareness*

"Stylish and streamlined, nostalgic... More, please."
                       —Mark Sanderson, *The Times* (London)

"A tiny boarding school on the coast in the South of France is the setting for Musso's new thriller, which has already been a hit in Europe but will mark the author's US debut... Despite the ticking-clock premise, Musso takes time to set the atmosphere, with lush details that transport the reader to a locale that's at once glamorous and also laced with a deep, abiding sadness."
                                                   —*CrimeReads*

"Intense nostalgia and simmering guilt drive this evocative mystery from Musso... He moves effortlessly between the violent past and the increasingly dangerous present as complicated relationships and tragic misunderstandings unfold... Readers interested in the dark side of the good life on the Côte d'Azur will be satisfied."
                                             —*Publishers Weekly*

"A fun read, spiced with pop-culture references."
          —Laura Wilson, *The Guardian,* "Thrillers of the Month"

"A fine tale of suspense from France's bestselling author... News of a reunion at an international school on the Côte d'Azur is terrifying for two of its graduates... What happened in 1992 is revealed

gradually, revolving around vibrant, enigmatic Vinca Rockwell, Thomas's first love."
                                                  —Michele Leber, *Booklist*

"School reunions are a tried-and-true setting, and this one brings the bonus of being set at an expat school on the glamorous Côte d'Azur...Musso, a prolific French writer, was born on the French Riviera and brings this storied area to life."
                                                  —Sarah Murdoch, *Toronto Star*

"Hugely enjoyable and beautifully staged, with an audacious authorial coup at the death that is simply breathtaking."
                                                  —Declan Hughes, *Irish Times*

THE
REUNION

THE REUNION

A NOVEL

GUILLAUME MUSSO

TRANSLATED FROM THE FRENCH BY FRANK WYNNE

BACK BAY BOOKS

Little, Brown and Company

New York   Boston   London

Copyright © 2019 by Guillaume Musso
Translation copyright © 2019 by Frank Wynne

Back Bay Books / Little, Brown and Company
Hachette Book Group
1290 Avenue of the Americas, New York, NY 10104
littlebrown.com

First Back Bay trade paperback edition, July 2020
Originally published in France as *La Jeune Fille et la Nuit* by Guillaume Musso ©
Calmann-Lévy, 2018

First English-language edition: July 2019
Published simultaneously in the United Kingdom by Weidenfeld and Nicholson, July 2019

Back Bay Books is an imprint of Little, Brown and Company, a division of Hachette Book Group, Inc. The Back Bay Books name and logo are trademarks of Hachette Book Group, Inc.

The publisher is not responsible for websites (or their content) that are not owned by the publisher.

The Hachette Speakers Bureau provides a wide range of authors for speaking events. To find out more, go to hachettespeakersbureau.com or call (866) 376-6591.

Extract from *Letter to an Amazon*
Marina Tsvétaïéva, *Mon frère féminin: Lettre à l'Amazone,*
coll. Le Petit Mercure, Gallimard, 1979.
Translated by Sonja Franeta, *The Harvard Gay and Lesbian Review,* 1994.

ISBN 978-0-316-49014-6 (hc) / 978-0-316-49021-4 (pb)
LCCN 2019931412

10 9 8 7 6 5 4 3 2 1

LSC-C

Printed in the United States of America

To Flora,
in memory of our
conversations
that winter during those
four-in-the-morning
feedings . . .

The problem of the night remains intact.
How to come through it?

Henri Michaux

LYCÉE SAINT-EXUPÉRY

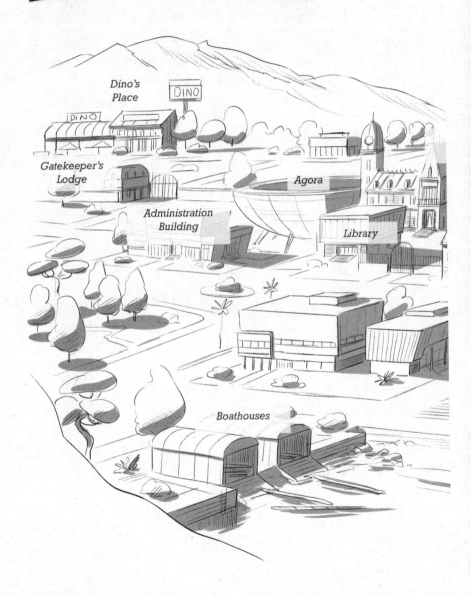

Dino's Place

DINO

DINO

Gatekeeper's Lodge

Agora

Administration Building

Library

Boathouses

Eagle's Nest

Staff Quarters

Historic Halls

Place des Marronniers

Gym

Head Teacher Quarters

Nicolas de Staël Building

The Lake

SMUGGLERS' WAY

The Maiden
Pass by! Oh, pass me by!
Go, cruel man of bones!
I am yet young! Leave me, dear one,
And touch me not.
Death
Give me thy hand, thou fair and gentle
    creature!
I am a friend, and come not to chastise.
Take heart! I am not cruel;
Softly shalt thou sleep in my arms!

Matthias Claudius (1740–1815),
"Death and the Maiden"

2017
Southernmost point, Cap d'Antibes, May 13

Manon Agostini parked her patrol car at the end of the chemin de la Garoupe. She slammed the door of the battered old Renault Kangoo, inwardly railing at the chain of events that had led her here.

At about nine p.m., a security guard of one of the most opulent mansions on the cape had called the precinct in Antibes to report hearing a firecracker or possibly a gunshot—some strange noise— coming from the rocky coastal path. The Antibes Precinct attached little importance to the call and relayed the information on to the local police, who could think of nothing better to do than radio *her*, even though she was not on duty.

At the point when her superior officer called to ask her to check out the coast road, Manon was already in an evening dress and preparing to go out. She wanted to tell him to fuck off, but she felt she could not say no to him. Just that morning, he had given her permission to use the Kangoo outside working hours. Manon's own car had recently died, and she desperately needed a car that Saturday night to go to an event that was important to her.

The school she had attended, the Lycée Saint-Exupéry, was celebrating its fiftieth anniversary and there was to be a reunion of her former classmates. Manon secretly hoped she might run into a guy she had been smitten with long ago, a boy who was not like the others but whom she had stupidly passed over at the time, preferring to date older guys who had all turned out to be utter shits. There was nothing rational about her hope—she could not be sure that he would be there, and besides, he had probably forgotten that she existed— but she needed to believe that *something* was finally going to happen in her life. Manicure, haircut, clothes shopping; Manon had spent all afternoon getting ready. She had blown three hundred euros on a designer dress—midnight-blue lace with a silk bodice—borrowed a pearl choker from her sister and a pair of sling-backs (Stuart Weitzman suede pumps that pinched her feet) from her best friend.

Tottering on her high heels, Manon flicked on her phone's flashlight setting and headed down the narrow trail that hugged the coast as far as the Villa Eilenroc. She knew the area like the back of her hand; when she was a child, her father used to take her here to fish in the streams. Locals once called this area Smugglers' Way; later, it appeared in guidebooks under the intriguing name of sentier de Tire-Poil—Hair-Pluck Lane. These days, it was known by the prosaic, anodyne term "the coastal path."

After some fifty meters, Manon came to a barrier with a warning sign: DANGER—NO ENTRY. Earlier in the week, a powerful storm had lashed the coast, and the waves had caused landslides that had cut off certain sections of the path.

Manon hesitated for a moment, then scrambled over the barrier.

1992

Southernmost point, Cap d'Antibes, October 1

Vinca Rockwell blithely hopped and skipped as she passed La Joliette Beach. It was ten p.m. To get here from the high school, she had had to sweet-talk a friend from her class who owned a moped into driving her as far as the chemin de la Garoupe.

As she set off down Smugglers' Way, she could feel butterflies fluttering in the pit of her stomach. She was going to meet Alexis. She was going to meet the love of her life!

A fierce gale was blowing, but the night was so beautiful, the sky so cloudless, she could see almost as well as in daylight. Vinca had always loved this place because it was so wild, so unlike the clichéd image of the French Riviera. When the sun shone, you were dazzled by the tawny-white glare of the limestone crags, the myriad shades of blue that bathed the narrow inlets. Once, while gazing out toward the Lérins Islands, she had seen a pod of dolphins.

On nights like tonight, when the wind howled, it was a very different place. The sheer rock face loomed dangerously; the olive and pine trees seemed to writhe in pain, as though trying to uproot themselves. Vinca did not care. She was going to meet Alexis. She was going to meet the love of her life!

2017

For fuck's sake!

The heel of one of Manon's pumps had snapped off. *Jesus.* She'd now have to stop off at her apartment before she went to the reunion, and the friend who'd lent her these shoes would rip her a new one tomorrow. She slipped them off, shoved them into her bag, and continued barefoot.

She was still following the narrow, paved path that overlooked the cliffs. The air was pure and invigorating. The mistral had cleared the night sky of clouds and scattered it with constellations.

The view was breathtaking, sweeping from the old city walls of Antibes across the bay of Nice, framed by the mountainous inland. Here, in the shelter of the pine forests, were some of the most lavish properties on the Côte d'Azur. The air quivered with the crash of waves, sending up sea spray. She could feel the brute force of the sea.

Time was, the area had seen many tragic accidents. The roiling waves had swept away fishermen, tourists, even couples who had come to make love by the shore. The resulting outcry had forced the authorities to secure the path; they built concrete steps and erected barriers to thwart any hiker's impulse to get too close to the edge. But it took only a few hours of high winds to turn it into dangerous terrain once more.

Manon reached a spot where a fallen Aleppo pine had blocked the path. Impossible to go any farther. She considered turning back. There was not a living soul around—the gale-force mistral had kept ramblers away.

Get the hell out, girl.

She stood motionless and listened to the wind blowing. It was like a plaintive howl, at once close and distant. A muted threat.

Although she was barefoot, she leaped up onto a boulder, skirted the obstruction, and walked on, with only her phone to light the way.

A dark shape was silhouetted some distance down the cliff face. She peered into the gloom. No, she was too far away to make out what it was. With great care, she tried to climb down. She heard a tearing sound. The hem of her lace dress had ripped, but she ignored it. Now she could see the shape that had caught her eye. It was a body. The corpse of a woman sprawled on the rocks. As she moved closer, she felt terror grip her. This was no accident. The woman's face had been beaten to a bloody pulp. *God Almighty*. Manon felt her legs start to give. She knew she was about to collapse. She keyed the security code into her phone to call for help. There was no signal, but still the screen said Emergency calls only. She was about to press Call when she realized that she was not alone. A little farther away, a man sat, sobbing. Slumped over, he wept, his face buried in his hands.

Manon was terrified. In that moment, she regretted coming out unarmed. Warily, she approached him. The man sat up, and when he raised his head, Manon recognized him.

"It was me…this is my fault," he said, pointing at the corpse.

1992

Lithe and graceful, Vinca Rockwell bounded over the rocks. The wind was gusting more fiercely. But Vinca reveled in it, the swell, the danger, the heady sea air, the steep crags. Nothing in her life had ever been as intoxicating as meeting Alexis. A profound, all-consuming magnetism, a joining of minds and bodies. If she lived to be a hundred, nothing would ever compare to that memory. The prospect of seeing Alexis secretly, of making love in some rocky crevice, was exhilarating.

She could feel the warm wind envelop her; it whipped around her legs, lifted her skirt like a prologue to the long-awaited embrace. Her heart was beginning to race, the wave of heat coursing through her, the pulse of blood, a throbbing that made every inch of her body quiver.

Alexis was this thunderstorm, this night, this moment. Deep down, Vinca knew she was making a mistake, knew that things would end badly. But she would not have traded the thrill of this moment for anything in the world. The anticipation, the wild madness of love, the painful pleasure of being engulfed by the night.

"Vinca!"

Suddenly, the figure of Alexis was silhouetted against the clear moonlit sky. Vinca stepped forward to greet the shadow. In the blink of an eye, Vinca could almost feel the pleasures that were to come. Intense, burning, overpowering. Bodies melding and dissolving until they became one with the wind, the waves. Cries mingling with those of the gulls. The tremor, the overwhelming blast, the blinding flash that trills through the body and makes it feel as though one's whole being has shattered into a thousand pieces.

"Alexis!"

As Vinca finally embraced her lover, she heard the inner voice again, whispering that this would not end well. But the girl cared nothing for the future. Love is everything, or it is nothing.

All that mattered was *now*.

The blazing, baleful beauty of the night.

YESTERDAY AND
TODAY

50TH ANNIVERSARY OF THE LYCÉE INTERNATIONAL SAINT-EXUPÉRY

(NICE-MATIN—Monday, May 8, 2017)

by Stéphane Pianelli

The flagship school of the Sophia Antipolis technology park will celebrate its fiftieth anniversary next weekend.

Founded in 1967 by the Secular Mission to Provide Schooling for the Children of Expatriates, the international lycée is an exceptional institution on the Côte d'Azur. Renowned for its academic excellence, it is modeled around the teaching of foreign languages. Its bilingual departments allow students to study for international qualifications, and today it welcomes more than a thousand French and foreign students. The celebrations will begin on Friday, May 12, with an open day where students and teaching staff will demonstrate their artistic talents in a series of photography exhibitions, films, and theater projects conceived to mark the occasion.

The following day, the festivities will continue with a cocktail party for alumni and staff. The reception will see the laying of the foundation stone for a new building dubbed the Glass Tower, a five-story structure that will stand on the site of the gymnasium, which will be demolished. This state-of-the-art building will welcome students taking preparatory courses for the Grandes Écoles. Later that evening, graduates from the classes of 1990 through 1995 will attend the Alumni Prom and have the honor of being the last to visit the gym.

The current headmistress, Madame Florence Guirard, hopes that as many alumni as possible will join in the celebrations. "I warmly invite all former students and staff to come and take part in this wonderful evening. Shared experiences and memories are a reminder of where we came from and are crucial to deciding where we are heading," Guirard said before mentioning that a private Facebook group has been created to mark the occasion.

FOREVER YOUNG

1

CHERRY COKE

1.

Sophia Antipolis, Saturday, May 13, 2017

I parked the rental under the pine trees, near the gas station, about three hundred meters from the entrance to the school. I'd driven straight from the Nice Airport after a red-eye flight from New York during which I hadn't slept a wink.

I'd left Manhattan in a hurry the day before after someone had e-mailed me an article about the fiftieth anniversary of my old school. The e-mail, forwarded to me by my publisher, was from Maxime Biancardini—my best friend once upon a time, though I hadn't seen him now in twenty-five years. There was a French phone number, and although at first I was reluctant to call back, I realized that there was nothing else I could do.

"Did you get the article, Thomas?" Maxime asked, skipping the small talk.

"That's the reason I'm calling."

"You do realize what it means?"

His voice hadn't changed over the years, but it was distorted now by fear.

I didn't answer his question right away. Yes, of course I knew what it meant. It meant the end of life as we knew it. It meant we'd be spending a chunk of the future behind bars.

"You've got to get over here, Thomas," Maxime said after a moment's silence. "We've got to think of some way to stop this. We've got to do *something*."

I squeezed my eyes shut as I considered the potential fallout: the magnitude of the scandal, the criminal implications, the shock wave that would hit our families.

Deep inside, I'd always known this day would come. For twenty-five years, I'd lived—or tried to live—with this sword of Damocles hanging over my head. Sometimes, in the dead of night, I'd wake up in a cold sweat thinking about what had happened back then and about the prospect that one day someone would find out. On nights like that, I'd pop a bromazepam and wash it down with a Karuizawa single malt, but I rarely managed to get back to sleep.

"We have to do *something*," my old friend said again.

I knew he was kidding himself. The bomb that was now threatening to blow our lives apart was one that we had built ourselves one night in 1992.

We both knew there was no way to defuse it.

2.

After locking the car door, I walked toward the gas station. There was a sort of American drugstore there that everyone called Dino's place. Behind the gas pumps was a colonial-style clapboard building with a small shop and a nice café with a large terrace sheltered by an awning.

I pushed open the swinging door. The place hadn't really changed. At the back of the shop, a few high stools were set around a painted wooden counter lined with colorful cakes under glass domes. The rest of the room was filled with benches and tables that extended out onto the terrace. The walls were hung with vintage enamel signs for long-defunct brands and posters of the Riviera in the 1920s. To squeeze in more people, the owners had gotten rid of the pool table and the arcade games—*Out Run, Arkanoid, Street Fighter II*— that used to guzzle my pocket money. Only the foosball table had survived, an old Bonzini competition model, its paint now peeling and chipped. I couldn't resist stroking the heavy beech frame— this was where Maxime and I had spent hours replaying the great Olympique de Marseille matches. A slew of random images came to me: Papin's hat trick in the '89 Coupe de France; Vata's hand ball against Benfica; Chris Waddle's left-foot goal against AC Milan the night when the floodlights in the Vélodrome suddenly went out. Sadly, we didn't celebrate the long-awaited victory—winning the 1993 UEFA Champions League—together. By then, I'd already left the Côte d'Azur to go to business school in Paris.

I let the atmosphere of the café wash over me. Maxime hadn't been the only person I came here with after school. My most vivid memories were of Vinca Rockwell, the girl I was in love with back then, the girl every boy was in love with back then. It was only yesterday. It was a lifetime ago.

As I walked up to the counter, I felt the hair on my arms bristle as snapshots came into focus in my mind: Vinca's bright laugh, the gap between her front teeth, her floaty dresses, her paradoxical beauty, the detached gaze she affected. At Dino's place, she drank Cherry Cokes in summer and mugs of hot chocolate with marshmallows in winter.

"What can I get you?"

I couldn't quite believe it; the café was still run by the same

Polish-Italian couple, Dino (obviously) and Hannah Valentini. Dino had gained weight and gone bald, and Hannah's blond hair had faded and her face was lined. But with age, they seemed somehow better suited to each other. This is the leveling effect of time: dazzling beauty fades while more banal features acquire a luster and a patina.

"Coffee, please. A double espresso."

I let the words hang in the air for a moment, then stirred up the past, conjuring Vinca's ghost: "Oh, and a Cherry Coke—ice and a straw."

For a second I thought that one of the Valentinis might recognize me. Both my father and mother had been deans of the faculty at Saint-Exupéry from 1990 to 1998. He managed the lycée and she ran the preparatory classes for the Grandes Écoles, which meant they were entitled to campus housing, so I was often to be found holed up in Dino's. For a couple of free rounds of *Street Fighter*, I'd help Dino clean up the stockroom or make the famous frozen custard recipe he'd gotten from his father. But when the elderly Italian took my money and handed me the drinks, there was no spark of recognition in his weary eyes.

The place was three-quarters empty, which, even for a Saturday morning, was surprising. Back in my day, there were a lot of boarders at Saint-Ex, some of whom stayed through the weekend. I made the most of the empty room and sat at the table Vinca and I had always preferred, the one at the end of the terrace, under the sweet-scented pines. Just as celestial bodies are drawn to each other, so Vinca had always taken the chair facing the sun. Now, tray in hand, I sat down in my usual spot, facing away from the trees. I took my cup of coffee and set the Cherry Coke in front of the empty chair.

The PA system was playing an old REM hit, "Losing My Religion." Most people think it's a song about faith; actually, it's about the pain of unrequited love. The helplessness of a boy saying to the girl he loves, *Hey, look, I'm here! Why can't you see me?* A neat summary of my own life story.

A light wind made the branches quiver; sunlight glittered on the deck. For a few seconds I was magically transported back to the early nineties. In the sun's rays filtering through branches, I saw Vinca's ghost appear before me, heard the echo of our heated conversations. I could hear her talking to me eagerly about *The Lover* and *Dangerous Liaisons*. I would respond with *Martin Eden* and *Belle du Seigneur*. This was the table where we would discuss for hours the movies we watched on Wednesday afternoons at the Star in Cannes or the Casino in Antibes. She was obsessed with *The Piano* and *Thelma and Louise*. I liked *A Heart in Winter* and *The Double Life of Véronique*.

The song began to fade. The ghostly Vinca put on her Ray-Bans and sipped Cherry Coke through a straw; from behind the tinted lenses, she gave me a wink. Her image dissolved and vanished completely, bringing our enchanted interlude to an end.

Gone was the heat of the carefree summer of '92. I was alone, sad and breathless from chasing the dreams of my lost youth. It had been twenty-five years since I had seen Vinca. Twenty-five years, in fact, since *anyone* had seen her.

3.

On Sunday, December 20, 1992, nineteen-year-old Vinca Rockwell ran off to Paris with her twenty-seven-year-old philosophy teacher, Alexis Clément, with whom she was having a secret affair. They were last seen the following day in a hotel in the seventh arrondissement near the Basilica of Sainte-Clotilde. After that, all trace of their presence in Paris was lost. They never reappeared, never contacted friends or family. They quite literally vanished.

That, at least, was the official version.

From my pocket, I took out the crumpled copy of the article from *Nice-Matin* I had read a hundred times. Although on the face of it, it seemed banal, it nonetheless contained a piece of information that would upend everything that people knew about the story. These days, everyone talks about *truth,* about *transparency,* but truth is rarely what it seems, and in this specific case, it would bring no comfort, no closure, no real justice. Truth would leave in its wake only calamity, a manhunt, and slander.

"Oops! Sorry, m'sieur!"

A loutish teenager running between the tables had just knocked over the Cherry Coke with his backpack. I managed to catch the glass before it hit the ground and shattered. I wiped down the table with a wad of paper napkins, but my pants were spattered. I walked through the café to the bathrooms. It took me a good five minutes to get rid of the stains and five more to get my pants dry. Best not to show up at a school reunion looking like I'd pissed myself.

I went back to the table to pick up my jacket, which was hanging on the chair. When I saw the table, I felt my heart race. In my absence, somebody had carefully folded the printout of the article and set a pair of sunglasses on top of it. Ray-Ban Clubmasters with tinted lenses. Who could have played such a horrible trick? I looked around. Dino was talking to someone next to the gas pumps; Hannah was watering the geraniums on the far side of the terrace. A few garbage collectors were taking a coffee break at the counter, and the handful of other customers were all students working on MacBooks or chatting on their phones.

Shit...

I had to pick up the glasses to make sure that this was not a hallucination. As I did so, I noticed that someone had written on the newspaper article a single word in meticulous cursive:

Revenge.

2

TOP OF THE CLASS
AND THE "BAD BOYS"

1.

"Paint It Black," "No Surprises," "One"...

At the gates to the grounds, the school band was welcoming guests with cover versions of Rolling Stones, Radiohead, and U2 songs. The music—as horrendous as it was jaunty—could be heard as far as the place des Marronniers, where the morning's celebrations were scheduled to take place.

Straddling the borders of several districts (including Antibes and Valbonne) and often dubbed the French Silicon Valley, the Sophia Antipolis technology park was a lush green oasis amid the concrete jungle of the Côte d'Azur. Thousands of start-ups and major corporations specializing in cutting-edge technologies had chosen to base their headquarters in these five thousand acres of pine forest. The area had many benefits that attracted executives from all over the world: the glorious weather (sunshine three-quarters of every year), the proximity to the blue Mediterranean and the ski resorts of Mercantour, the first-class sporting facilities, and the top-flight international schools, of which the Lycée Saint-Exupéry was the exemplar, the pinnacle of academic institutions in Alpes-Maritimes. This was where all parents hoped they might one day send their offspring, trusting in the future pledged by the school's motto, *Scientia potestas est*—Knowledge Is Power.

Having passed the gatekeeper's lodge, I walked by the administration offices and the staff quarters. Constructed in the mid-sixties, the school buildings were beginning to show their age, but the campus as a whole was still exceptional. The architect had wisely taken advantage of the unique natural setting of the Valbonne plateau. On that Saturday morning, the air was mild, the sky a deep turquoise. Set between scrubland and forest, amid rocky crags and uneven terrain, the concrete, glass, and steel structures merged with the undulating landscape. Farther down, set near the large lake, half hidden by trees, were the small two-story buildings that housed the boarding students, each one painted a different color and bearing the name of an artist associated with the Côte d'Azur: Pablo Picasso, Marc Chagall, Nicolas de Staël, F. Scott Fitzgerald, Sidney Bechet, Graham Greene...

Between the ages of fifteen and nineteen, I'd lived here with my parents in the staff quarters. My memories of my time here were still vivid, particularly the joy of waking every morning to the sight of the pine forest. From my bedroom, I could see the same spectacular view that I was now admiring again: the shimmering lake, the pontoon bridge, and the boathouses. Having spent two decades living in New York, I'd managed to convince myself that I preferred the electric-blue sky over Manhattan to the drone of the mistral and the cicadas, preferred the bustle of Brooklyn and Harlem to the scent of eucalyptus and lavender. *But is that still true?* I wondered as I rounded the Agora, an early 1990s glass building next to the library that housed a number of lecture halls and a movie theater.

I came to the "historic" red-brick Gothic buildings that evoked an American university. Architecturally, they were anachronistic and entirely out of keeping with the otherwise coherent style of the campus, but they had always been the pride of Saint-Ex, since they gave the school an Ivy League luster and made the parents feel like they were sending their brats to the local Harvard.

"Well, well, if it isn't Thomas Degalais...looking for inspiration for your next novel, are you?"

2.

The voice startled me. When I spun around, I saw the smiling face of Stéphane Pianelli; with his long hair, his goatee, his round John Lennon glasses, and the bag slung across his chest, the journalist from *Nice-Matin* looked exactly as he had as a student. His sole concession to the present day was that the T-shirt beneath his sleeveless jacket was emblazoned with the φ logo of Jean-Luc Mélenchon's populist left-wing party, La France Insoumise.

"Hey, Stéphane," I said, shaking his hand.

We walked a little way together. Pianelli was my age, and, like me, a local boy. We'd been in the same class right up to our final year. I remembered him as a loudmouth, a brilliant debater with a keen sense of logic who often unsettled our teachers. He was one of the few students in the school who had a political conscience. After taking the *baccalauréat,* although his grades had been good enough to get him a place in the Saint-Ex preparatory course for Sciences Po, he decided to study arts at the Nice Faculté des Lettres, a university my father dismissed as an "unemployment factory" and my mother scorned as being filled with a "bunch of leftist slackers." But Pianelli had always wanted to be seen as a rebel. At Carlone, the arts college there, he walked a delicate line between the National Students' Union and the Young Socialist Movement. He had his first moment of glory one spring evening in 1994 during an episode of *Demain les Jeunes,* a youth-culture program that gave dozens of students a platform to rail against proposals by the government to slash student grants. I'd recently rewatched the program online and was struck by Pianelli's self-assurance. When he was called on to speak, he used his time to heckle and humiliate seasoned political pundits twice his age. He was hardheaded and not cowed by anyone.

"What did you think about Macron getting elected?" he asked suddenly. He was clearly still obsessed with politics. "It's good news for guys like you, huh?"

"Writers?"

"No, filthy-rich fuckers!" he said with a twinkle in his eye.

Pianelli was a joker and he could be malicious, but I liked him. He was the only guy from Saint-Ex I was still regularly in touch with, although that was because he interviewed me for *Nice-Matin* whenever I published a new novel. He'd never aspired to a career in the national media, as far as I knew. He preferred being a jack-of-all-trades, the "Swiss army knife of journalism," he called it. At *Nice-Matin* he was given free rein to write about whatever he liked—politics, the arts, city life—and it was this freedom that he really appreciated. Being a hack armed with a pen always in search of a scoop didn't keep him from maintaining a certain objectivity. I read his reviews of my books because he could read between the lines. They weren't always positive, but even when he had reservations, Pianelli never forgot that a novel—or a film or a play—was the result of years of hard work, of doubts, of rewrites. He might be critical, but he believed it would be cruel and arrogant to dismiss a novel in a few lines. "The average piece of bad writing is probably more meaningful than our criticism designating it so," he once told me, freely adapting the line by Anton Ego, the food critic in *Ratatouille.*

"Joking apart, what the hell are you doing here, Mr. Potboiler?" he asked.

Though pretending not to be interested, he was a journalist

sniffing out the territory, putting out feelers, drawing me out. He knew bits and pieces about my past. Maybe he could tell I was nervous from the way I was fumbling in my pocket, toying with the scribbled threat I had received fifteen minutes earlier and the pair of sunglasses that were just like the ones that Vinca used to wear.

"Doesn't hurt to go back to your roots, does it? As we get older, we—"

"Cut the shit." He sniggered. "This alumni reunion is exactly the kind of thing you loathe, Thomas. Look at you, with your Charvet shirt and your Patek Philippe watch. D'you really expect me to believe that you flew here from New York to bond over nineties TV shows and shoot the shit with guys you despise?"

"You're wrong—I don't look down on anyone." That much was true.

Pianelli regarded me suspiciously. Then something in his eyes shifted imperceptibly. They began to shine as though the penny had just dropped.

"Oh, I get it," he said, nodding. "You came because you read my article!"

The remark left me as winded as a punch in the stomach. How did he know? "What article?"

"Don't play dumb. You know what I mean."

I affected an offhand tone: "Listen, I live in Tribeca—I read the *New York Times* over my morning coffee, not your local rag. What article? You mean the one about the fiftieth anniversary?"

From his puzzled look, I could tell we weren't talking about the same article. But my relief was short-lived.

"I meant the article about Vinca Rockwell."

This time, I was so shocked that I froze.

"So you really haven't heard?" he said.

"Heard what, for fuck's sake?"

Pianelli shook his head and took a notepad from his bag. "I've gotta go do some work," he said as we reached the main square. "I've got an article to write for my local rag."

"Stéphane! Wait!"

Satisfied with the effect he had produced, Pianelli stalked off. "Let's talk later," he said with a little wave.

3.

The place des Marronniers was humming with the music of the school band and the murmur of small groups engaged in lively conversations. If there had ever been chestnut trees on the square, they had long since been killed off by some parasite, and although it was still called the place des Marronniers, it was now adorned with date palms, their graceful silhouettes conjuring images of exotic holidays and idleness. Buffet tables had been set up in the huge marquees hung with garlands of flowers and furnished with rows of chairs. Outside in the crowded square, waiters in straw hats and striped shirts performed an intricate ballet as they moved around refilling glasses.

I grabbed a glass from a passing tray, took a sip, and immediately tipped the rest into a flowerpot. Clearly the school's idea of a welcome cocktail did not stretch beyond ginger iced tea made with foul-tasting coconut water. I wandered over to the buffet. Here, too, administrators had evidently opted for a sort of low-calorie feast. It felt like being back in America, specifically in California or in certain areas of Brooklyn where the cult of healthy living reigned supreme. There were no stuffed vegetables *niçoise,* no courgette-flower beignets, no Provençal pizzas. Nothing but miserable carrot and cucumber *crudités,* shot glasses filled with low-fat desserts, and cheese on certified gluten-free toast.

I walked away from the buffet tables and went to sit at the top of the huge polished-concrete steps that circled part of the square like the seats in an amphitheater. I put on my sunglasses and, hidden from prying eyes, observed my former schoolmates with interest.

They were making toasts, slapping each other on the back, showing off cute photos of their toddlers or their teenage children, swapping e-mail addresses and cell phone numbers, friending each other on social media. Pianelli had been right—I was an outsider in this world; there was no point pretending otherwise. I didn't feel nostalgic about my school years and I was essentially a loner, always walking around with a book in my pocket, and with no Facebook presence, I was a square ill-suited to an era of Like buttons. And I had never worried about the passing of time. I hadn't freaked out when I turned forty, when I started to go gray at the temples. To be honest, I was eager to be old, because it meant distancing myself from a past that, far from being a lost paradise, was the setting of a tragedy I had been running from ever since.

4.

My first observation about my classmates was that most of those who had bothered to show up were from the sort of wealthy backgrounds where people are determined not to put on weight. The main scourge of the men was baldness. Nicolas Dubois's hair transplant wasn't exactly convincing; Alexandre Musca was trying to hide his bald patch with a comb-over; Romain Roussel had opted to shave his head completely.

I was pleasantly surprised by my powers of recollection—I could put a name to most of the faces from my generation of students. It was amusing, even fascinating, in some cases, to watch them, since for many, the reunion seemed to be an opportunity to get revenge for the past. Take Manon Agostini, for example, a plain, painfully shy girl who had grown up to be a beautiful, self-confident woman. Christophe Mirkovic had undergone a similar transformation. He was no longer the nerd—not that we used the word back then—the pimply, bespectacled punching bag I remembered, and I was happy for him. Like an American, he now brazenly flaunted his success;

he bragged about the merits of his Tesla and spoke English to his girlfriend, twenty years his junior, who was turning heads.

Éric Lafitte, however, had clearly had a rough time of it. I remembered him as a demigod, a kind of raven-haired angel, like Alain Delon in *Purple Noon*. Now, Éric the King had become a pathetic, potbellied guy with a pockmarked face who looked more like Homer Simpson than the star of *Rocco and His Brothers*.

Kathy and Hervé Lesage arrived holding hands. They had started dating in junior year and married as soon as they had finished their studies. Kathy had been Katherine Laneau. I remembered her because she used to have magnificent legs—she probably still did, though she had swapped her plaid miniskirt for a pantsuit—and a perfect command of English. I used to wonder how a girl like her could fall in love with a guy like Hervé Lesage. We used to call him Nigel, Christopher Guest's character in *This Is Spinal Tap*. He was pasty-faced, pea-brained; he made off-color jokes and asked teachers questions that were entirely beside the point. But most of all, he seemed blissfully unaware that his girlfriend was completely out of his league. Twenty-five years later, with his suede jacket and his smug grin, he looked every bit as dumb as he had back then.

But when it came to clothes, Fabrice Fauconnier took the cake. Fabrice "the Falcon" was sporting his Air France pilot's uniform. I watched him strut among the women with their blond hairdos, high heels, and boob jobs. He had remained handsome; his build was still athletic and his graying mane, forceful gaze, and evident vanity already designated him as a silver fox. A few years earlier, I'd come across him on a short-haul flight. He'd wanted to show off and thought it would please me to be invited into the cockpit for the landing, treating me like an excitable five-year-old.

5.

"Bloody hell, Falcon's looking rough, isn't he?"

Fanny Brahimi gave me a wink and kissed me warmly. She had changed considerably herself. Originally from Algeria, she was petite with short blond hair and pale eyes; she was squeezed into skintight jeans and wore a belted trench coat and high heels. Back in school, she'd been a die-hard grunge fan who'd traipsed around in Doc Martens, lumberjack shirts, patched cardigans, and ripped 501s.

She was clearly more resourceful than I was—she had somehow unearthed a glass of champagne.

"Didn't manage to find any popcorn, though," she said, sitting next to me on the step.

She had a camera around her neck, just like she used to, a Leica M, and she started taking pictures of the crowd.

I'd known Fanny forever. She, Maxime, and I had been together at La Fontonne Elementary School, known locally as the "old school," whose striking late-nineteenth-century buildings stood in stark contrast to the prefab structures of the École René-Cassin built decades later by the Antibes city council. As teenagers, the three of us had been close. Fanny was the first girl I'd ever dated, back when I was fourteen and in the ninth grade. We went to see a Saturday matinee of *Rain Man,* and, on the bus back to La Fontonne, both listening to the headphones of my Sony Walkman, we exchanged four or five awkward kisses between Jean-Jacques Goldman singing "Puisque tu pars" and Mylène Farmer crooning "Pourvu qu'elles soient douces." We stayed together until junior year, at which point we drifted apart, though we remained friends. She was one of those mature, liberated girls, and in our final year, she started sleeping with guys, no strings attached. This was pretty unusual at Saint-Ex, and a lot of people criticized her for it. But I always respected her—to me, she was the embodiment of freedom. She was a friend of Vinca's, a brilliant student, and a wonderful human being, three qualities that endeared her to me. After completing her degree in medicine, she traveled around a lot, working in combat zones and with various humanitarian missions. A few years ago, we'd met up again by chance in Beirut, where I was attending the Francophone Book Fair, and she'd told me that she was planning to move back to France.

"Have you spotted any of our old teachers?" she asked.

I nodded toward Monsieur N'Dong, Monsieur Lehmann, and Madame Fontana, who had taught us math, physics, and biology, respectively.

"A fine bunch of sadists," Fanny said, snapping their photos.

"Can't argue with that. Are you working in Antibes?"

She nodded. "I've been in the cardiology unit at La Fontonne Hospital for the past two years. I've been looking after your mother there—didn't she mention?"

From my silence, she could tell I knew nothing about this.

"We've been monitoring her since the minor heart attack, but it's all good," Fanny said reassuringly.

I was completely taken aback. "Me and my mother...well, it's complicated," I said evasively.

"That's what all boys say, isn't it?" she said, then let the subject drop. Fanny pointed out another teacher. "Now, she was cool!" she said.

It took me a moment to recognize Miss DeVille, an American who taught English literature to those preparing for the Grandes Écoles.

"And she's still a knockout too!" Fanny whispered. "She looks like Catherine Zeta-Jones!"

Miss DeVille was a good five feet eleven inches and had long straight hair that fell to her shoulders. She was wearing high heels, tight leather pants, and a collarless jacket. Her lithe, svelte figure made her look younger than some of her former students. How old had she been when she first came to Saint-Ex? Twenty-five?

Thirty at most. She had never taught me but I remembered that her students were very fond of her, and some of the boys all but worshipped her.

For a few minutes, Fanny and I continued spying on our former classmates and reminiscing. As I listened to her talk, I was reminded why I'd always liked her. She radiated a sort of positive energy, and she had a sense of humor, which was always a bonus. But she hadn't had an easy start in life. Her mother, a pretty, blond, olive-skinned woman with eyes that could be either tender or lethal, worked as an assistant in a clothes shop on the Croisette in Cannes. When Fanny was in second grade, her mother had walked out on her husband and three children and run off to South America with her boss. Before becoming a boarder at Saint-Ex, Fanny and her brothers had lived for nearly a decade with their father, who'd been paralyzed in an accident on a construction site. The four of them lived in a run-down housing project on the boulevard du Val Claret—not the sort of place mentioned in guidebooks to Antibes Juan-les-Pins.

Fanny delivered a few more stinging but good-natured barbs ("Good to see Étienne Labitte still looks like a dickhead"), then stared at me, a curious smile playing on her lips. "Life might have reassigned certain roles to others, but you're still the same as ever." She snapped a picture of me with the Leica and continued, "Top of the class, preppy, clean-cut in your flannel jacket and your nice blue shirt."

"Coming from you, I'm pretty sure that's not a compliment."

"You'd be surprised."

"Girls only go for bad boys, don't they?"

"At sixteen, maybe. Not when they've turned forty!"

I shrugged, squinting and shading my eyes with my hand.

"Looking for someone?"

"Maxime."

"Our future member of Parliament? I had a quick cigarette with him behind the gym where we're supposed to be having our big class party. He didn't seem too interested in pressing the flesh. Fucking hell, have you seen the state of Aude Paradis? Poor thing looks like shit! See if you can find some popcorn, Thomas. I could sit here for hours!"

But her enthusiasm waned the moment she saw a couple of staff members setting up a microphone on a small platform.

"Sorry, I'm going to skip the official speeches," she announced, getting to her feet.

On the steps across from us, Stéphane Pianelli was taking notes as he talked to the mayor. When he saw me, he gave a wave that meant something like *Don't move—I'll be right over.*

Fanny dusted off her jeans and, in typical fashion, dropped a final zinger.

"You know what? I think you're one of the few men at this party that I haven't slept with."

I wanted to say something witty, but nothing came to mind, because her words were not intended to be funny. They were sad and melodramatic.

"But back then, you were head over heels in love with Vinca," she remembered.

"True," I admitted. "I was in love with her. Like pretty much everyone else here, right?"

"Yeah, but you always idealized her."

I sighed. After Vinca's disappearance and the revelation about her affair with the teacher, she had quickly become a Laura Palmer–like character in a remake of *Twin Peaks* set on the Côte d'Azur.

"Fanny, don't you start too."

"Whatever you say. I'm sure it's easier to keep your head in the sand."

She slipped her camera into her bag, looked at her watch, and handed me the half-full glass of champagne.

"I'm running late and I really shouldn't have drunk that. I'm on duty this afternoon. See you, Thomas."

6.

The headmistress was giving her speech, the sort of vacuous homily that is a specialty among middle managers in France's national education system. Madame Guirard hailed from Paris, and she had not been in this post for very long. What she knew about the school was strictly theoretical, so she confined her remarks to vague platitudes. As I listened to her, I wondered why my parents hadn't come. As former deans of the faculty, they would certainly have been invited. I scanned the crowd, puzzled by their absence.

When the headmistress had finished her lecture about "the universal values of tolerance, equal opportunity, and dialogue between cultures that this institution has cherished since its inception," she went on to talk about the "notable figures" who had attended the school. I was mentioned with a dozen or so others, and when she said my name, a few heads turned in my direction. I gave an embarrassed smile and made a vague gesture of thanks.

"That's it, your cover's been blown, Mr. Potboiler," said Stéphane Pianelli, sitting down beside me. "Give it a few minutes and they'll be getting you to autograph books."

I was careful not to encourage him, but he continued.

"They'll ask why you killed off the hero at the end of *A Few Days with You*. They'll ask where you get your ideas, and—"

"Give me a break, Stéphane. What is it you want to talk about? What's this business about an article?"

Pianelli cleared his throat. "When did you get here?" he asked.

"I flew in this morning."

"Okay. Have you heard of the Ice Saints?"

"No, but I'm guessing there are no statues of them in Antibes Cathedral."

"Very funny. Actually, it's a meteorological term for the late frost you sometimes get in spring." He took an e-cigarette from his jacket as he spoke. "The weather on the Côte has been completely shit this spring. First freezing cold, then days of torrential rain—"

I cut him off. "Keep it short, Stéphane, I don't want to hear weeks' worth of weather reports!"

He jerked his chin toward the colorful boarders' buildings, shimmering in the sunshine. "Some of the dorm basements were flooded."

"That's nothing new. Have you seen how steep the slope is? Even back in our day, they flooded every other year."

"Yes, but on the weekend of April eighth, the water rose as high as the ground-floor entrance halls. The school had to have the basements cleared out as an emergency measure." Pianelli puffed on his e-cigarette, releasing plumes of vapor scented with grapefruit and verbena. Compared to Che Guevara chomping his cigar, a revolutionary vaping herbal tea was faintly preposterous.

"During the clear-out, they brought up some old rusty lockers that had been there since the mid-nineties. A moving company was contracted to take them to the dump, but before they could, a bunch of students thought it might be fun to open them up. You'll never guess what they found."

"Tell me."

Pianelli paused for as long as possible for effect.

"A leather sports bag containing a hundred thousand francs in hundreds and two-hundreds! A small fortune that had been stashed away for twenty years."

"So the cops came to Saint-Ex?"

I imagined the turmoil created at the school by the gendarmes showing up.

"You could say that! Like I say in my article, they were pretty worked up about the whole business. A cold case, a stack of cash, a prestigious school; it didn't take much to persuade them to search the whole place with a fine-tooth comb."

"What did they find?"

"They haven't released the information, but from my contacts, I know that they found two clear sets of fingerprints on the bag."

"And?"

"One set of prints was on file."

I held my breath as Pianelli prepared to land the next blow.

"They were Vinca Rockwell's."

I blinked several times as I took this in; I tried to work out what it might mean, but my mind was a blank. "So what do you figure, Stéphane?"

"I figure that I was right all along!" Pianelli said triumphantly.

Aside from politics, the subject that most obsessed Stéphane Pianelli was the Vinca Rockwell affair. About fifteen years ago, he'd even written a book about it, *Death and the Maiden,* the title a nod to Schubert. It was a meticulous, exhaustive investigation, but it contained no stunning revelations about the disappearance of Vinca and her lover.

"If Vinca really did run away with Alexis Clément, she would have taken the money with her. At the very least, she'd have come back for it!" he said.

I wasn't convinced. "Who's to say it was hers?" I said. "Just because her fingerprints were on the bag doesn't mean the money belonged to *her.*"

He nodded. "Yeah, but you've got to admit, it's pretty crazy. Where did all this cash come from? A hundred thousand francs! That was a fortune in those days."

I'd never really worked out what his theory about the Vinca Rockwell case was, but he didn't accept the idea that she'd run off. Though he had no concrete proof, Pianelli believed that there had been no word of Vinca since then because she was dead, and he thought that Alexis Clément had probably killed her.

"What does that mean in terms of criminal charges?"

"No idea," he said, making a face.

"But the investigation into Vinca's disappearance was closed years ago. Whatever they find now, surely it's past the statute of limitations?"

He thoughtfully rubbed his beard with the back of his hand. "Not necessarily. There's quite a lot of complex case law on the subject. These days, there are cases where the statute of limitations doesn't depend on when the crime was committed but on when the body was discovered."

He stared at me and I held his gaze. Pianelli was constantly looking for a scoop, but I'd often wondered what lay behind his fascination with this particular case. From what I remembered, he and Vinca had never been close. They'd never spent time together, and they had almost nothing in common.

Vinca's mother was Pauline Lambert, an Antibes-born actress with close-cropped red hair—a dead ringer for Marlène Jobert—who had played minor roles in 1970s films directed by Yves Boisset and Henri Verneuil. The highlight of her career was a twenty-second topless scene with Jean-Paul Belmondo in *La Scoumoune*. In 1973, in a nightclub at Juan-les-Pins, Pauline met Mark Rockwell, an American race-car driver who had briefly been with the Lotus F1 team and had competed several times in the Indianapolis 500. Rockwell was the youngest son of a prominent Massachusetts family who owned a large stake in a major supermarket chain on the East Coast. Knowing that her career was going nowhere, Pauline followed her new lover to America, where they married. Their only daughter, Vinca, was born in Boston shortly afterward and lived there until the age of sixteen, when she was sent to Saint-Ex after the tragic death of her parents. In the summer of 1989, Mark and Pauline Rockwell had been among the victims of a plane crash. Their plane underwent an explosive decompression shortly after taking off from a Hawaii airport. When the fuselage was breached, the six rows of business-class seats had been torn from the plane. Twelve people had died in the accident, and, for once, it was the rich who suffered, a detail that must surely have pleased Pianelli.

Given her background and her manner, in theory, Vinca epitomized everything Pianelli despised: a daddy's girl from a wealthy American family, a brainy, snobbish heiress interested in Greek philosophy, the films of Tarkovsky, and the poetry of Lautréamont. Slightly pretentious and astonishingly beautiful, she was a girl who did not really live in this world but in a world of her own. A girl who was, unwittingly, somewhat contemptuous of young men like Pianelli.

"For fuck's sake, don't you even care?" he snapped.

I sighed, shrugged, and pretended to be uninterested. "It was all a long time ago, Stéphane."

"A long time ago? But Vinca was your friend! You worshipped her, you—"

"I was eighteen; I was a kid. I've moved on."

"Bullshit, Mr. Potboiler, you haven't moved on at all. I've read your novels, and Vinca's in every single one of them. She's there in most of your female characters!"

Pianelli was starting to piss me off.

"Enough with the pop psychology. It belongs on your rag's horoscope page."

Now that the tone of the discussion had become heated, Stéphane Pianelli seemed electrified. You could see the excitement in his eyes. Vinca had driven him mad, just as she had other boys before him, though for different reasons.

"Say what you like, Thomas, I'm taking up the investigation again. Seriously this time."

"You didn't get very far fifteen years ago," I said.

"The discovery of the money changes everything! That much cash must be hiding something. I think there are only three possibilities: drugs, corruption, or serious blackmail."

I rubbed my eyes. "It's like you're writing a screenplay for a B movie, Pianelli."

"So you're saying that there is no Rockwell case?"

"Oh, there is. It's a clichéd story of a girl who ran away with the guy she loved."

He pulled a face. "Even you don't believe that theory for a second. Take my word for it, Vinca's disappearance is like a tangle of wool. Someday, someone's going to pull the right thread and the whole thing's going to unravel."

"And people will find out what, exactly?"

"Something much bigger than anyone ever imagined."

"You're the one who should write novels. Maybe I can help you find a publisher." I looked at my watch. I needed to find Maxime urgently.

Suddenly calm, Pianelli got to his feet too and patted me on the shoulder. "Later, Mr. Potboiler. I'm sure we'll see each other again."

He sounded like a policeman releasing a prisoner on bail. I buttoned up my jacket and walked down a step, hesitated for a second or two, and turned around. So far, I hadn't put a foot wrong. I had to make sure I didn't give him anything useful, but there was one question I was dying to ask. I tried to adopt as nonchalant a tone as possible.

"You said they found the money in an old locker?"

"Yeah."

"What did it look like?"

"It was canary yellow. The same color as the Henri Matisse dorm."

"Vinca didn't even live in that dorm!" I said triumphantly. "Her room was in the Nicolas de Staël dorm, the blue one."

"I know, I already checked. For someone who's moved on, that's some memory you've got."

He stared at me again, eyes glittering, as though he had tricked me, but I held his gaze and advanced another pawn.

"And this locker, did it have a name on it?"

He shook his head. "After so many years, obviously any writing had worn off."

"Aren't there any records detailing who the lockers were assigned to?"

"Back then, no one bothered with things like that. At the start of the school year, students bagged any locker they liked, first come, first served."

"But in this case, which particular locker was it?"

"Why do you want to know?"

"Just curiosity. You know, that thing journalists are famous for."

"They published the photo next to my article. I don't have it on me, but it was locker A one. Top left, first one. Ring any bells?"

"No, none. So long, Stéphane."

I turned on my heel and walked away quickly so I could leave the square before the end of the headmistress's speech.

On the platform, she was in the closing stages of her address and had mentioned the imminent demolition of the gym and the laying of the foundation stone for "the most ambitious building project in the history of this institution." She thanked the generous donors, without whom this project, thirty years in the planning, would not have been possible; it would include "a building devoted to preparatory classes for the Grandes Écoles, a landscaped garden, and a new sports center with an Olympic-size pool."

If I'd had any doubts about what lay ahead, they were now dispelled. I had lied to Pianelli. I knew perfectly well who had used the locker where the money had been found.

It was me.

3

WHAT WE DID

1.

The gym was a concrete building set on a raised platform surrounded by the pine forest. It was accessed by a steep ramp flanked by large opalescent limestone boulders that blindingly reflected the sunlight. When I got to the parking lot, I saw a bulldozer and a dumpster parked next to a modular building, and my anxiety level rose a notch. The Algeco modular structure contained all kinds of tools: jackhammers, concrete breakers, alligator shears, grappling hooks, and demolition excavators. What the headmistress had said about the imminence of the project was no lie—the old gym was on borrowed time. Construction work was about to start and with it the beginning of our downfall.

I walked around the sports center looking for Maxime. Although we hadn't kept in touch over the years, I'd followed his career with genuine interest and a certain sense of pride. The Vinca Rockwell affair had had a very different effect on his life than it'd had on mine. While it had devastated me and stopped me in my tracks, for Maxime, it had broken down barriers, released him from a strait-jacket, and left him free to write his own story.

After what happened, I was never the same. I lived in fear and in a constant state of mental anguish that led me to disastrously fail my final exams. By the summer of '93, I had already left the Côte d'Azur for Paris, where, to my parents' disappointment, I enrolled in a second-rate business school. I spent four years languishing in Paris, skipping half my classes and spending my days hanging out in the cafés of Saint-Michel, leafing through books in Gibert Jeune, buying CDs at the FNAC in Montparnasse, and watching movies at the Paramount.

In the fourth year, the business school required students to do a six-month placement abroad. While most of my classmates found internships at prestigious companies, I accepted a more modest job as assistant to Evelyn Warren, a New York feminist intellectual. Though she was eighty at the time, Warren was still giving lectures at universities all over the United States. She was extraordinarily brilliant but also autocratic and capricious, and she was constantly losing her temper. She took a liking to me, God knows why. Maybe because I didn't react to her volatile moods, didn't let her get to me. Though she did not think of herself as a substitute grandmother to me, she asked me to continue working for her after I completed my studies, and she helped me get a green card. This is how I came to work with her, living in a wing of her Upper East Side apartment.

During my free time—and I had a lot—I did the one thing that brought me calm: I wrote stories. Since I could not control my own life, I invented radiant worlds free of the fears that plagued me. There *is* such a thing as a magic wand—in my case, it took the form of a ballpoint pen. For a dollar fifty, I had access to a device that could transform reality, set it right, even refute it.

In 2000, I published my first novel, which, through word of mouth, made it onto the bestseller lists. I have written a dozen more since, and writing and promoting my novels has become my full-time job. Though my success was real enough, my family did not consider writing fiction a *serious* profession. "To think, we used to dream you'd grow up to be an engineer!" my father said once with his customary tact. Gradually, my visits to France became more infrequent, and these days they were confined to little more than a week spent there doing promotions and signings. I barely saw my older sister and brother. Marie had graduated from the École des Mines and now had an important job at the National Directorate of External Trade Statistics. I had no idea what she did, but it didn't sound like much fun. As for Jérôme, he was the family hero—a pediatric surgeon who had been working in Haiti since the 2010 earthquake, coordinating operations with Doctors Without Borders.

2.

And then there was Maxime.

The former best friend I had never replaced. My brother from another mother. We'd known each other forever; my mother's family and his father's family both hailed from Montaldicio, an Italian village in Piedmont. Before my parents were offered housing on the campus of Saint-Ex, we had been next-door neighbors on the chemin de la Suquette in Antibes. Our houses offered a sweeping view of the Mediterranean; our gardens, separated only by a low drystone wall, provided the venue for our games of soccer and our parents' barbecues.

Unlike me, Maxime had not been very good at school. Though far from stupid, he was a little immature and more interested in sports and blockbuster movies than the subtleties of *L'Éducation sentimentale* and *Manon Lescaut*. During summer vacation, he would work as a beach attendant at the Batterie du Graillon in Cap d'Antibes. He cut a handsome figure: sculpted torso, shaggy, surf-rat hair, Rip Curl trunks, and laceless Vans. He had the blond, wistful innocence of a teenager in a Gus Van Sant movie.

Maxime was the only son of Francis Biancardini, a well-known contractor in the area who had built up an empire at a time when regulations about the awarding of public contracts were more relaxed. Because I knew him well, I could tell that Francis was a complex, ambiguous, intensely private individual. But to most people he seemed like a boor, with his coarse bricklayer's hands, his potbelly, his rough manners, and the drunken ramblings that often echoed the rhetoric of the National Front. It didn't take much for him to get going. He lined up in his sights those he believed responsible for the country's decadence—"Arabs, commies, feminazis, and faggots." He was a bigoted white alpha male who hadn't yet realized that his world had disappeared.

Having spent years in the shadow of a father he both worshipped and despised, Maxime struggled to carve out a place for himself. Only after the events of December 1992 did he manage to break free of his father's grip. His metamorphosis spanned twenty years and occurred in stages. Once a second-rate student, Maxime began to study hard and earned an engineering degree in building and public works. He then took the reins of his father's business and transformed it into a leader in green construction techniques. He was involved in setting up Platform77, the biggest start-up incubator in southern France.

Around the same time, he came out as gay. In the summer of 2013, a few weeks after the same-sex marriage bill was passed, he and his partner, Olivier, were married at the Antibes city hall. Olivier Mons, another Saint-Ex alumnus, was director of the city's multimedia library. Now, in 2017, they were raising two little girls, born to a surrogate mother in the United States.

All this I had gleaned from the websites of *Nice-Matin* and

Challenges and from an article about the "Macron generation" in *Le Monde*. Maxime had gone from being a lowly city councilor to joining the party Macron founded and running his regional campaign during the presidential election. Now he was running for a seat in Parliament as a Macron candidate. Although the district of Alpes-Maritimes was historically right-wing, in recent years, residents had consistently voted for centrist, no-nonsense candidates. A year ago, the idea that the locals would shift their political allegiance seemed unthinkable, but it now seemed as though the Macron wave might sweep up everything in its path. It would be a close-run contest, but Maxime looked to have every chance of ousting the incumbent.

3.

When I spotted Maxime, he was outside the old gym chatting to the Dupré sisters. I studied him from afar—the baggy cotton pants, the white shirt, the linen jacket; the tanned, slightly rugged face, the clear-eyed gaze, the sun-bleached hair. Léopoldine and Jessica were hanging on his every word as he tried to convince them that the proposed hike in social security contributions would increase the spending power of average earners.

"Well, look who it is!" Jessica called out when she spotted me. I kissed each of the twins and gave Maxime a man-hug. Maybe my mind was playing tricks, but I thought he still smelled of the coconut hair gel he used to wear when we were at school.

For another five minutes, we had to suffer the twins' blathering about organizing the Alumni Prom, among other things. At some point, Léopoldine told me how much she *adored* my novels, "especially the Trilogy of Evil series."

"I rather enjoyed it myself," I said, "even if I didn't write it. But I'll pass on your comments to my friend Chattam."

Léopoldine was mortified. After an awkward silence, she muttered something about problems with the strings of lights and left, dragging her sister along.

I was finally alone with Maxime. Now that he did not have to put up a front for the twins, he looked distraught.

"I'm completely shattered."

His agitation only increased when I showed him the sunglasses that had been left on my table at Dino's and the handwritten word on the *Nice-Matin* article: *Revenge*.

"The exact same message on that same article was delivered to my campaign office the day before yesterday," he said, massaging his temples. "I should have mentioned it over the phone. I'm really sorry I didn't, but I thought it might put you off coming."

"Any idea who sent them?"

"Not the faintest, but even if we managed to find out, it wouldn't change things." He nodded at the bulldozer and the site office filled with tools. "Demolition starts Monday. Whatever we do, we're fucked."

He took out his phone and showed me pictures of his daughters: Louise, four, and Emma, two. Despite the grim circumstances, I congratulated him. Maxime had achieved everything I had failed to: he'd started a family, built a career, was serving his community.

"And now I'm going to lose everything," he mumbled.

"Hang on, hang on, let's not panic before we have to," I said in a vain attempt to reassure him. I paused for a moment, then said: "Have you been inside?"

"No," he said. "I was waiting for you."

4.

Together, we went into the gym.

The building was as vast as I remembered, more than two thousand square meters divided into two separate sections, a sports hall with a climbing wall and a basketball court surrounded by bleachers. In preparation for the ghastly Alumni Prom mentioned in the article, the tatamis, the mats, the goalposts, and the baskets had been stored away, making room for a dance floor and a stage for the band. Tablecloths were draped over Ping-Pong tables and the space was festooned with paper garlands and handmade decorations. As we walked across the linoleum floor, I couldn't help but think that as some band played old hits by INXS and the Chili Peppers, couples would be dancing next to a corpse.

We walked to the wall dividing the sports hall from the basketball court and the bleachers. Sweat was beaded on Maxime's temples, and dark stains were spreading under the arms of his linen jacket. As we took the last few steps, he faltered and finally froze, as though unable to move, as though the concrete wall were physically repelling him. I pressed my hand against the wall, trying to keep my emotions in check. This was not a mere partition; it was a one-meter-thick load-bearing wall that spanned the twenty-meter width of the gym. Images once more flashed through my mind; for twenty-five years, generations of teenagers had come here to train, to sweat, oblivious to the dead body hidden in this gym.

"Since I'm a city councilor, I was able to talk to the contractor doing the demolition," Maxime said.

"How do they plan to go about it?"

"First thing Monday, the mechanical shovels and the wrecking balls will get to work. These guys are pros, they're going to raze this place in less than a week."

"So, in theory, the body might be discovered the day after tomorrow."

"Yeah," he whispered, putting a finger to his lips.

"Is there any chance they might miss it?"

"You're kidding, right? There's no way." He rubbed his eyelids. "The body was wrapped in a double layer of tarp. Even after twenty-five years there'll be a pile of bones. All work will be immediately stopped while the police search for clues."

"How long will it take to positively identify the remains?"

"I'm no cop." Maxime shrugged. "But with DNA and dental records, I'd say a week, tops. Problem is they'll have found my knife and your crowbar long before then. And probably a bunch of other things. We were too fucking sloppy! Given today's technology, they'll probably find our DNA, maybe even fingerprints. And even if they don't, my fucking name is on the murder weapon."

"A present from your dad," I said.

"Yeah, a Swiss army knife." Maxime nervously tugged at the skin on his neck. "I've got to get in front of this," he muttered. "I'll resign this afternoon. The party will be able to select another candidate. I don't want to be the first scandal of Macron's presidency."

"Take your time. I'm not saying we can sort things out this weekend, but we've got to at least try and work out exactly what's happening to us."

"What's happening to us? We killed a guy, for fuck's sake, we killed a man and we walled him up in the fucking gym."

4

THE DOOR OF MY UNDOING

1.

Saturday, December 19, 1992

It had been snowing since early morning. The weather, as exceptional as it was unexpected—and coming during the Christmas vacation—was causing chaos. "Complete pandemonium," as people said around here. On the Côte d'Azur, a light dusting of snow is usually enough to bring everything grinding to a halt. But this was not a few snow-flakes; it was a bona fide blizzard, something no one here had seen since the storms of January '85 and February '86. The forecast was for fifteen centimeters of snow in Ajaccio, ten in Antibes, eight in Nice. Only a handful of flights were taking off, most trains had been canceled, and the roads were almost impassable, and in addition to all that, random power outages were disrupting local life.

From my bedroom window, I looked out at the campus glazed with frost. It was surreal. Snow had shrouded the scrubland, transforming it into a vast white expanse. The olives and the citrus trees were bowed by the weight of the snow, and the stone pines looked as though they had been transplanted into a scene from a Hans Christian Andersen fairy tale.

Fortunately, most boarders had left the night before. Christmas vacation was the one time of year when Saint-Ex was deserted. The only people still on campus were a few students who had requested permission to stay for the holidays and study because they were applying to the Grandes Écoles and had difficult exams ahead and three or four teachers who had missed their flights or their morning trains.

I had been sitting at my desk for half an hour, my vision blurring, staring at a convoluted algebra problem. I was eighteen and taking a foundation course for a science degree. Since this term had started, my life had been a living hell. I felt like I was drowning, and I was barely getting four hours of sleep a night. The grueling coursework left me exhausted and demoralized. Of the original forty students in my class, fifteen had already dropped out. I was desperately trying to cling on, but it was no use. I loathed math and physics, but given the course I had chosen, I found myself spending most of my days studying them. I was drawn to literature and the arts, but as far as my parents were concerned, there were only two worthwhile careers, medicine and engineering.

But if my classes were excruciating, they were far from being the only source of my suffering. What was really killing me, what had reduced my heart to ashes, was my unrequited love for a girl.

2.

Morning and night, I thought about Vinca Rockwell. We'd known each other for three years, ever since her grandfather Alastair had sent her to school in France to get her away from Boston after her parents' death. Vinca was not your average teenage girl; she was sophisticated, vibrant, witty. She had a shock of red hair, eyes that were of two different colors, delicate features. She was not the most beautiful girl at Saint-Ex, but she had a magnetic charm, a mysterious allure that drew you in and drove you insane. An indefinable quality that made you think that if you could just have Vinca, you would have the whole world.

For a long time, we were partners in crime, completely inseparable. I introduced her to the places I most loved—the botanic gardens in Menton, the Villa Kerylos, the Maeght Foundation, the winding lanes of Tourrettes-sur-Loup. We roamed the area, talking for hours on end. We hiked the Via Ferrata at La Colmiane, munched *socca* flatbread in the Antibes market, set the world to rights while sitting at the foot of the Genoese tower at Cap d'Antibes.

We could almost read each other's minds. I was constantly amazed by the connection between us. Vinca was the person I'd been desperately longing to meet ever since I was old enough to desperately long for anything.

As far back as I could remember, I had always felt alone, somehow disconnected from the world, from its bustle, from a mediocrity as infectious as a disease. At one time, I convinced myself that books might cure me of this feeling of ennui, but it is foolish to ask too much of books. Books tell us stories, they allow us to vicariously live out snippets of other lives, but they cannot take you in their arms and comfort you when you're scared.

Vinca had strewn my life with stars, but she had also instilled in me a fear: the fear of losing her. Which is what had just happened on that snowy day.

Although we were both preparing for the Grandes Écoles, we had barely seen each other since the beginning of the term. She was studying humanities, and I was taking advanced math, but it was more than that; I felt as though she was avoiding me. She no longer answered my calls and letters, and she ignored my

suggestions for things we could do together. A few of her classmates
warned me that she was infatuated with Alexis Clément, a young
philosophy teacher. There was even a rumor that their flirtation
had blossomed into a full-blown affair. At first, I refused to believe
it, but I was being slowly eaten up by jealousy. I needed to know
the truth.

3.

One Wednesday about ten days earlier, while the humanities students
were taking a mock exam, I'd blown off study period to go see the
school caretaker, Pavel Fabianski. Pavel liked me. I came by every
week to give him my copy of *France Football* after I'd read it. That
afternoon, while he was getting a can of Coke from his fridge to
thank me, I pocketed a bunch of keys to the student dorm rooms.

Then, clutching the master keys, I raced over to the blue Nicolas
de Staël building where Vinca lived and searched her room.

I know, love doesn't give someone carte blanche, and I know I'm a
scumbag, probably worse than that. But, like most people consumed
by their first love, I was convinced I'd never feel this deeply about
anyone ever again. And that, unfortunately, would prove true.

The other mitigating circumstance was my thinking that I knew
all there was to know about love because I'd read novels when, in
fact, the only thing that truly teaches us about life is a punch in the
face. By December 1992, I had long since drifted from the shores
of romantic love and entered the turbulent waters of passion. And
passion has little if anything to do with love. Passion is a no-man's-
land, a bombed-out war zone situated somewhere at the intersection
of sorrow, madness, and death.

Searching for proof of a relationship between Vinca and Alexis
Clément, I flicked through every book on my friend's shelf. From
between the pages of a Henry James novel, two neatly folded sheets
fluttered to the floor. Hands trembling, I picked them up and was

struck by the lingering scent, at once fresh, woody, and spicy. I unfolded the paper. They were letters from Clément. I had been looking for proof, and what I had found was irrefutable.

December 5

Vinca, my love,

What a glorious surprise you gave me in taking the risk of coming to spend last night with me!

When I opened the door of my apartment and saw your beautiful face, I thought I might die of happiness.

Those few scant hours we spent together were the most passionate I have ever experienced, my love. The whole night, my heart was racing— our mouths, our bodies, were one. My blood trilled in my veins.

When I woke this morning, the sea-scent of your kisses still lingered on my skin, the sheets still exhaled the vanilla of your perfume, but you were gone. I could have wept. I had wanted to wake up in your arms, to fuse my body with yours once more, to feel our breath mingle, to hear the passion in your voice. I wanted your soft tongue to once again explore every inch of my body.

I wish that it would never end, that I could forever remain drunk on your desire, your kisses, your caresses.

I love you,
Alexis

December 8

My darling Vinca,

Today, you have held sway over my every thought. Today, everything I have done has been a pretense: teaching classes, talking to colleagues, feigning interest in a play performed by my students . . . I went through the motions, but my mind was utterly consumed by tender, febrile memories of our last night together.

By noon, I could not bear it any longer. I had to sneak off between classes to smoke a cigarette on the staff-room terrace, and it was here that I saw you from afar, sitting on a bench, chatting to your friends. When you noticed me, the little wave you gave me warmed my poor heart. Whenever I see you, my whole being quivers and the world around you melts away. At one point, I almost threw caution to the wind and walked over to take you in my arms so everyone might see my love blaze. But we must keep our secret a little longer. Fortunately, freedom is at hand. Soon we will be able to break these bonds. You have chased away the shadows that loomed over me, Vinca. You have given me faith in a radiant future. My every kiss is eternal. My tongue, when it touches your skin, brands you with my incandescent love and marks out the borders of a new world, a lush, fertile land of freedom where soon we will raise our own family. Our child will seal our twin fates forever. Our child will be blessed with your angelic smile, your silvery eyes.

I love you,
Alexis

4.

Discovering the letters left me traumatized. I couldn't eat, I couldn't sleep. I was broken, overwhelmed by an anguish that drove me mad. My teachers and my family were concerned by my plummeting grades. When my mother grilled me about it, I had no choice but to tell her why I was so crushed—I confessed my feelings for Vinca and told her about the letters I'd found. She coldly responded that no girl was worth ruining my education over and told me to pull myself together.

I sensed that I would never really crawl from the abyss into which I had fallen. At the time I couldn't possibly have known that the real nightmare lay ahead.

To be honest, I could see why Vinca was attracted to Clément. He'd taught me the year before, and although I personally found him shallow, I had to admit he looked the part of a lover. It was hardly a fair fight, given my age. In the blue corner, Alexis Clément, twenty-seven, devilishly handsome, tennis pro, driving an Alpine A310 and quoting Schopenhauer in the original German; in the red corner, Thomas Degalais, eighteen, slogging away at a math course, all of seventy francs in pocket money a week, riding a Peugeot 103 moped (without even a souped-up engine), and spending his scant free time playing *Kick Off* on his Atari ST.

I never thought of Vinca as *mine*. But Vinca was made *for me,* just as I was made for her. I was convinced that I was the right person for her, even if this was not the right time. I felt that the day would come when I would have my revenge on guys like Alexis Clément, though it might be years before the tables were turned. And while I waited for that day, my mind was flooded with images of her sleeping with this man. It was unbearable.

When the phone rang that Saturday afternoon in December, I was home alone. The day before, the official start of the vacation, my father had flown to Papeete with my sister and brother. My paternal grandparents had been living in Tahiti for about ten years and we visited them every other Christmas. This year, I had decided to stay home to tackle my falling grades. My mother had decided to spend Christmas in the Landes with her sister Giovanna, who was slowly recovering from major surgery. She was planning to go the next day, and right now she was overseeing the whole campus, manning the tiller of the storm-tossed ship.

Our phone had been ringing all morning because of the snow-storm. In those days, there were no salt spreaders or snowplows to clear the roads of Sophia Antipolis. My mother had been called in to deal with an emergency—a delivery truck had skidded on the icy road and was blocking the gate next to the caretaker's lodge. In despair, she had turned for help to Maxime's father, Francis Biancardini, and he had promised to come as quickly as possible.

I picked up the ringing phone, assuming it was another emergency or maybe Maxime calling to cancel our plans. We usually met up at Dino's on Saturday afternoons to play foosball, watch videos, and swap CDs, or sometimes we'd hang around outside McDonald's in the Carrefour parking lot on our mopeds before heading home to watch the soccer highlights on *Jour de Foot*.

"Thomas, can you come over, please?"

I felt a pang in my heart. It was not Maxime—it was Vinca, sounding slightly choked. I had assumed she'd flown back to Boston to be with her family, but she said that she was still at Saint-Ex, that she wasn't feeling well, and that she wanted to see me.

I was all too conscious of the fact that, when it came to Vinca, I was completely pathetic. Every time she called, every time she spoke to me, hope surged anew and I rushed off to be with her. Which was what I did then, cursing my weakness and my nonexistent self-respect, wishing I had the moral courage to pretend not to care.

5.

The predicted late-afternoon thaw was taking its time to arrive. It was bitterly cold, and the mistral whipped the powdery snow into eddies. In my haste, I'd forgotten to wear boots, and my Air Maxes sank into the snow. Wrapped up in my fleece jacket and hunched against the wind, I looked like Jeremiah Johnson in pursuit of a ghostly grizzly bear. Despite my best efforts, and though the student dorms were only a stone's throw from my parents' apartment, it took me almost ten minutes to reach the Nicolas de Staël building, its blue faded to a gray spectral mass in the iridescent mist.

The building was cold and deserted. The sliding doors leading to the students' common room had been closed off. I kicked the snow from my shoes and took the stairs four at a time. I knocked on Vinca's door several times. When there was no answer, I pushed it open and stepped into a room that smelled of vanilla and benzoin, the characteristic perfume of Armenian paper incense.

Her eyes tightly shut, Vinca huddled in her bed, her long red hair almost invisible beneath the white quilt that reflected the snowy sky. I walked over, brushed her cheek, and laid a hand on her forehead. She was feverish. Without opening her eyes, she mumbled a few words. I decided to let her sleep while I rummaged in the bathroom for something to reduce the fever. The medicine cabinet was stuffed with sleeping pills, tranquilizers, powerful painkillers, and an assortment of other pills, but I couldn't see any paracetamol.

I had stepped out of her room, intending to knock on the door at the end of the corridor, when Fanny Brahimi's face appeared.

"Hey, Thomas," she said, taking off her glasses.

She was wearing ripped jeans, a battered pair of Converse sneakers, and a baggy mohair sweater. Thick mascara blotted out the pale beauty of her eyes. The goth makeup went well with the Cure album on her record player.

"Hey, Fanny, I need a hand."

I explained the situation and asked if she had any paracetamol. While Fanny went to look, I lit her little gas stove and put some water on to boil.

"I found some Doliprane," she said when she reappeared.

"Thanks. Could you make Vinca some tea?"

"Yeah, lots of sugar so she doesn't get too dehydrated. I'm on it."

I went back to Vinca's room. She opened her eyes and propped herself up on her pillow.

"Take these," I said, handing her two tablets, "you're burning up."

Though she wasn't delirious, she was in a bad way. When I asked her why she had phoned, she burst into tears. Even feverish, haggard, and bathed in tears, Vinca was powerfully attractive; she had an ineffable dreamlike aura. Like the pure, crystalline sound of a celesta in a 1970s folk song.

"T...Thomas..." she stammered.

"What is it?"

"I'm a terrible person."

"Come on. Why would you say that?"

She leaned over to the bedside table and picked up something I thought at first was a pen and then realized was a pregnancy test.

"I'm pregnant."

As I looked at the little blue bar indicating a positive result, I remembered fragments of Alexis's letter that had revolted me: *Soon we will raise our own family. Our child will seal our twin fates forever. Our child will be blessed with your angelic smile, your silvery eyes.*

"You've got to help me, Thomas."

I was too shocked to realize what she was asking me to do.

"I didn't want to, you know...I never wanted to," she stuttered.

I sat next to her on the bed, and between ragged sobs, she whispered, "It's not my fault! Alexis forced me."

Stunned, I asked her to repeat what she'd said.

"Alexis forced me. I didn't want to sleep with him!"

This is what she said. Word for word. *I didn't want to sleep with him.* That bastard Alexis Clément had forced himself on her.

I jumped up from the bed, determined to do something. "I'll fix this," I said, heading for the door. "I'll come back and see you later." As I left, I almost bumped into Fanny arriving with the tea tray.

Though I did not know it then, I had just told two lies. I would not "fix this"; I would make things much worse. And I would not go back and see Vinca. Or, rather, by the time I came back, she would be gone for good.

6.

Outside, the snow had stopped, but steel-gray clouds lowered over the scene. The sky was dark, oppressive, a foretaste of the gathering night.

I had raced out of Vinca's room furious and sickened by what she had told me, determined to rescue her. At last, everything made sense. Alexis was a fraud and a rapist. Vinca still cared about me, and she had turned to me when she needed help.

The teachers' residence was close by. As an on-campus teacher at Saint-Ex, Alexis Clément was entitled to housing in the small building that overlooked the lake. To get there, I had to cut through the construction site where the new gym was being built. The foundations, the cement mixers, the half-finished walls were all but buried by a thick layer of pristine snow.

I deliberated over my choice of weapon and eventually picked up a crowbar a builder had left in a wheelbarrow next to a pile of sand. I can't pretend that what I did was not premeditated. Something was stirring in me, an ancient, primal violence that spurred me on. It is something I have felt only once in my life.

To this day, I still remember the intoxicating air that trilled through me. I was no longer an asthmatic student grumbling about a math problem—I was a warrior, a soldier marching to the front lines. By the time I reached the teachers' building, night had almost fallen. Far off, the dark waters of the lake shimmered with the reflected sky.

In the daytime—even on weekends—it was possible to access the building without a key. Like the student dorms, the building was cold, silent, lifeless. Doggedly, I climbed the stairs. I knew I would find Alexis Clément there because I had heard my mother take a call from him earlier saying that his flight home to Munich had been canceled.

I pounded on the door of his room. Inside, a radio was playing. When Alexis opened the door, he suspected nothing.

"Oh—hey, Thomas!"

He looked like Cédric Pioline, a hulking French tennis pro with long, dark, curly hair. Alexis had a good four inches on me, and he was much brawnier, but in that moment, I was not intimidated by him.

"What's the deal with this weather?" he said. "There I was, planning to go skiing in Berchtesgaden, but I bet there's less snow there than there is here!"

The room was sweltering. A large suitcase stood next to the door. From the radio came the velvet voice of Jean-Michel Damian wrapping up his show: "That's all from me for this evening, but stay tuned to France Musique for jazz with Alain Gerber . . ."

Only after he had ushered me in did Alexis Clément notice the crowbar.

"What the . . ." He stared, wide-eyed.

This was no time for hesitation or discussion.

The first blow came almost by itself, as though someone had swung the bar in my stead. It hit him squarely in the chest, knocking the wind out of him and sending him reeling. The second smashed his knee. He howled.

"How dare you touch her, you fucking creep?"

Alexis reached for the counter that divided the room from the kitchenette but it collapsed with him; a pile of plates and a bottle of San Pellegrino crashed to the floor. Still I did not slow down.

I was completely out of control. By now Alexis was sprawled out in front of me, but I continued to beat him mercilessly. I rained down blows furiously, urged on by something I could not stop.

Blows with the crowbar gave way to kicks. The images whirling in my mind of this bastard raping Vinca fueled my rage. I knew I was doing something that could not be undone, yet I could not regain my self-control. Caught in a spiral of violence, I was now the pawn of some malevolent, vengeful god.

I'm not a murderer.

The words echoed inside my head. Faintly. The prospect of a way out. A last wake-up call before the point of no return. Suddenly, I dropped the crowbar and stood, paralyzed.

Alexis made the most of my hesitation. Summoning all his strength, he grabbed my leg, and my slippery shoes made me lose my balance and fall to the floor. Though badly beaten, he scrabbled on top of me in an instant, turning from prey to predator. He leaned his full weight on me, gripping me with his knees so that I couldn't move.

I opened my mouth to scream, but Alexis had already picked up a broken bottle. Helplessly, I watched as he raised his arm to drive home the shard of glass. Then time disintegrated and I felt life ebbing away. It was a second that seemed to drag on for several minutes. A second that would change the course of many lives.

Then the world sped up again. A crimson stream of warm blood splashed across my face. Alexis's body slumped, and I managed to extricate one arm from under him and wipe my eyes. When I opened them, everything was blurry, but looming above the figure of the philosophy teacher was the shadowy figure of Maxime, the blond hair, the Adidas tracksuit, the gray baseball jacket with red leather sleeves.

7.

Maxime had needed only a single stab, a quick thrust with a glittering blade no bigger than a scalpel that looked as though it had merely grazed Alexis Clément's jugular.

"We have to call an ambulance!" I screamed, scrabbling to my feet.

But I knew it was too late. He was already dead. And I was covered in his blood. It was on my face, in my hair, on my shoes. There was blood on my lips, on the tip of my tongue.

For a moment, Maxime and I stood there, exhausted, drained, devastated. Unable to speak.

It was not an ambulance we needed to call. It was the police.

"Wait! My father might still be on campus," Maxime said, snapping out of his daze.

"Where?"

"Down by the caretaker's lodge."

He raced out of Alexis's apartment, and I heard him hurtling downstairs, leaving me with the body of this man we had just killed.

How long was I left alone? Five minutes? Fifteen? In the enveloping silence, I felt as though time had stopped. I remember standing by the window, my nose against the glass so I would not have to look at the body. The tremulous surface of the lake was now plunged into darkness, as though someone had flipped a switch. I tried to focus on something, anything, but I was lost in the iridescent snow.

This dazzling abyss was our future. I knew that our lives had been changed forever. I knew this was not a new chapter, not the end of an era—this was the gaping maw of hell blazing from beneath the snow.

Suddenly, I heard a sound on the stairs and a door slamming. Francis Biancardini stepped into the room; he was followed by his foreman and Maxime. Francis looked as he always did; his gray-streaked hair was disheveled, his paint-spattered leather jacket strained to enclose his barrel chest and potbelly.

"You all right, son?" he said, looking me in the eye.

I was in no fit state to answer. His hulking form seemed to fill the whole room, but his careful, feline steps contrasted with his thickset figure.

Francis stood in the middle of the floor and slowly surveyed the situation, his stony face betraying not a flicker of emotion. It was as though he had always known this day would come. As though this was not the first time he had dealt with such bloody carnage.

"Okay, from here on out, I'm in charge," he said, looking from me to Maxime.

I think it was in this moment, as I listened to his calm and measured voice, that I realized that the crude, proto-fascist mask he wore in public was a cover for his true personality. Right now, the man towering over me seemed like a ruthless gangster, like someone out of *The Godfather*—but if there was even the faintest chance that he could help us, then I was ready to pledge my allegiance to him.

"We're going to clean this place up," he said, turning to Ahmed, the foreman. "But first, go and get some tarps from the van."

The blood had drained from Ahmed's face and his eyes were wide with fear. "What's the plan, boss?"

"We're going to concrete him into the wall," Francis said, jerking his chin toward the corpse.

"Which wall?" asked Ahmed.

"The wall of the new gym."

5

THE LAST DAYS OF VINCA ROCKWELL

1.

May 13, 2017

"I never talked to my father about it ever again," Maxime said, lighting a cigarette.

A ray of sun caught his lighter, a Zippo in a lacquer case with a reproduction of Hokusai's *The Great Wave off Kanagawa*. We had left the stifling atmosphere of the gym for the heights of the Eagle's Nest, a narrow, flower-strewn ridge that ran along a rocky outcropping overlooking the lake.

"I don't even know exactly where he walled up the body."

"Don't you think maybe this is the time to ask him?" I said.

"My father died last winter, Thomas."

"Shit... I'm really sorry." The shadow of Francis Biancardini loomed over our conversation. I had always thought of Maxime's father as indestructible. A rock on which all those foolish enough to attack him met their fate. But death is an exceptional adversary. It always wins in the end. "What happened?"

Maxime took a long drag off his cigarette. "It's a pretty grim story," he said. "In recent years, he had been spending a lot of time at his villa in Aurelia Park—you know where that is?"

I nodded. I knew the opulent gated community in the hills above Nice.

"Late last year, there was a spate of burglaries in the complex, some of them pretty violent. The burglars often burst into the villas in broad daylight when residents were there. There were a number of home invasions where they tied up the victims."

"And Francis was one of them?"

"Yeah. Over Christmas. He always had a gun in the house, but he didn't have time to use it. He was tied up and beaten by the intruders. He died of a heart attack brought on by the beating."

Burglaries were one of the many plagues of the Côte d'Azur, along with the concrete sprawl, the permanent traffic jams, the crowds brought by mass tourism.

"Did they ever catch the guys who did it?"

"Yeah, it was a Macedonian gang, really well organized. The cops caught a couple of them and they're behind bars now."

I leaned on the guardrail. The rocky half-moon terrace afforded a stunning view of the lake. "Other than Francis, who else knew that Clément was murdered?"

"You and me, no one else," Maxime said. "And you know my father, he wasn't the type to talk."

"What about your husband?"

Maxime shook his head. "Fuck no, that's the last thing I'd want Olivier to know about me. I've never talked about what we did to anyone."

"What about Ahmed Ghazouani, the site foreman?"

Maxime looked skeptical. "I don't know anyone more tight-lipped than Ahmed. And besides, why would he have talked about it when he himself was an accomplice?"

"Is he still alive?"

"No. He got cancer and went home to Tunisia to die."

I put on my sunglasses. It was almost noon. From high in the sky, the sun beat down on the Eagle's Nest. Ringed only by a wooden guardrail, the place was as dangerous as it was beautiful. The students of Saint-Ex had never been allowed to come up here, but being the son of two deans, I had special privileges, and I remembered spending several magical evenings here with Vinca, smoking and drinking *mandarinello* as the moon glistened on the lake.

"Whoever's sending us those messages has got to know what we did!" Maxime said. He took one last drag on the cigarette as the glowing ember reached the filter. "Did he have any family, this Alexis Clément guy?"

I knew Clément's family tree by heart. "He was an only child, and his parents were pretty old even back then. They're bound to be dead by now. Besides, that's not where the threat is coming from."

"Who, then? Stéphane Pianelli? The guy's been trailing me for months. Since I started campaigning with Macron, he's been investigating me from every angle. He's dug out old case files about my father. And he wrote that book about Vinca, remember?"

Maybe I was naive, but I could not imagine Stéphane Pianelli going this far to flush us out.

"He's an interfering hack," I said, "but I don't see him writing anonymous threats. If he did suspect us, he'd splash it on the front page. But he did mention something that got me worried—that cash they found in the old locker."

"What are you talking about?"

Maxime had missed the news story. I summarized it: the floods, the discovery of a hundred thousand francs in a sports bag, and the two sets of fingerprints, one of them belonging to Vinca.

"The problem is that the money was found in what used to be my locker."

Somewhat bewildered, Maxime frowned. I explained a little more.

"Before my parents were appointed deans at Saint-Ex, I had a dorm room here for a year."

"Yeah, I remember."

"When my folks were hired, they were offered housing on campus, and they insisted I give up the room so that another boarder could have it."

"And you did, didn't you?"

"Yeah, but the guy who took the room never used the locker and never asked me for the key. So I kept it—not that I had much use for it. But a couple of weeks before Vinca disappeared, she asked me for it."

"And she didn't tell you she was planning to stuff it full of cash?"

"Obviously not! I completely forgot about the locker. Even after Vinca disappeared, I didn't make any connection with her asking me for the key."

"When you think about it, it's unbelievable that they never managed to find a trace of her."

2.

Maxime pushed himself off the drystone wall and took a few steps to join me in the sunshine. He echoed something that I had heard several times that morning: "Thing is, we never really knew who Vinca was."

"Of course we did. She was our friend."

"Okay, then, we knew her without really knowing her," he insisted.

"What do you mean?"

"Everything points to her being in love with Alexis Clément—the letters you found, the photos of them together . . . you remember that photo taken at the winter dance where she's making eyes at him?"

"So what?"

"So why would she claim a couple of days later that the guy had raped her?"

"You think I lied to you?"

"No, but..."

"Spit it out, Maxime!"

"What if Vinca is still alive? What if she's the one sending us the messages?"

"I thought about that," I said. "But why would she?"

"Revenge. Because we killed the guy she loved."

"For fuck's sake!" I exploded. "She was terrified of him, Maxime, I swear. She told me. In fact, it's the last thing she ever said to me: *Alexis forced me. I didn't want to sleep with him!*"

"She could have been high. She was a bit of a druggie back then. She was dropping acid and taking any other shit she could get her hands on."

"No." I drew a line under the discussion. "She said it twice. The guy was a rapist."

Maxime's face was expressionless. For a moment, he stared at the lake, then he turned back to me. "At the time, you told me that she was pregnant."

"Yeah, that's what she said. She even showed me the test."

"If that's true, and if she gave birth, her kid would be about twenty-five now. There could be a son or a daughter out there trying to avenge the father's death."

The idea had occurred to me. It was a possibility, but it struck me as more fantasy than reality, the sort of twist you might find in a second-rate thriller. Which is what I said to Maxime, but he did not seem entirely convinced. I decided to tackle the subject that seemed most important right now.

"There's something else I need to tell you, Max. In early 2016, when I was about to fly back to the States after a tour promoting my new book, I had a run-in with a border control officer at Roissy Airport. This asshole thought it was funny to humiliate a trans woman, calling her 'monsieur.' The whole thing got pretty heated, and I was in custody for a couple of hours…"

"They took your fingerprints!"

"Yeah, I'm in the police database. That means we don't have much time. If they find a single fingerprint when they dig up the body and the crowbar, my name will pop up and I'll be taken into custody and questioned."

"What difference does that make?"

I told him what I had decided on the red-eye flight the night before. "I won't mention you. Or your father. I'll take the blame. I'll tell them I killed Clément and I got Ahmed to help me get rid of the body."

"They're never going to believe you. And besides, why would you do it? Why would you take the rap?"

"I have no kids, no wife, no life. I've got nothing to lose."

"No, it doesn't make sense," he said, shaking his head.

There were gray bags under his eyes; his face was crumpled, as though he had not slept in days. Far from reassuring him, my suggestion had only made him more jittery. I pressed him and found out why.

"The cops already know something, Thomas. I'm convinced. You can't get me off the hook. Last night, I got a call from the Antibes Precinct, from the chief of police himself, Vincent Debruyne."

"Debruyne? Like the former public prosecutor?"

"Yeah, his son."

This was not particularly good news. In the 1990s, the Jospin government had appointed Yvan Debruyne public prosecutor to the Nice District with the stated purpose of putting an end to political racketeering on the Côte d'Azur. "Yvan the Terrible," as he liked to be called, had arrived in a blaze of glory like a knight in shining armor. He'd held the post for more than fifteen years, waging war against the Freemasons and corrupt elected officials. Many were relieved when he finally announced his retirement. A lot of people in the region loathed Debruyne and his bravado, but even his critics admitted that he was fiercely tenacious. If the son took after his old man, we would be dealing with a shrewd, stubborn cop with an innate suspicion of elected officials and anyone remotely connected to Macron's campaign.

"So what did Debruyne say exactly?"

"He asked me to come and see him urgently, because he had a few questions for me. I told him I'd drop by this afternoon."

"Well, go as soon as you can—that way we'll know what the situation is."

"I'm scared shitless."

I put a hand on his shoulder and summoned all my powers of persuasion in an attempt to reassure him. "You haven't been issued an official summons. Maybe Debruyne's been brainwashed. He's probably fishing for information. If he had any concrete evidence, he would have acted on it by now."

Panic oozed from every pore in Maxime's body. He opened the top button of his shirt and wiped the sweat from his forehead. "I can't go on living like this. Maybe if we tell them the whole story—"

"No, Max! Try to hang in there, at least until after the weekend. I know it's tough, but someone out there is trying to scare us, to throw us off balance. Let's not walk into the trap."

He took a deep breath, and with considerable effort seemed to regain his composure.

"Let me do a little digging of my own," I said. "Everything's up in the air right now. Let me try and find out what happened to Vinca."

"All right." He nodded. "I'll go to the precinct and I'll let you know how it goes."

I watched as Maxime walked down the rocky steps and along the path that wound its way between tall thickets of lavender, his slim figure growing smaller and hazier until it finally disappeared, engulfed by the mantle of purple.

3.

Before leaving campus, I stopped in front of the Agora, the curved glass-and-steel building that encircled the historic library.

The midday bell had just rung, and students were beginning to stream out. Although an ID card was now required to access the lecture halls, I avoided the problem by hopping over the turnstile, a trick I had seen performed in the Paris Métro by vagrants, cash-strapped students, and presidents of the French Republic.

When I came to the checkout desk, I recognized the librarian. Her name was Eline Bookmans, though everyone on campus called her Zélie. Originally from the Netherlands, she was a rather self-important bluestocking with a well-rehearsed opinion about practically everything. The last time I'd seen her, she had been a flamboyant forty-something who made the most of her lithe figure. Age had transformed her into a sort of hippie grandmother—square face, double chin, gray hair pulled into a chignon, round glasses, baggy sweater with a Peter Pan collar.

"Hello, Zélie."

In addition to running the library, Eline Bookmans managed the campus cinema, the school radio station, and the Sophia Shakespeare Company, a pretentious name for the school drama club that my mother used to run when she had been a head teacher.

"Well, hello there, pencil pusher," she said as though we had seen each other only yesterday.

Zélie was a woman I had never quite been able to figure out. I had briefly suspected her of being my father's lover, but from what I could remember, my mother had always liked her. When I was a student at Saint-Ex, all the students adored her—it was Zélie this, Zélie that, and they treated her as a confidante, a social worker, a voice of conscience. And Zélie used and abused her position. Always "strong when dealing with the weak and weak when dealing with the strong," she had her favorites, and certain students—usually the more brilliant or the more extroverted—got special treatment. I remembered that she had adored my brother and sister but had never deemed me worthy of her interest. Which suited me fine; the antipathy was mutual.

"What brings you here, Thomas?"

Since the last time we had spoken, I had written a dozen novels that had been translated into twenty languages and sold millions of copies all over the world. One might think that would mean something to a librarian who had watched me grow up. Not that I was necessarily expecting a compliment, but I did think she'd offer a token sign of interest. Which did not come.

"I'd like to borrow a book," I said.

"I need to check that your library card is still valid," she said, acting as if she were taking me seriously.

She belabored the joke, pretending to search her computer database for a library card.

"Ah, found it! Exactly as I thought—you still have two overdue books, *Distinction,* by Pierre Bourdieu, and Max Weber's *The Protestant Ethic and the Spirit of Capitalism.*"

"You're kidding, right?"

"I am. So, how can I help?"

"I'm looking for Stéphane Pianelli's book."

"He had a piece in the *Manual of Journalism,* published by—"

"Not that one, the one he wrote about the Vinca Rockwell case, *Death and the Maiden.*"

She keyed the title into the computer. "We don't have it anymore."

"What do you mean?"

"The book was published in 2002 by a small independent press. The first edition sold out and it's never been reprinted."

I stared at her calmly. "How can you not have a copy?"

Zélie turned the computer screen so that I could see it; the book was not listed.

"I don't understand. Pianelli is an alum. Surely you bought several copies when it was first published?"

She shrugged. "I suppose you think we buy several copies of your novels."

"Just answer the question, please."

A little embarrassed, she squirmed in her baggy sweater and took off her glasses. "The administration recently decided to remove Stéphane's book from the shelves."

"Why?"

"Because twenty-five years after her disappearance, that girl had become something of a cult figure among certain students at the school."

"That girl? You mean Vinca?"

Zélie nodded. "Over the past three or four years, we've noticed that Pianelli's book has been constantly out on loan. We did have a number of copies, but there was a waiting list as long as your arm. Vinca often cropped up in conversations with the students. The Heterodites even put on a show about her last year."

"The Heterodites?"

"A group of rather brilliant young women, radical feminists. A sort of sorority that follows the precepts of an early-twentieth-century New York feminist group. Many of them have rooms in the Nicolas de Staël building, and they wear the tattoo that Vinca used to have on her ankle."

I remembered the tattoo. The letters GRL PWR discreetly inked onto her skin—*girl power.* As she was talking, Zélie double-clicked a file on her computer. It was a poster for a musical, *The Last Days of Vinca Rockwell.* The poster reminded me of a Belle and Sebastian album cover, a black-and-white photo with a pink overlay and artsy typography.

"That's not all. There were nighttime vigils in the room where Vinca used to stay, a morbid cult devoted to certain relics, and a commemoration of the day of her disappearance."

"Why on earth would millennials be so obsessed by Vinca?"

Zélie rolled her eyes. "I imagine that a number of girls identify with her, with her storybook love affair with Clément. To them, she embodies a sort of illusory ideal of freedom. And when she disappeared at the age of nineteen, she was frozen in the amber of eternity."

Zélie got up from her chair and looked through the metal book-shelves behind the reception desk. Eventually, she came back with a copy of Pianelli's book.

"I kept one. If you want to flip through it." She sighed.

I ran my hand over the cover. "I can't believe you're censoring books in 2017."

"It's in the best interests of the students."

"Yeah, sure. Censorship in Saint-Exupéry—you would never have seen that in my parents' time."

Zélie stared at me very calmly for a moment. "As I recall, your parents' time didn't end very well..."

I felt rage course through my veins, but I managed to control myself. "What exactly are you referring to?"

"Nothing," she said prudently.

I knew precisely what she was talking about. In 1998, my parents' roles at the lycée came to an abrupt, and very unjust, end when they were formally charged with some obscure breach of the regulations relating to granting public contracts.

It was a perfect example of collateral damage. Yvan Debruyne, the public prosecutor at the time, had gotten it into his head to bring down a number of local bigwigs he suspected of taking kickbacks from contractors, particularly from Francis Biancardini. Debruyne had had the contractor in his sights for a long time. Although most of the rumors about Francis were ridiculous—there were people who claimed he laundered money for the Calabrian Mafia—others seemed well founded. He had probably greased the palms of local politicians in order to be awarded public contracts. It was in trying to take down Francis that Debruyne had come across my parents' names in a file. Francis had secured a number of contracts at the lycée without entirely respecting the bidding process. During the investigation, my mother had spent twenty-four hours in custody in the squalid Auvare police station. The following morning, there was a picture of my parents on the front page of the local paper, the sort of black-and-white shot that would not look out of place in a slideshow on serial murderers between Bonnie and Clyde and the Lonely Hearts Killers.

Shaken by this unexpected ordeal, my parents both resigned from their teaching positions.

I was no longer living on the Côte d'Azur at the time, but the case had an effect on me. Although my parents had their faults, they were honest people. As teachers, they had spent their careers doing what was in the best interests of their students, and they deserved better than an ignominious resignation that cast a shadow over everything they had achieved. A year and a half after the investigation began, all charges against them were dropped. But by then the damage had been done.

I glared at Zélie until she looked down at her keyboard.

"Can I take it?" I asked, nodding at Pianelli's book.

"No."

"I'll bring it back Monday, promise."

"No." Zélie was obdurate. "It is the property of the library."

I ignored her comment and slipped the book under my arm, and as I turned on my heel, I said, "I think you might be mistaken about that. Check your database. You'll see that there's no mention of the library owning a copy."

I left the library and walked around the Agora. I took the path through the lavender beds that led to the main gate of the campus. The lavender had bloomed early this year, but the aroma seemed different, as though something had gone awry. The coppery, metallic scent drifting on the breeze had the pungent smell of blood.

6

SNOWSCAPE

1.

Sunday, December 20, 1992

I woke up late the day after the murder. The night before, I had popped two sleeping pills I'd found in the family medicine cabinet. That morning, the house was empty and freezing cold. My mother had set off before dawn for the Landes and at some point a fuse had blown, so the radiators were not working. Still groggy, I spent a quarter of an hour tinkering with the fuse box before I managed to get the electricity going again.

In the kitchen on the door of the fridge, I found a little note from my mother, who had made me some French toast. Outside the window, the sunlight glittering on the snow made me feel as though I were in Isola 2000, the ski resort in Mercantour where Francis had a chalet to which he invited us most winters.

Reflexively, I turned the radio on to *France Info*. Overnight, I had become a murderer, but the world was still turning—massacres in Sarajevo, starving Somali children, bloody clashes at the match between Paris Saint-Germain and Olympique de Marseille. I made some black coffee and wolfed down the French toast. I was a murderer, but I was ravenous.

In the bathroom, I stayed in the shower for half an hour and threw up everything I had just eaten. I scrubbed myself with soap as I had the night before, but it felt as though Alexis Clément's blood were caked on my face, my lips, my skin. And as though it would be there forever.

After a while, overcome by the scalding steam, I almost fainted. I was twitchy, my neck felt stiff, my legs were shaky, my belly burned from regurgitated acid. My mind was overwhelmed. Unable to face the situation, I felt my thoughts slither away. It had to stop. I could not keep going as though nothing had happened. When I stepped out of the shower, I had decided to go to the police station and come clean, but I changed my mind at the last minute; if I confessed, I would bring down Maxime and his family, people who had helped me, who had risked everything for me. Eventually, to keep fear from engulfing me completely, I pulled on a tracksuit and went out running.

2.

I ran around the lake three times, sprinting until I was exhausted. The whole world was silvery with frost. I was fascinated by this snowy scene. For as long as I cleaved through the air, I felt as though I was at one with nature, as though the trees, the snow, the wind were assimilating me into their crystalline cortex. All around me, everything was luminous and infinite. An icy parenthesis, an unspoiled, almost unreal territory. The blank page on which I once again believed I might write the next chapters of my life.

On my way home, my legs still numb from exertion, I stopped

by the Nicolas de Staël building. The deserted halls made the place seem like a ghost ship. I knocked long and loud, but neither Fanny nor Vinca was in. Although Fanny's door was closed, Vinca's was ajar, which made me think that she had popped out for only a minute. I went in and stayed for a long time in the warm, downy cocoon. Everything in the room radiated Vinca's presence, an atmosphere that was melancholy, intimate, almost timeless. The bed was rumpled; the sheets still exhaled a smell of perfume and fresh grass.

Vinca's whole world was contained within these fifteen square meters. Pinned to the wall were posters for *Hiroshima mon amour* and *Cat on a Hot Tin Roof*. Black-and-white photos of writers—Colette, Virginia Woolf, Rimbaud, Tennessee Williams. A page clipped from a magazine with an erotic Man Ray photograph of Lee Miller. A quote from Françoise Sagan, copied out on a postcard, that talked of speed, sea, and dazzling blackness. On the windowsill there was a Vanda orchid and the reproduction of Brancusi's *Mademoiselle Pogany* that I'd given her for her birthday. On a shelf above her desk was a pile of CDs, classical (Satie, Chopin, Schubert), classic rock (Roxy Music, Kate Bush, Procol Harum), and more impenetrable recordings that she'd played for me and I'd found hard to understand (Pierre Schaeffer, Pierre Henry, Olivier Messiaen).

On the nightstand, I spotted the book I had seen the day before, a collection of poems by Marina Tsvetaeva. On the flyleaf, the elegantly phrased dedication by Alexis Clément once again plunged me into despair.

For Vinca,
I wish I were an incorporeal soul
that I might never leave you.
To love you is to live.
Alexis

I waited for a few minutes longer. I felt fear gnawing at my gut. To calm myself, I turned on the CD player. "Sunday Morning," the first track on the legendary *Velvet Underground and Nico*. A song that seemed appropriate for this particular moment—diaphanous, ethereal, toxic. I waited and I waited some more until I finally realized that Vinca was not coming back. Ever. Like a junkie, I lingered in the room, breathing in the last wisps of her presence.

In the long years that followed, I have often wondered about the nature of the hold Vinca had over me, the fascinating yet painful fever she triggered in me. And every time, I'm reminded of a drug. Even when we spent time together, even when I had Vinca all to myself, I was already feeling the eventual withdrawal. There were magical moments, lyrical, harmonious sequences that had the perfection of certain pop songs. But that weightlessness never lasted. Even as I was living them, I knew that these perfect moments were like bubbles. Always about to burst.

And Vinca slipped away from me.

3.

I headed back home so that I would not miss the phone call from my father; he had promised to get in touch after the long flight from Paris to Tahiti, around one p.m. Since long-distance calls were expensive, and he was never very talkative, our conversation that afternoon was short and a little cold, which rather summed up our relationship.

I managed to eat the chicken curry my mother had left and not throw up. Then I tried to focus on what I was actually supposed to be doing: studying math and physics. I tried to work my way through a number of differential equations but soon gave up. I could not concentrate. I could feel a panic attack coming on. My mind teemed with images of the murder. By early evening, when my mother called, I was in a terrible state. I was determined to confess everything, but she never gave me the chance. She suggested I come and join her in the Landes. On reflection, she had decided that it was not good for my morale to be on my own for two weeks. It would be less of a chore to study with family around, she argued.

I accepted the suggestion, if only to stop myself from foundering completely. In the snowy darkness in the early hours of Monday morning, I caught the first train, a commuter train from Antibes to Marseille, then a crowded Corail train that arrived in Bordeaux two hours late. By that time, the last regional train had already left and I had to take a bus to Dax. After a hellish journey, I arrived sometime after midnight.

My aunt Giovanna lived in a cottage out in the countryside. The old stone building was overgrown with ivy, the roof was beyond repair, and there were leaks everywhere. In the winter of 1992, it rained constantly in the Landes. By five in the afternoon, it was pitch-dark, and the sun never seemed to rise.

I have no clear memories of the two weeks I spent with my mother and my aunt. A strange atmosphere hung over the house. The days passed—short, cold, bleak. It felt as though all three of us were convalescing. My mother and my aunt looked after me as much as I did them. Sometimes, in the sluggish afternoons, my mother would make crepes and we would slump in front of the television watching old episodes of *Columbo* and *The Persuaders* or the umpteenth screening of *Who Killed Santa Claus?*

All the time I was there, I didn't open a math or a physics book once. To shake off my fears, to escape the present, I did what I had always done: I read novels. That's the only thing I remembered about those two weeks, the books I read. That winter, I suffered with the twins in Ágota Kristóf's *The Notebook* as they struggled to survive the inhumanity of man in a city ravaged by war. I wandered the Creole neighborhood of Fort-de-France in Patrick Chamoiseau's *Texaco*, crossed the Amazon rain forest in Luis Sepúlveda's *The Old*

Man Who Read Love Stories, and was surrounded by tanks during the Prague Spring as I contemplated *The Unbearable Lightness of Being.* These novels did not heal me, but they briefly relieved me of the burden of being myself. They were like a decompression chamber. Like a dike raised against the waves of terror crashing over me.

On those days when the sun never rose, I woke each morning thinking it would be my last day of freedom. Whenever I heard a car approaching, I was convinced the police had come to arrest me. The one time the doorbell rang, determined not to go to prison, I climbed onto the roof so that, if necessary, I could throw myself off.

4.

But no one came to arrest me. Not in the Landes, not on the Côte d'Azur.

In January, when I went back to the Lycée Saint-Exupéry, life returned to normal. Almost. Although everyone was talking about Alexis Clément, people were not lamenting his death but droning on about the rumors that Vinca and the philosophy teacher had been having a secret affair and had run away together. As with most salacious stories, this one enthralled the academic community. Everyone had something to add—an opinion, a little secret, an anecdote. They reveled in the scandal. Even some of the teachers whose open-mindedness I had always admired got involved, vying with one another to come up with the wittiest comments and making me physically sick. A handful remained dignified, including Jean-Christophe Graff, my French teacher, and Miss DeVille, who taught English literature. Although I was not in her class, I heard her in my mother's office saying, "We should not lower ourselves to wallow in mediocrity. It is an infectious disease."

I took comfort in that sentence, and for a long time it became my touchstone when I had a difficult decision to make.

The first person other than me to worry about Vinca's disappearance was Alastair Rockwell, her grandfather and legal guardian. Vinca had often described him as a tight-lipped, authoritarian patriarch. The epitome of an industrialist, he was a self-made man who saw his granddaughter's disappearance as a kidnapping and therefore an attack on his whole family. The parents of Alexis Clément also began to ask questions. Their son was supposed to join some friends for a week of skiing in Berchtesgaden but had not shown up, nor had he visited them, as he usually did, to celebrate the new year.

Although the families worried about these disappearances, it took some time before the police launched a serious investigation. That was partly because Vinca was over eighteen and partly because the prosecutor was reluctant to initiate proceedings, since it was a legal nightmare as to who had jurisdiction. Vinca held both French and American citizenship. Alexis Clément was German. It was not known where or when they had disappeared. Was one of them the aggressor, or were they both victims?

It was at least a week after the start of the school term before the police showed up at Saint-Ex, and even then, their investigation was limited to brief interviews of Vinca's and Alexis's close friends. They conducted fairly minimal searches of their rooms and then had them sealed, though they did not call in a forensics team.

It was only much later, when Alastair Rockwell flew to France toward the end of February, that the pace of the investigation picked up. The industrialist made the most of his contacts and told the media that he had hired a private detective to find his granddaughter. There was another visit by the cops, this time the Nice Serious Crimes Unit. They questioned a number of people—including me, Maxime, and Fanny—and collected DNA evidence from Vinca's room.

Gradually, from witness statements and from documents they seized, they were able to get a clearer sense of what had happened on Sunday and Monday, December 20 and 21, the days when Vinca and Alexis had vanished into thin air.

In his statement, Pavel Fabianski, the school caretaker, insisted that on Sunday, December 20, at about eight in the morning, he had raised the gate to allow an Alpine A310 driven by Alexis Clément to leave the grounds. Fabianski was positive that Vinca Rockwell was in the passenger seat and had rolled down her window and waved to thank him. Some minutes later, at the Haut Sartoux traffic circle, two council workers clearing snow saw Clément's car; it skidded slightly as it approached the intersection, then took the road toward Antibes, and it was on the avenue de la Libération that the car was found, parked outside a launderette near Antibes train station. A number of passengers on the Paris TGV remembered seeing a red-haired girl with an older man wearing a soccer cap emblazoned with the name of Clément's favorite team, Mönchengladbach. On Sunday evening, the night porter at the Hôtel Sainte-Clotilde on the rue de Saint-Simon in Paris stated that a Mademoiselle Vinca Rockwell and a Monsieur Alexis Clément took a room for the night. The reservation had been made by telephone the previous day, and they paid in cash. They consumed a bottle of beer, two cans of Pringles, and a bottle of pineapple juice from the minibar. The porter went on to say that the girl had called down to the front desk to ask whether they had any Cherry Coke, and he had told her that they didn't.

Up to this point, the story of lovers running away together made sense. But after that, investigators could find no trace of them. Vinca and Alexis had not had breakfast in their room or in the hotel restaurant. A chambermaid had seen them in the corridor early in the morning, but no one could say for sure when they left. A toiletry bag containing makeup, a toothbrush, a Mason Pearson hairbrush, and a bottle of perfume was found in the en suite bathroom and put in a storeroom where the hotel kept lost property.

And that's where the investigation ended. No credible witness ever came forward to say he or she saw Vinca and Alexis after that. At the time, most people expected them to reappear as soon as the fires of passion guttered out. But Alastair Rockwell's attorneys persisted. In 1994, they obtained a court order to have the toothbrush and the hairbrush left in the hotel tested for DNA. The results confirmed that they belonged to Vinca, though this did not move the investigation forward. It's possible that some single-minded cop later made a token attempt to reopen the case so that it would not be closed under the statute of limitations, but as far as I know, that was the final act of the investigation.

In 2002, Alastair Rockwell fell ill and passed away. I remembered meeting him a few weeks before 9/11 on the forty-ninth floor of one of the towers of the World Trade Center, where he had his New York offices. He told me that Vinca had often talked to him about me, that she described me as a kind, generous, sensitive boy. Three adjectives that, on the old man's lips, did not sound like compliments. I felt like telling him that I was so sensitive that I had beaten a man half to death with a crowbar, but I bit my tongue. I had asked to meet with him to find out whether the private detective he had hired had come up with any new leads about the whereabouts of his granddaughter. He said no, although I never knew whether this was the truth.

Time passed, and, with the years, almost everyone stopped worrying about what had become of Vinca Rockwell. I was one of the few people unable to move on. Because I knew the official story was a lie. And because one question had haunted me ever since: Was Vinca's hasty departure connected to the death of Alexis Clément? Was I to blame for the disappearance of the girl I'd loved so much?

For twenty years, I had been trying to shed some light on this mystery. And I still did not have the faintest idea.

DIFFERENT FROM
OTHER BOYS

7

THE STREETS OF ANTIBES

1.

When I arrived in Antibes, I drove to the parking lot of Port Vauban, where some of the most beautiful yachts in the world are moored. It was in this parking lot in July 1990—just before I turned sixteen—that I had my first summer job. Not much of a job, to be honest. I raised the barrier after relieving tourists of thirty francs so they could park out of the blazing sun. This was the summer that I read *Swann's Way*—the Folio paperback edition, with Monet's painting of the Rouen cathedral on the cover—the summer I fell dreamily in love with a Parisian girl with wavy blond hair cut in a bob who went by the glorious name of Bérénice. On her way to the beach, she would always stop off at the sentry box for a little chat, though I quickly realized she was more interested in Glenn Medeiros and New Kids on the Block than she was in Charles Swann and Odette de Crécy.

These days, the summer parking-lot attendant jobs had given way to an automated barrier. I took my ticket, found a space near the harbormaster's office, and walked along the quays. Many things had changed in twenty years; the entrance to the harbor had been completely redesigned, the road had been widened, and most of the area had been pedestrianized. But the view was the same. For me, it is one of the most beautiful on the Côte d'Azur: the blue sea in the foreground, a vast, reassuring silhouette of the Fort Carré rising behind the forest of masts, the azure sky sweeping everything away, and the pale mountains just visible in the distance.

The mistral was blowing hard today, and I loved it. Everything came together to reconnect me with my past, to make me feel rooted in this place I loved, this place I had left for tragic reasons. I had no illusions—the city was no longer what it had been when I was a teenager, but as with New York, I liked my idea of Antibes. A place apart, sheltered from the tawdry glitz of many towns on the Côte. The city I had once introduced Vinca to was the city of jazz, of the Lost Generation, one that had welcomed almost every artist who mattered to me. Maupassant had moored his yacht *Le Bel-Ami* here. In the 1920s, Scott and Zelda Fitzgerald had stayed at the Hôtel Belles Rives. Picasso had set up his studio in the Château Grimaldi, a stone's throw from the apartment where Nicolas de Staël executed his most beautiful paintings. Finally, Keith Jarrett, whose concerts provided the soundtrack for all of my novels, still regularly played at La Pinède.

I walked through the stone arch of the Porte Marine, the ancient ramparts dividing the harbor from the old walled city. It was a spring weekend; the place was buzzing, but the tidal wave of tourists that robbed the city of its atmosphere had yet to arrive. It was possible to walk along the rue Aubernon without being jostled. On the Cours Masséna, grocers, florists, cheesemongers, and local craftsmen were packing up their stalls, but the covered market still shimmered with a myriad of colors. People chatted in patois, solving the world's problems amid a symphony of scents: black olives, candied lemons, mint, sun-dried tomatoes. Outside city hall, the last wedding of the morning was ending, and a beaming couple was coming down the steps to a shower of cheers and fluttering rose petals. Although my life was far removed from such festivities—these days, the idea of being married made no sense to me—I let myself be swept along by the whoops of joy and the wide smiles.

I walked down rue Sade, the narrow alley where my father had lived as a child, toward the Place Nationale and strolled as far as Le Michelangelo—known to locals as Mamo, after its owner—one of the restaurants that defined the city. There were a few free tables on the terrace, so I sat down and ordered the local specialty, a *citron pressé* with pastis and basil.

2.

I have never had an office. Ever since elementary school, I have loved working in bright, open spaces—my parents' kitchen, the reading rooms of public libraries, the cafés in the Latin Quarter. In New York, I did my writing in Starbucks, in hotel bars, in parks and restaurants. I felt that I could think more clearly amid the bustle; I was swept along by the conversations and the hum of life. I laid Stéphane Pianelli's book on the table of the restaurant and, while waiting for my aperitif, checked my phone for voice mail. There was an irritable message from my mother, who did not bother with small talk: "Zélie tells me you're here for the fiftieth anniversary of Saint-Ex. What were you thinking, Thomas? You didn't even tell me you're in France. Come over for dinner tonight. We've invited the Pellegrinos. They'd love to see you." I typed a curt response: *I'll call later, Mom.* I downloaded the iPhone app for *Nice-Matin* and bought the issues from April 9 to April 15.

I skimmed through them and quickly found the article I was

looking for—Stéphane Pianelli's piece on how students had found a sports bag stuffed with cash in an old locker. There was little new in the article and I was disappointed that there were no photographs of the sports bag, only an aerial view of the school campus and a photo of the rusty locker, but it did say that "a number of students shared pictures of the money on social media before being told by police to delete them so as not to obstruct the investigation."

I thought for a moment. There would be some trace online somewhere, but I was not clever enough to find it without wasting time. The Antibes offices of *Nice-Matin* were only a few steps away, next to the bus station on the Place Nationale. After a moment's hesitation, I decided to call Pianelli.

"Hey, Stéphane, it's Thomas."

"Can't live without me, can you?"

"I'm down on the terrace at Mamo and I thought if you were in the area, I could buy you lunch. We could split a shoulder of lamb."

"You put in the order and I'll be there as soon as I've finished with this piece."

"What's it about?"

"The retirement and leisure exhibition at the conference center. Not something that's likely to win me Journalist of the Year, I'll grant you."

While I waited for Pianelli, I picked up his book and was yet again struck by the photograph on the cover: Vinca and Alexis Clément on a dance floor. It had been taken in mid-December, a week before Alexis was murdered and Vinca disappeared. I had always found it painful to look at. Captured at the height of her innocence, her beauty, Vinca was gazing at her partner. Her eyes were filled with love, admiration, and a feverish desire to please. As the pair of them danced the twist, the photographer froze them forever in a graceful, sensual pose. It was like *Grease* photographed by Robert Doisneau.

Who had taken the photograph? I had never thought to wonder before now. A student? A teacher? I looked for a photo credit on the back of the book, but it simply said © *Nice-Matin, all rights reserved*. I used my camera to take a picture of the cover and texted it to Rafael Bartoletti, a celebrated fashion photographer who lived on the same street as me in Tribeca. The man was an artist. He had a comprehensive knowledge of photography, an eye that noticed even the tiniest detail, and a way of analyzing things that was singular and remarkable. For years, he had taken all of my promotional photographs and those that appeared on the dust jackets of my books. I loved his work because he always managed to find in me an innocence that I might have had a lifetime ago but had lost. His portraits depicted a *better* me, happier, less tortured, the man I might have been if life had been kinder.

Rafael called me right away. He spoke French with a slight Italian accent that many people found irresistible.

"*Ciao*, Thomas. I'm in Milan doing a shoot for Fendi. Who's the beauty in the photograph you just sent me?"

"A girl I was in love with long ago. Vinca Rockwell."

"I remember—you've talked about her."

"What do you think of the photograph?"

"Did you take it?"

"No."

"Technically, it's a little out of focus, but the photographer certainly knew how to capture a moment. That's all that matters. *The decisive moment*. You know what Cartier-Bresson said: 'Photography must seize upon the moment at which the elements in motion are in balance.' Well, your guy did that. He captured a fleeting moment and transformed it for all eternity."

"You always say that there is nothing more deceptive than a photograph."

"And that's true!" Rafael said. "But I don't see any contradiction."

On the other end of the line, someone turned up the music. I heard a woman's voice urging Rafael to hang up.

"Gotta go," he said. "I'll call you back."

I opened the book and began to leaf through it. It was full of information. Pianelli had had access to police files. He had personally corroborated the statements given by witnesses. I had read the book when it first came out and had conducted my own investigation, interviewing every imaginable witness. I spent twenty minutes skimming through the book. The various memories of different witnesses all told the same story, the one that, over time, had become the official version: Vinca and Alexis had left Saint-Ex in the Alpine, the "young woman with flame-red hair" on the train to Paris next to the older man "wearing a German soccer cap with some unpronounceable name on it"; they'd checked in at the hotel on the rue de Saint-Simon and later "the young lady phoned down to ask for Cherry Coke"; the chambermaid had glimpsed them in the corridor the following morning; and then they'd disappeared—"When the receptionist came to take over from the night watchman, the room keys were lying on the front desk." The book asked questions and highlighted a number of gray areas but offered no compelling evidence for a credible alternative theory. I had an advantage over Pianelli; while he simply had a hunch that the official story was false, I *knew* it was. Clément was dead. He could not have spent those two days with Vinca. She had run away with another man, with a ghost I had spent twenty-five years vainly trying to track down.

3.

"I see you've finally decided to read a good book!" Pianelli said as he took the chair opposite.

I looked up, still a little dazed from wandering through my labyrinthine past. "Did you know your book's been banned by the Saint-Ex library?"

Stéphane speared a black olive from the little bowl. "Yeah, by that old bat Zélie! Not that it stops people who want to read it from downloading the PDF and passing it around."

"How do you explain the current students' obsession with Vinca?"

"Just look at her!" he said, flipping to the photo section of the book.

I did not even look down. I didn't need to see the photographs to know exactly what Vinca had looked like. The almond eyes, her stylishly tousled hair, her pouting lips, her mischievous expressions that flickered between ladylike and lascivious.

"Vinca created a very distinct image," Pianelli said. "She embodied what people used to call French chic, somewhere between Brigitte Bardot and Laetitia Casta. Most of all, she symbolized freedom." He poured himself a glass of water. "If Vinca were twenty years old today, she'd be an It girl with six million followers on Instagram."

The restaurant owner personally brought out the lamb shoulder and carved it for us. After a mouthful or two, Pianelli continued his lecture. "Obviously, all this went right over her head. I can't pretend that I knew her better than you did, but behind that façade, she was pretty dull, wasn't she?"

When I did not respond, he taunted me: "You idealize her because she disappeared when she was nineteen. But just suppose that the two of you had gotten married back then. Can you imagine what things would be like now? You'd have three kids, she'd be fat with saggy tits, and—"

"Shut up, Stéphane!"

I had raised my voice. He backpedaled and apologized, and we spent the next five minutes polishing off the lamb and the salad without talking. In the end, I was the one who broke the silence.

"Do you know who took this photo?" I asked, nodding at the cover.

Pianelli frowned and his face froze, as though I had caught him out. "I, um..." He checked the copyright credit. "I suppose it's part of the *Nice-Matin* archives from way back."

"Could you check?"

He took out his phone and began tapping. "I'll text Claude Angevin. He was the journalist who worked on the story back in 1992."

"Does he still work for the paper?"

"Are you joking? The guy's seventy! These days, he's sunning himself down in Portugal. Why do you want to know who took the photo?"

I ignored the question. "Speaking of photographs, I read in your article that the kids who found the hundred grand in a rusty old locker posted photos on social media."

"Yeah, but the cops made them take them down."

"Surely you kept copies."

"You know me so well."

"Could you send them to me?"

He looked for the photos on his phone. "I thought you weren't interested in the story," he said sarcastically.

"Of course I'm interested, Stéphane."

"What's your e-mail?"

As I gave it to him, something became clear to me. I no longer had any contacts in the area, while Pianelli had lived here all his life, so if I wanted to find out what had happened to Vinca and who was threatening me and Maxime, my only option was to team up with him.

"Would you be interested in collaborating on something?"

"What do you have in mind, Mr. Potboiler?"

"We do a little investigating into Vinca's disappearance and pool our findings."

He shook his head. "You wouldn't play fair."

I had expected his response. To earn his trust, I decided to take a risk. "Okay, to prove I mean it, I'll tell you something that no one knows."

I sensed his every muscle strain. I knew I was walking a tightrope, but then I felt as though I had lived my whole life on a high wire. "Vinca was pregnant by Alexis when she disappeared."

Pianelli stared at me, half incredulous, half concerned.

"Fuck . . . how do you know that?"

"Vinca told me herself. She even showed me the pregnancy test."

"Why didn't you say anything at the time?"

"Because it was her private life. And because as far as the investigation was concerned, it wouldn't have changed anything."

"Of course it goddamned would have!" He bridled. "There would have been three lives to save, not two. With a baby in the mix, there'd have been a hell of a lot more media attention."

Perhaps he was right. To tell the truth, I'd never really thought of a blue line on a piece of plastic as a baby. I was barely eighteen at the time.

I could see the wheels turning in his mind as he shifted in his chair. He opened his notepad and began scribbling. It was some time before he turned back to me.

"Why are you so interested in Vinca if you think she was so dull?" I asked.

"I'm not interested in Vinca, I'm interested in the person or persons who killed her."

"You really think she's dead?"

"People don't just disappear like that. Nineteen years old and all alone—or practically—with no resources."

"So what's your theory, then?"

"Ever since they found the money, I've been convinced that Vinca was blackmailing someone. Someone who didn't like being threatened and did a little threatening of his own. Maybe the kid's father. Could be Clément, could be someone else . . ."

As he closed his notepad, a couple of tickets fluttered to the ground. A smile lit up his face. "I've got tickets to a Depeche Mode concert tonight!"

"Where?"

"Parc des Sports. Want to come with me?"

"Meh. I was never really a synth fan."

"Synths? You obviously haven't listened to the latest albums."

"They never did much for me."

He narrowed his eyes and delved into his memories. "In the late eighties, Depeche Mode was the biggest band in the world. I saw them in Montpellier in '88 at the Zénith. The sound—they were shit hot."

His eyes glittered. I decided to tease him.

"In the late eighties, the biggest rock group in the world was Queen."

"Oh, please! I wouldn't mind, but you're being serious. Now, if you'd said U2, maybe..."

For a few minutes we both lowered our guard, and in that moment, we were seventeen again. Stéphane tried to convince me that Dave Gahan was the greatest singer of his generation and I argued that nothing could top "Bohemian Rhapsody."

Then, as quickly and unexpectedly as it had occurred, the spell was broken.

Pianelli glanced at his watch and jumped to his feet. "Shit, I'm late! I'm supposed to be in Monaco!"

"Another story?"

"Yeah, the heats for the Formula E Grand Prix. The biggest electric-car race in the world." He picked up his bag and gave me a wave. "Talk later."

I ordered a coffee. My mind was in a whirl, and I dimly felt that I had not played my hand well. At the end of the day, I had given Stéphane ammunition and had learned nothing in exchange.

I signaled for the check, and while I waited, I picked up my phone to look at the photographs Stéphane had sent me. I had asked for them just for the heck of it. I didn't expect that they would reveal much.

I was wrong. Within seconds, my hand was trembling so fiercely that I had to put down the phone. I recognized the leather sports bag that had been stuffed with cash—I'd often seen it lying around my house.

8

THE SUMMER OF
THE BIG BLUE

1.

In front of the curtain wall, the Pré-des-Pêcheurs esplanade was teeming with people. In a carnivalesque atmosphere, multicolored floats revved to life for the traditional battle of the flowers. A joyful throng was gathered behind the steel barriers: toddlers with their parents, teenagers in costumes, old men who had left their games of *pétanque*.

When I was a child, the battle of the flowers moved through the whole city. These days, security measures meant that there was a cop every ten meters and the floats went around in circles on the avenue de Verdun. The air was charged with excitement and apprehension. The crowd longed to have fun, to let themselves go, but the memory of the July 14 terrorist attack in Nice was on everyone's mind. As I watched the children brandishing bouquets of carnations behind the barricades, I felt a surge of pain and anger. The threat of terrorist attacks had destroyed our impulsiveness, our spontaneity. Though we pretended otherwise, the fear was with us constantly, a dark shadow looming over every joy.

I pushed my way through and walked back to the parking lot at Port Vauban. The Mini Cooper was exactly where I had left it, but someone had stuffed a thick brown envelope under one of the windshield wipers. No name, no address. I waited until I was in the driver's seat before examining it. My stomach was in knots as I tore open the envelope. Good news rarely comes via anonymous letters.

Inside the envelope were a dozen photographs, yellowing and faded by time. Staring at the first snapshot, I felt an abyss open up inside me—it showed my father kissing Vinca full on the lips. I felt a buzzing in my temples; my heart lurched into my throat. I opened the door of the car and spewed bile.

Dazed with shock, I studied the pictures in more detail. They were all much the same. Not for a second did it occur to me that they might be faked. Deep down, I knew the scenes captured in these images had taken place. Maybe some part of me was not entirely surprised. It felt like a secret I had never been told but that was nonetheless buried deep in my subconscious.

My father was in every photograph. Richard Degalais, known as "Richard the Lionheart" or simply "Rick." Back in the early nineties, he had been around the same age I was now. I did not take after my father. He was elegant, distinguished. In the photos, he was slim with shoulder-length hair, his shirt unbuttoned to reveal his chest. Rakishly handsome, silver-tongued, a gambler and a roué, my father was not so different from Alexis Clément except that he was fifteen years his senior. He loved beautiful women, sports cars, classic cigarette lighters, and Smalto jackets. It was depressing to admit, but in the pictures, he and Vinca made quite a couple.

The photos had been taken in at least two different locations. The first I immediately recognized as Saint-Paul de Vence, out of

season—the Café de la Place, the old oil mill, the city walls overlooking the countryside, the old cemetery where Marc Chagall lies
buried. In the photos, Vinca and my father were strolling hand in
hand, and there could be no doubt that they were in a romantic relationship. The second location was more difficult to identify. At first,
the only thing I could make out was my father's Audi 80 convertible
parked on a hard shoulder that was surrounded by gleaming white
boulders. A set of steps was carved into the rock. In the distance, a
steep island glittered like quartz. The penny dropped: Les Calanques
at Marseille. The sheltered cove behind the embankment was the
beach near the Baie des Singes, a secluded spot where my father had
taken us many times as a family and that, apparently, also served as a
setting for his secret trysts.

My mouth was dry. Although I felt disgusted, I studied the
pictures as closely as possible. There was something artistic, something creative about them. Who had sent me these photos? Who had
taken them? Back then, zoom lenses had been much more primitive;
in order to capture this much detail, the photographer would have
had to be close to his subjects, so close that, for a moment, I
wondered whether the shots could really have been taken without
their knowing. It seemed clear that my father had not known he was
being photographed, but what about Vinca?

I closed my eyes and imagined a scenario. Someone had used
these photos to blackmail my father. This explained what I had
discovered only minutes earlier when I looked at the screenshots
Pianelli had sent and realized that the leather bag had once belonged
to my father. If Rick had given Vinca a bag stuffed with a hundred
thousand francs, it could only be because she was threatening to tell
people about their relationship.

Maybe even about the fact that she was pregnant.

I needed some fresh air. I turned the key in the ignition, rolled
down the roof, and headed toward the sea. I could no longer

postpone the showdown with my father. As the car sped along, I could barely concentrate on the road ahead. The photographs of Vinca were engraved in my mind. For the first time, I noticed a sadness, an uncertainty in her eyes. Had she been afraid of my father? Had Vinca been a victim or a devious manipulator? Perhaps she'd been both.

I came to La Siesta—the most famous nightclub in Antibes—and stopped at the intersection where the road turns off toward Nice. The traffic lights hadn't been updated and they still took an age to change. When I was fifteen and riding my old moped, I had decided *just once* to run a red light here, and I was immediately stopped by cops. I was issued a seven-hundred-and-fifty-franc fine that my parents droned on about for months afterward. The curse of being a nice guy.

I dismissed this embarrassing memory, but another image appeared in my mind unbidden. *Click-click.* The girl with the Leica. *Click-click.* The girl who was mentally taking photographs of people even when she did not have her camera slung around her neck. I heard someone lean on the horn. The light was green. Suddenly, I knew who had taken the photos of my father and Vinca. I shifted gears and headed for La Fontonne Hospital.

2.

Situated to the east on the site of the market gardens that had once been the pride of Antibes, La Fontonne was a neighborhood on the outskirts of the city. Seen on a map, it looked like an idyllic spot set next to the beaches of the Mediterranean, but the reality was less promising. Although there was indeed a shingle beach, the nearby houses were cut off from the sea by the highway and the railway lines. In the mid-1980s, I had attended the local school, the Lycée Jacques Prévert, of which I had terrible memories; academic standards were poor, the atmosphere was toxic, and violence was endemic. The more

gifted students were miserable there. A handful of heroic teachers
managed the school as best they could. Without them and without
my friends Maxime and Fanny, I think I might easily have gone astray.
When the three of us were accepted at Saint-Ex, it changed our lives
dramatically. For the first time, we could go to school without feeling
terrified all the time.

Since then, the reputation of the school had improved and the area
had been completely transformed. Near Bréguières, one of the main
gates to the hospital, the old hothouses had been demolished to make
way for housing developments and blocks of luxury apartments.
There was no tourism here; this was a residential area sprinkled with
small neighborhood shops.

I pulled in to the hospital parking lot. Not for the first time today, I
was returning to a place that immediately evoked memories.

Winter 1982. I am eight years old. I'm chasing my sister in the
garden—she's stolen my Big Jim to turn him into a slave for her
Barbie doll. I accidentally knock over one of the metal benches on
the patio and the sharp edge of the bench slices off a piece of my big
toe. At the hospital, after giving me several stitches, a bungling junior
doctor forgets to use a gauze pad and sticks the surgical tape directly
onto my skin. The wound becomes infected, and for months, I'm
not allowed to play any sports.

I still have the scar to this day.

The second memory was more pleasant, although it, too, started
out badly. Summer 1988. Some guy from one of the rougher areas
of Vallauris attacks me on the soccer field after I score a goal from
a free kick. He snaps my left arm and pushes me down, and I end
up having to stay in the hospital under observation for two days
because he knocked me unconscious. I remembered Maxime and
Fanny coming to visit. They're the first to write on my cast. Maxime
simply scrawls *Marseille FC forever!* and *Back of the net!* because, at that
point in our lives, nothing was more important than soccer. When

it is Fanny's turn, she takes a little more time. I can picture the scene now. It's the end of the school year—maybe summer vacation has started already. The summer of *The Big Blue*. I can picture her, framed against the light, leaning over my bed, the sun streaming through her blond hair. She writes out a line of dialogue from the movie that the three of us saw two weeks earlier, Johana's response to Jacques Mayol at the end of the film when he says, "I've got to go and see." The moment when the audience realizes that he is going to dive and never come back up again:

See what? There's nothing to see, Jacques. It's dark down there. It's cold! You'll be alone. And I'm here! I'm real! I exist!

I might be over forty, but that line breaks my heart every time I think about it. More so today than it ever did.

3.

The hospital was a maze made up of a jumble of ill-assorted buildings. I somehow managed to find my way through the conflicting signage. Extensions had grown up over the decades around the main hospital building, which had been constructed in 1930 of dressed stone. Each extension offered a glimpse of what the best and worst architecture had produced over half a century: dark brick cubes, concrete blocks erected on piles, cubes with steel cladding, green spaces...

The cardiology department was in the newest addition, an ovoid building whose façade was a clever mix of glass and bamboo. I strode through the bright lobby to the front desk.

"How can I help, monsieur?"

With her bleached-blond hair, her frayed denim skirt, her extra-extra-small T-shirt, and her leopard-print tights, the receptionist looked like a Debbie Harry clone.

"I'd like to see the head of cardiology, Dr. Fanny Brahimi."

Blondie picked up the phone. "Who should I say is asking for her?"

"Thomas Degalais. Tell her it's an emergency."

The girl told me to wait in the small atrium. I gulped three glasses of icy water from the cooler and then slumped into one of the sofas that seemed to float on the floor. I closed my eyes. Pictures of Vinca and my father still flickered on my closed eyelids. I had been caught unawares by this nightmare, which further complicated and tarnished my memories of Vinca. I remembered what people had been saying to me all morning: "You never really knew Vinca." They were way off. I would never claim to truly know *anyone*. I was a firm believer in Gabriel García Márquez's maxim that "everyone has three lives: a public life, a private life, and a secret life." And yet I could not help but notice that, for Vinca, the third of these was uncharted territory.

I was not naive. I was well aware that my image of Vinca had been fashioned by my passionately romantic teenage self. I knew that it was an image that responded to what I'd most longed for at the time: to experience true love with a starry-eyed heroine straight from the pages of *Le Grand Meaulnes* or *Wuthering Heights*. I had created an image of Vinca as I wished her to be, not as she *actually* was. I had projected onto her things that existed only in my imagination. But I could not bring myself to admit that I had been wrong from beginning to end.

"Shit, I forgot my cigarettes. Would you mind getting my handbag from my locker?"

Fanny's voice roused me from my contemplation. She lobbed a key ring to Debbie, who caught it in midair.

"What's up, Thomas? We haven't spoken in years and now, suddenly, you can't live without me?" she said as she walked toward a vending machine.

It was the first time I'd seen Fanny in her role as a doctor. She wore a doctor's coat over pale blue cotton scrubs and a surgical cap. Her expression seemed much harder than it had been this morning. Behind her blond bangs, her pale eyes shone with a dark, flickering flame. A warrior of light waging war against illness.

Who was Fanny? Was she an ally or the devil's right hand? What if Vinca was not the only person from my past whom I had been wrong about?

"I've got something to show you, Fanny."

"I don't have much time."

She put coins into the machine and irritably thumped it when it didn't deliver her bottle of Perrier quickly enough. She gestured for me to follow her out into the staff parking lot. She took off the surgical cap and the white coat, then sat on the hood of what must have been her car: a bloodred Dodge Charger that looked like something off the cover of an old Springsteen album.

"Someone left this under my windshield wiper," I said, handing her the brown envelope. "Was it you?"

Fanny shook her head, took the envelope, and weighed it, seemingly in no hurry to open it, as though she already knew what was inside. A minute earlier, her eyes had flashed green; now they were gray and mournful.

"Did you take those pictures, Fanny?"

She extracted the photographs from the cardboard sleeve. She looked down, glanced at the first two snaps, then handed them back to me.

"You know what you should do, Thomas? Get on a plane back to New York."

"Answer the question. You did take those photos, didn't you?"

"Yeah, I did. Twenty-five years ago."

"Why?"

"Because Vinca asked me to." She tugged at the neck of her scrubs and rubbed her eyes. "I know it was all a long time ago." She sighed. "But your memories of that time are very different from mine."

"What are you talking about?"

"You need to face the truth, Thomas. Sometime in late '92, Vinca completely lost it. She was out of control; she was in free fall. You have to remember, this was the beginning of all-night raves—the whole school was tripping on something. And Vinca didn't mind getting stoned out of her mind."

I thought back to the stash of tranquilizers, sleeping pills, ecstasy, and speed I'd seen in Vinca's bathroom cabinet.

"One night in October or November, Vinca showed up at my door. She told me she was screwing your father and she asked me to follow them and take pictures. She—"

The receptionist interrupted her confession. "Here's your bag!" Debbie called.

Fanny thanked her, took out a pack of cigarettes and a lighter, and set the handbag on the hood. It was woven leather, white and tan, and the onyx eyes of its snake-head clasp looked menacing.

"What did Vinca want to do with the photos?"

Fanny lit a cigarette and shrugged. "My guess is she planned to blackmail your father. Have you asked him about it?"

"Not yet." I could feel rage and disappointment welling up in me. "How could you go along with something like that, Fanny?"

She shook her head and took a long drag. Her eyes were misted with tears. She half closed them, as though fighting the urge to cry, but I did not let up.

"How could you do that to me?"

I had shouted this at her, but she jumped down from the hood, faced me, and shouted even louder.

"Because I was in love with you, okay?"

Her bag had fallen to the ground. Eyes blazing with anger, Fanny pushed me hard. "I've always been in love with you, Thomas, always! And you used to love me before Vinca came along and fucked things up."

She punched me in the chest.

"You gave up everything for her, to please her. You gave up

everything that made you who you were. All the things that made you different from other boys."

This was the first time I'd ever seen Fanny lose control. I stood there and took the punches, perhaps because I knew there was some truth in what she was saying, because I felt I deserved it. When I decided I had been punished enough, I gently took her wrists.

"Calm down, Fanny."

She pulled away from me and buried her face in her hands. Her legs were shaking. She looked utterly defeated.

"I agreed to take the photos because I wanted to show them to you, to show you what Vinca was really like."

"So why didn't you?"

"Because back then, it would have completely destroyed you. I was terrified you'd do something stupid. To yourself, to her, to your father. I didn't want to take that risk."

She leaned against the door of the car. I bent down and picked up her bag, carefully avoiding being bitten by the snake. The contents were scattered on the ground—a diary, a bunch of keys, a lipstick. As I was putting everything into the bag, I noticed a folded piece of paper, a photocopy of the article from *Nice-Matin* that had been sent to me and to Maxime. Scrawled across it in red marker was the same word: *Revenge.*

"What's this?" I said, straightening up.

She took it from me. "An anonymous note. I found it in my pigeonhole earlier this week."

Suddenly, the air became heavier, and I realized that the danger threatening Maxime and me was more insidious than I had thought. "Have you any idea why someone sent you this?"

Fanny slumped against the car. She was at a breaking point. I couldn't understand why she had been sent this note. She had had nothing to do with Alexis Clément's murder; why would whoever was stalking me and Maxime blame her?

I gently laid a hand on her shoulder. "Tell me, Fanny, please—do you have any idea why you were sent this?"

She looked up, and I stared at her crumpled, ashen face.

"Of course I fucking know!" she snapped.

Now I was the one who was confused. "Well . . . why?"

"Because there's a corpse walled up inside the gym."

4.

For a long moment, I stood there, speechless. Everything was unraveling. I was paralyzed.

"How long have you known?"

She looked punch-drunk, as though she had given up fighting and was simply waiting to fall.

"Since the day it happened," she whispered wearily.

Then she collapsed. Literally. She slid off the car and crumpled into a sobbing heap on the pavement. I rushed to help her to her feet.

"You had nothing to do with Clément's death, Fanny. It was me and Maxime, we're the ones to blame."

For a moment she stared up at me, dazed, before once more bursting into ragged sobs and burying her face in her hands. I hunkered down next to her and waited for her tears to stop, staring at our elongated shadows on the ground. Eventually, she wiped her eyes with the back of her hand.

"How did it happen?" she said. "How did he die?"

At this point, there was nothing to lose, so I poured out every detail of our terrible secret, reliving the traumatic incident that had made me a murderer. By the time I had finished, Fanny seemed to have recovered her composure. The confession had calmed us both. "What about you, Fanny, how did you find out?"

She struggled to her feet, took a deep breath, lit another cigarette, and smoked for a moment as she summoned old memories.

"December nineteenth, the Saturday of the snowstorm, I'd been up late studying. Back when I was trying to get into medical school, I was sleeping barely four hours a night. I think it drove me a little crazy, especially since I didn't have any money to buy food. That night, I was so hungry I couldn't sleep. A couple of weeks earlier, Madame Fabianski, the caretaker's wife, had taken pity on me and given me a spare key to the cafeteria kitchen."

In her pocket, Fanny's beeper buzzed, but she ignored it.

"So I headed out. It was three in the morning, and I was walking across the campus to the cafeteria. Obviously, all the buildings were locked, but I knew the code to the fire door and was able to get into the dining hall. It was freezing cold, so I didn't exactly hang around. I gobbled a box of cookies and left with half a loaf of bread and a bar of chocolate."

She was speaking in a monotone, as though hypnotized.

"It was only as I was heading back to my building that I noticed how beautiful the scene was. It had stopped snowing, the wind had whipped away the clouds, and the sky was scattered with stars. There was a full moon. It was so magical that I decided to walk around the lake. I can still remember hearing my shoes crunching on the snow, seeing the blue reflected moon gliding on the lake.

"I saw a strange glow up on the hill, and that broke the spell. It was coming from the building site where they were working on the gym. As I got closer, I realized it wasn't simply a glow—the whole site was lit up. I could hear the hum of an engine, the rumble of a machine. My instincts told me to stay well away, but curiosity got the better of me."

"What did you see?"

"I saw a cement mixer churning in the darkness. I was dumbfounded—why would anyone be mixing concrete at three in the morning in the freezing cold? I could feel someone nearby. I turned around and saw Ahmed Ghazouani, the guy who used to work for Francis Biancardini. He was almost as scared as I was. I screamed and ran back to my room as fast as I could, but I always thought that I'd seen something that night that I wasn't supposed to see."

"How did you know Ahmed was walling up Alexis Clément's body?"

"I didn't. It was Ahmed who told me...nearly twenty-five years later."

"How did it happen?"

Fanny turned and nodded at the hospital building. "Last year, he was admitted with stomach cancer. He wasn't my patient, obviously, but sometimes I'd pop in to see him after my shift. My father worked with him on the commercial port in Nice back in '79, and they'd kept in touch. Ahmed knew the cancer was terminal, and before he died, he wanted to ease his conscience. So he told me everything. Like you did just now."

My panic was reaching a fever pitch. "If he told you, maybe he told someone else. Can you remember who came to visit him?"

"Nobody, actually. Nobody came to visit him. He grumbled about it. All he wanted was to go back to Tunisia, to Bizerte."

I remembered that Maxime had said Ahmed had gone back to his native Tunisia to die.

"And I always assumed that's what he did," Fanny said. "He discharged himself to go back to Tunisia..."

"...where he died a few weeks later."

Fanny's beeper echoed in the deserted parking lot. "This time, I really have to get back to work."

"Of course, go ahead."

"Let me know when you've talked to your father."

I nodded and headed back to the visitors' parking lot. When I reached the car, I couldn't help but turn back. I had walked twenty meters, but Fanny was still there, staring at me. Framed against the light, her blond hair glowed like the filaments of a magic lantern.

Her face was hidden in shadow, and in that moment she might have been any age.

For a fleeting instant, I imagined she was once again the Fanny I'd known back in the summer of *The Big Blue*. And I was once again the boy who was "different from other boys."

The only version of Thomas Degalais I had ever liked.

9

THE LIVES OF ROSES

1.

With its meandering roads, its olive groves, and its neatly trimmed hedges, the district of La Constance had always reminded me of certain pieces of jazz, an easy, laid-back call-and-response where elegant motifs are repeated, embellished, and echoed.

My parents lived on the chemin de la Suquette, which took its name from the Occitan word for "hill." It was here, overlooking Antibes, that the Château de la Constance had once stood, a vast estate to the east of the city. Over time, the château had been converted into a sanatorium and later into luxury apartments. The surrounding lands had mushroomed with elegant villas and housing developments. My parents had moved here not long after I was born, when the road was little more than a flower-strewn dirt track. I could remember my brother teaching me to ride a bicycle here, and on weekends the locals would often organize games of *pétanque*. Now, it was a wide paved road clogged with traffic. It was not exactly a highway, but it was not far off.

I pulled up outside number 74, the Villa Violette, rolled down my window, leaned out, and pressed the entry-phone button. No one answered, but a second later, the electric gates glided open. I shifted gears and set off down the narrow driveway that snaked up toward my childhood home.

My father, I noticed, was still loyal to Audi, and his current car, an A4 Estate, was parked right outside the door, strategically placed so he could take off whenever he wanted to (an inclination that I felt entirely summed up Richard Degalais). I parked a little farther away on a gravel forecourt next to a Mercedes convertible I assumed belonged to my mother.

I stepped out into the sunlight, trying to collect my thoughts and figure out what I hoped to achieve here this afternoon. The house had been built at the brow of the hill, and I was mesmerized, as always, by the view: the slender silhouettes of the palm trees, the cloudless expanse of sky and sea, the vast sweep of the horizon. I brought my hand up to shield my eyes from the dazzling sun, and as I turned my head, I saw my mother standing on the porch, arms folded, waiting for me.

I hadn't seen her in almost two years. As I raced up the steps to her, I held her gaze and studied her closely. I always felt vaguely intimidated in her presence. I had spent a serene and joyful childhood close to her, but late adolescence and adulthood had driven a wedge between us. Annabelle Degalais—née Annabella Antonioli—was an ice queen, a Hitchcock blonde without the radiance of Grace Kelly or the impulsiveness of Eva Marie Saint. Tall and angular, her physique perfectly matched that of my father. She was wearing pants in a clean, modern cut with a matching jacket. Although her blond hair had faded to ash gray, it was not yet white. She had aged a little since my last visit.

"Hi, Mom."

"Hello, Thomas."

Her glacial eyes had never been so clear, so piercing. I was always hesitant to hug her. Each time, I felt as though she might take a step back. Today, I decided not to even risk it.

When she was a child, her schoolfriends had nicknamed her "the Austrian." Her family had had a troubled history, and this was the one excuse I had come up with to explain her coldness. During the war, my maternal grandfather, Angelo Antonioli, a peasant farmer in Piedmont, had been conscripted into the Italian Expeditionary Corps, two hundred thirty thousand soldiers who, from the summer of 1941 to the winter of 1943, had been posted to the Eastern Front, from Odessa to the banks of the Don to Stalingrad. Barely half of them made it home. My grandfather Angelo was one of those who didn't make it back; captured by the Soviets during the Ostrogozhsk-Rossosh Offensive, he was sent to a prisoner-of-war camp but died on the march to the gulag. This beaming boy from northern Italy had fallen in the icy cold of the Russian steppes, victim of a war that was not his. To add to the family's woes, during his absence, his wife had gotten pregnant and could scarcely hide the fact that it was the result of adultery. As the product of my grandmother's forbidden love for an Austrian laborer, my mother was born into scandal. The shame that attended her birth meant that she grew up to be uncommonly determined and dispassionate. I had always had the impression that nothing truly unsettled or upset her, a manner that starkly contrasted with my own sensitivity.

"Why didn't you tell me you were ill?" I blurted out the question almost without thinking.

"It wouldn't have made any difference."

"I just wish I'd known, that's all."

She had not always been so distant with me. Thinking back to my childhood, I remembered moments of genuine intimacy and affinity, especially when we talked about novels and plays. This was not my wounded pride rewriting history; I had seen countless pictures of myself as a child with my mother smiling, clearly delighted and proud to call me her son. Later, things went sour, though I never really understood why. These days, she still got along well with my brother and my sister but markedly less so with me. In an unhealthy way, I thought of it as a badge of honor. At least I had something my siblings did not.

"So, you've been at the fiftieth anniversary of Saint-Ex? I don't know why you'd bother..."

"It was good to see old friends."

"You didn't have any friends, Thomas. The only friends you had were your books."

This was true, but hearing it stated so baldly was still upsetting. "Maxime is my friend."

Standing motionless and unblinking, ringed by a shimmering halo of sunlight, she looked like a marble Madonna you might find in an old Italian church.

"Why are you here, Thomas?" she said. "You don't have a book to promote at the moment."

"Couldn't you at least pretend to be happy?"

"Is that what you're doing, pretending?"

I sighed. We were going in circles. Both of us had considerable unspoken bitterness. For a split second, I almost told her the truth: *I killed a man, his body is walled up in the school gym, and by Monday, I might be locked up for murder. Next time you see me, Mom, I might be flanked by two burly cops or behind the glass wall of a prison visiting room.*

It's unlikely that I would have done it, but she did not give me a chance. Without gesturing for me to follow her, she had turned and was on her way up the steps. She had obviously had enough, and so had I.

For a moment, I stood there alone on the terra-cotta tiles of the terrace. Hearing voices, I wandered over to the wrought-iron balcony overgrown with ivy. My father was talking to Alexandre, the elderly gardener who also took care of the swimming pool. The pool had sprung a leak. My father thought it was near the filter but Alexandre, more pessimistic, was talking about digging up the lawn to get to the pipework.

"Hey, Dad."

Richard looked up and gave a little nod as though he'd seen me yesterday. He was the reason for my visit, but as Alexandre wandered off, I decided to go and rummage in the attic.

2.

Well, an attic in a manner of speaking. The villa didn't have an actual attic, but it had an enormous cellar accessible from the garden, almost a hundred square meters that no one had ever thought to organize, so over the years it had turned into the family's junk room.

While every other room in the villa was elegant, immaculately polished, and tastefully furnished, the cellar was filled with a grotesque collection of random stuff and illuminated by flickering strip lights. Here were stored the repressed memories of the Villa Violette. I managed to clear a path through the chaos. There were old bikes, a scooter, and pairs of roller skates that probably belonged to my sister's kids. Next to a toolbox, half hidden by a tarpaulin, was my old moped. My father—always a gearhead—had completely refurbished it. The body had been stripped and beautifully repainted, and he had replaced the wheel rims and the tires—my pathetic old 103 MVL now looked properly hot. He had even managed to track down the original Peugeot stickers. Deeper into the room, there were toys, trunks, suitcases, and vast piles of clothes; my mother and father had never skimped on clothes. There were stacks of books gathering dust. These were the books the family actually read but that weren't *literary* enough to earn a place on the walnut bookshelves in the library— my mother's thrillers and love stories, the popular nonfiction my father liked. Handsome leather-bound editions of Saint-John Perse and Malraux lined the shelves upstairs, but in the cellar were the true manuals of our lives—Dan Brown and *Fifty Shades of Grey*.

Somewhere near the back I finally found what I had been looking for. On a battered Ping-Pong table were two boxes with my name scrawled on them, both filled with nostalgia. I hauled the boxes upstairs—it took two trips—and spilled out the contents to sort through them.

On the kitchen table, I laid out everything connected with the year 1992 that might prove useful to my investigation. A blue Eastpak backpack daubed with Wite-Out, three-ring binders full of notes, report cards that offered a portrait of the meek, model student I had once been: *Diligent, constructive attitude in class. An easygoing, assiduous student. Insightful and relevant contributions. A keen mind.*

I flicked through a number of essays that had been important to me: an essay on Rimbaud's "Le dormeur du val," another on the opening section of *Belle du Seigneur*. I even found some philosophy homework marked up by Alexis Clément, who had taught me my junior year. On my essay entitled "Can Art Exist Without Constraints?," he'd written, *Interesting and sophisticated reasoning skills—B*. And on one entitled "Can Passion Be Understood?," I received a glowing assessment from Clément: *Despite a few elementary errors, this is an excellent essay, showing a clear grasp of concepts and elucidated with examples that demonstrate a genuine comprehension of literature and philosophy—A-*.

Among the other treasures in the boxes were our senior-year class photographs and a series of mixtapes I'd painstakingly made for Vinca but never dared give her. I opened a cassette box at random and perused the song titles that were the soundtrack to my life. The Thomas Degalais I had been back then was utterly consumed by words and music. This was the soundtrack of someone who was still "different from other boys," gentle, a little unconventional, oblivious to fashion, in touch with his emotions: Samson François playing Chopin, Jean Ferrat singing "Les yeux d'Elsa," and Léo Ferré reciting "A Season in Hell," but also Van Morrison's "Moondance" and Freddie Mercury's "Love Kills." Almost a premonition...

There were books too. Old yellowing paperbacks of the titles I still quoted in every interview when I said that "books taught me at a young age that I would never be truly alone."

If only it were that simple.

One of the books here was not mine, the collection of Marina

Tsvetaeva's poems signed by Alexis that I'd taken from Vinca's room the day after the murder.

> For Vinca,
> I wish I were an incorporeal soul
> that I might never leave you.
> To love you is to live.
> Alexis

I gave an ugly laugh. At the time, I had been moved by this dedication. Now I knew the jerk had stolen the line from a letter by Victor Hugo to Juliette Drouet. A charlatan to the end.

"So tell me, Thomas, what the hell are you doing here?"

I spun around. My father had just stepped into the kitchen holding a pair of pruning shears.

3.

Despite not being particularly affectionate, my father was demonstrative and usually hugged me when he saw me, though this time I was the one who felt like taking a step back.

"How's things in New York?" he said as he carefully washed his hands in the sink.

"Can we go into your office?" I said, ignoring his question, "There something I want to show you."

My mother was prowling around somewhere and I did not want her sticking her nose in just now.

Richard dried his hands, grumbling about my showing up out of the blue and being mysterious. Then he led me up to his den, a study cum library decorated like an English gentlemen's club with a chesterfield sofa, African statues, and a collection of antique hunting rifles. Two huge picture windows bathed the room in light and offered the finest view from the villa.

I immediately handed him my phone. On the screen was the *Nice-Matin* article about students finding a bag of cash. "Have you seen this story?"

He picked up his glasses but did not bother to put them on. He merely glanced at the screen, then set his glasses down again.

"Yeah, it's completely insane." Arms folded, he stood in front of the windows and jerked his chin toward the holes in the lawn next to the swimming pool. "Those bloody Asian red-bellied squirrels are taking over the place. They chewed through the wires to the pump, can you imagine?"

I focused on the article.

"That money would have been stashed back there when you were still dean," I said.

"Maybe. I don't know," he said, frowning but not turning toward me. "Did you notice we've had to cut down one of the palm trees? Red palm weevils—"

"I don't suppose you know who owned the bag?"

"What bag?"

"The bag the money was found in."

"How would I know?" Richard bridled. "You're starting to get on my nerves."

"A journalist told me that the cops found two sets of fingerprints. One set belonged to Vinca Rockwell. Remember her?"

At the mention of Vinca's name, Richard turned back to me and sat down in a battered leather armchair.

"Of course. The girl who disappeared. She had...the freshness of a rose."

He screwed up his eyes, and, to my great surprise, the former French teacher began reciting François de Malherbe:

But she was of this earth, where all great beauty knows
a fate so forlorn;

And Rose, she did live as live the wild roses,
   the space of a morn.

He was silent for a moment. Then, for the first time, he asked a question.

"You said something about two sets of fingerprints?"

"The cops don't know who the other set belongs to yet. But I'd stake my life on them being yours, Dad."

"How dare you," he said, startled.

I sat facing him and showed him the screenshots of the bag that Pianelli had sent me.

"Remember this bag? It's the one you always had when we played tennis together. You loved the calfskin leather and the dark greenish patina."

He picked up his glasses again and peered at the phone. "I can't really see anything. The screen's too small."

He grabbed the remote control on the coffee table and turned on the TV as though saying the conversation was at an end. He flipped through the sports channels, watched a few seconds of the Giro d'Italia, then turned back to the Madrid Open semifinal between Nadal and Djokovic. "It's not the same without Federer."

I was not about to give up.

"Maybe you could take a look at these. Don't worry, this time they're all close-ups."

I handed him the brown envelope. He took out the photographs and studied them, keeping one eye on the tennis match. I expected him to be unnerved, but he simply shook his head and sighed.

"Who gave you these?"

"What does it matter? Tell me what they mean!"

"You've seen the photos. Do you really need me to draw you a diagram?"

He turned up the volume, but I snatched away the remote control and turned off the television.

"Don't think you're going to get off so lightly!"

He sighed again and fumbled in the pocket of his blazer for the half-smoked cigar he always carried with him.

"Okay, I got caught," he said, rolling the Cuban between his fingers. "That little slut was always hanging around. She got me all worked up and I couldn't resist. Then she blackmailed me. And I was dumb enough to give her a hundred grand."

"How could you do it?"

"Do what? She was nineteen. She was fucking everything that moved. I didn't force her. She came after me."

I got up and jabbed my finger at him. "You knew she was my friend!"

"What difference does that make?" he said. "When it comes to sex, it's every man for himself. Besides, if you want the truth, you didn't miss much. Vinca was a ballbuster and a lousy lay. She was only in it for the cash."

I didn't know what infuriated me more, his arrogance or his vindictiveness. "Just listen to yourself!"

Far from being unnerved or uncomfortable, Richard sniggered. I could tell that some part of him was enjoying this conversation. He probably got off on the idea of the proud father affirming his superiority over his son by humiliating him.

"You filthy pervert. You disgust me."

This finally riled him. He got to his feet and stepped toward me until he was only inches from my face.

"You have no idea what she was like, that girl! She was the enemy; she was the one threatening to destroy our family."

He nodded to the photographs on the table.

"Think what would have happened if your mother or the parents' association had seen those. You live in this romantic, literary world, but real life is nothing like that. Real life is brutal."

I was tempted to punch him in the face to prove that life could indeed be brutal, but it would not have achieved much. And I still needed information from him.

"So you gave Vinca the money," I said, forcing myself to sound calmer. "And then what happened?"

"What always happens with blackmailers—she wanted more, and I refused." Still toying with his cigar, he screwed up his eyes as he thought back. "The last time she showed up was the night before Christmas vacation. She even brought a pregnancy test to try and turn the screws."

"So the child she was carrying was yours!"

"Of course it wasn't," he spluttered angrily.

"How can you be sure?"

"The dates didn't fit with her cycle."

It was a pathetic defense. And in any case, Richard always had been a compulsive liar. And what made him dangerous was that, after a while, he ended up believing his own lies.

"If it wasn't yours, whose was it?"

"That asshole she was fucking on the sly," he said as though it were obvious. "That pretentious little philosopher...what was his name?"

"Alexis Clément."

"Clément, yeah, that's the guy."

"Do you know anything else about Vinca's disappearance?" I asked gravely.

"What could I possibly know? You don't think I was involved, do you? I was in Papeete with your brother and sister when she disappeared."

As an alibi, it was watertight.

"Why do you think she didn't take the money with her?"

"I honestly have no idea, and I don't give a damn."

He relit his cigar, which filled the room with acrid smoke, and picked up the remote. He turned up the volume. Djokovic was struggling against Nadal, who was leading 6 to 2, 5 to 4, and was now serving for a place in the final.

The air in the room was unbreathable. I needed to get out now, but Richard was not about to let me leave without giving me a last life lesson.

"It's about time you toughened up, Thomas, time you realized that life is war. Since you're such a fan of books, try rereading Roger Martin du Gard: 'All existence is a battle. Life is any victory that endures.'"

10

THE HATCHET

1.

The conversation with my father had made me feel sick, but it had not revealed anything I didn't already know. When I went back into the kitchen, my mother had moved the boxes and was busy cooking.

"I'm going to make you an apricot tart. It's still your favorite, isn't it?"

This was something I had never understood about my mother, something integral to her personality—her ability to blow hot and cold. Sometimes Annabelle would lower her defenses; she would relax, become gentler, warmer, more Mediterranean, as though Italy was suddenly prevailing over Austria. When she looked at me, her eyes would glitter with a spark akin to love. For a long time, I craved that spark, watched for it, waited for it, always hoping it would be the prelude to a more enduring blaze. But the flame never rose above a flicker. Over time, I learned not to be taken in.

"Don't put yourself to all that trouble, Mom," I said tersely.

"But it's my *pleasure*, Thomas."

I caught her eye and gave her a look that said *Why do you do this?* She had unknotted her chignon and her hair spilled out. Her aquamarine eyes shimmered, pure and translucent. On days like today, her eyes were as fascinating as they were inscrutable. My mother, the alien, even went so far as to venture a smile.

I studied her as she took the flour and a cake tin from the cupboard. Annabelle had never been the sort of woman whom men could easily pick up. Everything about her signaled that they would be blown off. She gave the impression that she was somewhere else, on a distant planet, utterly inaccessible. Growing up with her, I had always found her *too* much—too sophisticated for the mediocre life we lived, too brilliant to be sharing her life with Richard Degalais. To me she seemed as though she belonged in the heavens, among the stars.

The sound of the entry-phone buzzer made me flinch.

"That'll be Maxime," Annabelle said, pressing the button to open the gate.

Where had this sudden burst of joy come from? While she headed off to greet my friend, I went out onto the terrace. I put on my sunglasses and watched the maroon Citroën drive through the electric gates, go up the concrete driveway, and park behind my mother's convertible. As the car doors opened, I realized that Maxime had brought his children, two cute, dark-haired little girls who seemed to know my mother very well; they ran to her, arms outstretched, and hugged her with charming impulsiveness. Maxime must have just gotten back from meeting with Vincent Debruyne at the precinct. The fact that he was here and that he had brought his daughters obviously meant that the interview had not gone too badly. As he got out of the car, I tried to read the emotions on his face. I was about to wave when the phone in my pocket vibrated. I glanced at the screen. Rafael Bartoletti, my official photographer.

"*Ciao,* Rafa," I said, picking up.

"*Ciao,* Thomas. I'm calling about that photo of your friend Vinca."

"I had a feeling you'd find her fascinating."

"Oh yes. In fact, I was so intrigued that I got my assistant to enlarge the photo."

"And?"

"As I was looking at the enlargement, I realized what it was that bothered me."

I could feel a tingling in my stomach. "Tell me."

"I'm almost certain that she's not smiling at her partner. She's not even looking at him."

"I don't get it. Who is she looking at, then?"

"Someone about six or seven meters in front of her and a little to her left. If you want my opinion, Vinca's not even dancing with the guy in the photo; it's just an optical illusion."

"Are you saying it's been Photoshopped?"

"No, not at all, though it has obviously been cropped. Take my word for it, your pretty little *ragazza* is smiling at someone else."

Someone else . . .

I found this difficult to believe, but I thanked Rafa and promised to keep him in the loop. I texted Pianelli and asked whether he had managed to contact Claude Angevin, the former *Nice-Matin* editor who might know who had taken the photograph.

Then I went down the steps and joined my mother, Maxime, and his daughters on the lawn. The first thing I noticed was the thick file under his arm. I shot him a quizzical look.

"We'll talk later," he whispered, reaching for a bag containing a stuffed dog and a rubber giraffe on the back seat.

He introduced me to his children, two bouncing little girls with dazzling smiles, and for a few minutes, thanks to their antics, we were able to forget our troubles. Emma and Louise were funny and utterly delightful. From the way my mother treated them—and the way my father did when he eventually joined us—I realized that Maxime was a regular visitor to the house. Seeing my parents playing the role of grandparents was charming if faintly ridiculous and, for a moment, it occurred to me that Maxime had filled the vacuum in the family that I left when I moved away. But I did not feel bitter. On the contrary, I felt that it was all the more important to protect him from what we had done.

After about fifteen minutes, my mother took the girls into the kitchen to help her make the apricot tart—the secret ingredient was lavender seeds sprinkled over the fruit—and my father went back up to watch the Giro d'Italia.

"Right," I said to Maxime. "Time for a council of war."

2.

The place I loved most in the Villa Violette was the stone-and-timber pool house my parents had built as soon as they moved here. With an outdoor kitchen, a patio, and a canopy, it looked like a home within a home. It was my favorite spot, one where I had spent countless hours reading, curled up on the canvas sofa.

I sat down at the teak table under the arbor overgrown with Virginia creeper. Maxime sat next to me.

I didn't beat around the bush—I told him what Fanny had revealed, that, as Ahmed was dying and feeling the need to salve his conscience, he had told her how, on Francis's orders, he had walled up the body of Alexis Clément in the gym. If he had told Fanny, he might have told others. This was hardly good news, but at least it meant that we knew the identity of the traitor. Well, maybe not exactly a traitor, but the person responsible for our past coming back to haunt us.

"Ahmed died in November. If he'd talked to the cops, they would have had all the time in the world to x-ray the gym walls for a corpse," Maxime said.

Although his face was still lined with worry, he seemed less over-whelmed than he had been this morning, more in control of his emotions.

"Agreed. But he must have told someone else. What about you? How did things go down at the station?"

He ruffled the hair on the back of his neck. "Yeah, not bad. I saw Chief Debruyne. You were right, it had nothing to do with Alexis Clément."

"So what did he want?"

"He wanted to talk to me about my father."

"About what, exactly?"

"I'll explain, but first, you need to read this." He set the thick file he had brought in front of me. "Talking to Debruyne made me think about something: What if the death of my father was somehow connected to the murder of Alexis Clément?"

"You've lost me."

Maxime explained. "I think my father was murdered by the same person who's been sending the anonymous messages."

"This morning you said that Francis died during a burglary that went wrong."

"I know, but I didn't give you all the details, and after what I found out at the police station, I've got my doubts."

He nodded for me to open the dossier.

"Read that and then we'll talk. I'm going to make myself a coffee. Want one?"

I nodded. Maxime got up and went over to a recess that housed an espresso machine and some cups and saucers.

I immersed myself in the dossier, which comprised press cuttings about the wave of burglaries on the Côte d'Azur in late 2016 and early 2017. There had been about fifty incidents, all in the swanky neighborhoods of Alpes-Maritimes, from Saint-Paul de Vence to Mougins by way of mansions in Cannes and the countryside inland from Nice. The modus operandi was always the same: Four or five guys in balaclavas would burst into the house, spray the family with tear gas, tie them up, and lock them in a room. The gang was armed, violent, and dangerous. They were primarily interested in cash and jewelry. On several occasions they had not hesitated to rough up their victims to get PIN codes for credit cards or the combination to a safe.

The whole area had lived in fear of these home invasions, which had resulted in two deaths, a cleaning woman who died of a heart attack when the gang burst in, and Francis Biancardini. In Aurelia Park alone, the gated community where Maxime's father had lived, there had been three burglaries. It seemed almost inconceivable; Aurelia Park was one of the most heavily guarded estates on the Côte.

Among the robbery victims were a distant relative of the Saudi royal family and a prominent French art collector, patron, and dignitary. Although the latter had not been home during the incident, the furious gang, frustrated at not being able to find anything salable in the villa, had destroyed the paintings hanging on the walls. What they did not know was that among them was a very valuable work of art: *Dig Up the Hatchet,* by Sean Lorenz, one of the hottest painters on the market. The destruction of the work had sent shock waves through the contemporary art world, even in America. The *New York Times* and CNN mentioned the break-in and talked about Aurelia Park, once the flagship estate on the Côte d'Azur, as a dangerous area; in the space of three months, property prices had plummeted by 30 percent. To stem the panic, the regional serious crimes office had set up a dedicated team to track down the burglars.

From this point, the investigation moved quickly—DNA samples, phone tapping, high-level surveillance. In early February, the cops conducted a dawn raid on several homes in a small village on the Italian border and arrested a dozen Macedonian men, some without papers, others known to have been involved in similar crimes. A search of the houses uncovered jewelry, a significant amount of cash, firearms, ammunition, computer equipment, and fake passports. Officers also found balaclavas, knives, and a number of additional stolen items. Five weeks later, they tracked down the head of the gang, who was hiding out in a hotel in Drancy. He had already sold much of the loot in Eastern Europe. The suspects were transferred to Nice, where they were charged and held in custody to await trial. Most of them pleaded guilty to several charges but denied involvement in the raid on Francis's villa. This was hardly surprising, since a man who admitted to that could be charged with voluntary manslaughter and sent to prison for twenty years.

3.

I shuddered as I leafed through the press clippings, at once horrified and excited. The remaining documents related to the home invasion and the vicious assault on Francis Biancardini. Maxime's father had not been merely roughed up; he had been beaten to death. The articles described his grotesquely swollen face, numerous lacerations to his body, and deep cuts left on his wrists by handcuffs. I was beginning to understand what Maxime was getting at. In my mind, I fleshed out a scenario: Ahmed had confessed to someone who had then tracked Francis down and tortured him, perhaps to force him to confess. But confess to what? His role in the death of Alexis Clément? Ours?

I continued reading. Angélique Guibal, a journalist with the *Nouvel Observateur,* had managed to gain access to the police file. Although her article was primarily focused on the destruction of the Sean Lorenz painting, she mentioned the other break-ins in Aurelia Park. From what she had been able to discover, Francis Biancardini was still alive when his attackers left the villa; he had dragged himself to the window and tried to scrawl a name in blood on the glass. As though he had known his assailants.

The story made my blood run cold. I had been fond of Francis long before he helped us dispose of the body of Alexis Clément. He had always been kind to me. I felt sick at the thought of the horrors he endured in his dying moments.

I looked up from the dossier. "What was stolen in the break-in at your father's villa?"

"Just one thing, his collection of watches. Though according to the insurance, they were worth upward of three hundred thousand euros."

I remembered Francis's obsession with wristwatches, in particular his passion for Patek Philippe. He owned a dozen different models that were the pride of his collection. When I was a teenager, he loved to show them to me and tell me about them, and I inherited something of his passion. I still remembered the 1930s Calatrava, the Grand Complications, and the 1970s Nautilus designed by the legendary Gérald Genta.

A question had been nagging at me since the morning.

"How long had your father been living in Aurelia Park? I always assumed he still lived next door."

Maxime looked a little embarrassed.

"He had been shuttling between the two for years, even before my mother died. Aurelia Park was his project. He was one of the primary investors in the development early on, and he earmarked one of the most beautiful villas for himself. To be honest, I never wanted to set foot in the fucking place. Even after his death, I let the caretaker clear it out. It was a sort of bachelor pad where he took mistresses or call girls. I even heard he organized orgies there."

Francis had had a reputation as a womanizer. I knew he openly bragged about his conquests, though I didn't remember any names. Despite this—and despite myself—I still liked the man. He seemed to me a tortured, neurotic character. I had always felt there was something exaggerated and histrionic about his racist tirades and his macho, antifeminist rants. They seemed completely at odds with his behavior. Most of his laborers hailed from North Africa, and they worshipped him. He was an old-fashioned boss, a little paternalistic, maybe, but they knew they could count on him. As for his attitude toward the female sex, it was my mother who once pointed out that most of the senior figures in his company were in fact women.

A memory resurfaced in my mind, and it was quickly followed by a second.

The first: Hong Kong, 2007. I'm thirty-three. I've just published my third novel. My agent has organized a promotional tour of Asia— the French Institute in Hanoi, a bookstore called Le Pigeonnier in Taipei, the prestigious Ewha University in Seoul, Parenthèses, the famous French bookshop in Hong Kong. I'm sitting with a journalist in the bar on the twenty-fifth floor of the Mandarin Oriental. Outside the window, the Hong Kong skyline rolls away into the distance, and yet for several minutes, I have been oblivious to the view, staring at a man sitting several tables away. It is Francis Biancardini, though I barely recognize him. He is reading the *Wall Street Journal,* wearing an elegant tailored suit (*spalla con rollino* shoulders, Parisian *bocca di lupo* lapels), and he is clearly fluent enough in English to discuss the relative merits of Japanese and Scotch whiskeys with the waiter. At some point, the journalist realizes that I am no longer listening to her and becomes irritated. I quickly recover; I pretend to think hard and then offer a perceptive response to her question. When I look up again, Francis has disappeared.

The second: It's spring 1990. I'm fifteen. I'm studying French for my *baccalauréat.* I'm alone in the house—my parents are on vacation in Spain with my brother and sister. I enjoy the solitude. I spend all day buried in the books on the syllabus: *Les liaisons dangereuses, L'éducation sentimentale, Aurélien*...every book leads to another book, every discovery urges me to explore the music, the art, and the ideas of the period. Late one morning, I collect the mail and notice that the mailman has accidentally included a letter addressed to Francis. I decide to bring it to him. Since there is no fence between the two houses, I go around the back and walk across the lawn. One of the French doors is standing open. Without calling out, I walk into the living room, intending to simply leave the letter on a table. Suddenly, I see Francis sitting in an armchair. He hasn't heard me over the Schubert impromptu playing on the stereo (curious in itself in a house more accustomed to Michel Sardou and Johnny Hallyday). Even more improbably, Francis is reading. And it is not just any book. I can see the cover reflected in the window: *Memoirs of Hadrian,* by Marguerite Yourcenar. I am stunned. Francis likes to boast that, aside from the sex scenes in Gérard de Villiers's racy spy novels, he doesn't read. He openly rails against the arty types and intellectuals living in their ivory towers while he has been breaking his back working on building sites since the age of fourteen. I tiptoe out of the room, my mind swirling with questions. I have often seen morons try to pass themselves off as intelligent, but this is the first time I have seen an intelligent man try to pass himself off as a moron.

4.

"Papa! Papa!"

I was roused from my memories by shouts. From the far end of the lawn, Emma and Louise were running toward us with my mother trailing behind. Instinctively, I snapped shut the dossier and the horrors it contained.

As the little girls clambered over their father, my mother said, "I'll leave the girls with you. I'm going to buy some more apricots at Vergers de Provence."

She waved the keys to the Mini Cooper that I'd left on the hall stand when I arrived. "I'll take your car, Thomas. Maxime's car is blocking mine."

"That's okay, Annabelle, I'll move it."

"No, no, don't worry. I need to pop by the shopping center and I'm already running late."

She turned to me and said pointedly, "And this way, Thomas can't sneak off like a thief or turn his nose up at my apricot tart."

"But I need to go somewhere. I need my car!"

"You can take mine. The keys are in the ignition."

Without giving me time to protest, my mother turned on her heel. My phone started to vibrate. Unknown number. I hesitated, then took the call. It was Claude Angevin, former editor of *Nice-Matin* and Stéphane Pianelli's mentor.

He was a nice enough guy but impossible to shut up. He told me that he had moved to Portugal, to the Douro, and then spent at least five minutes trying to sell me on the wonders of the region. Eventually I steered him back to the Vinca Rockwell case and tried to get a sense of what he thought of the official story.

"I think it's horseshit, but we'll never be able to prove different."

"Why do you think that?"

"Call it a hunch. I always thought that everyone—the cops, the press, the families—missed something in the investigation. Actually, to be honest, I think the whole investigation was flawed."

"In what way?"

"From the start, we missed out on something crucial. I'm not talking about details here, I'm talking about something big. Something no one noticed. And we all ended up heading down the wrong path. Do you get what I'm saying?"

Although what he was saying was vague, I did understand, and I agreed with him.

"Stéphane told me you wanted to know who took the prom photo," he said.

"Yeah—do you know?"

"*Claro que sei!* It was one of the parents, Yves Dalanegra."

The name rang a faint bell. Angevin refreshed my memory.

"I looked him up. He was the father of Florence and Olivia Dalanegra."

I vaguely remembered Florence, a sporty girl who had been half a head taller than me. We had been in the same year for the *baccalauréat*. She took mostly science subjects and I was studying literature, but we were in the same PE class. I probably even played with her on the coed handball team. But I had no memory of her father.

"He was the one who offered us the photo back in '93, after we published the first article about Vinca and Alexis Clément. We were happy to buy the rights. We ended up using it a lot."

"Did someone at *Nice-Matin* crop the photo?"

"No—at least, not as far as I remember. I think we published exactly what we were given."

"Have you any idea where Yves Dalanegra lives these days?"

"Yeah, I just dug up the information. Give me your e-mail and I'll send it to you, but prepare yourself for a surprise."

I gave him my e-mail address and thanked him for his help. Angevin asked me to keep in touch if I made any headway in my investigation.

"Vinca Rockwell isn't someone you can just forget," he said.

By the time I hung up, the coffee that Maxime had made was ice cold. I got up to make another cup. Once Maxime was sure the girls were occupied, he joined me by the coffee machine.

"You still haven't told me why Debruyne wanted you to come to the police station."

"He wanted me to identify something linked to the death of my father."

"Don't be so damned coy. Identify what, exactly?"

"Last Wednesday night, there was a high wind off the coast. The tide brought in a lot of seaweed and other junk. The day before yesterday, a public-health team was sent down to clean up the beach."

Staring vaguely at his daughters, he took a sip of coffee.

"On Salis Beach, one of them found a canvas bag washed up by the tide. You'll never guess what was inside."

I shook my head.

"My father's watches, the whole collection."

I tried to take in the magnitude of this revelation.

The Macedonians had had nothing to do with the death of Francis. There had been no burglary. Whoever had murdered Francis had been clever enough to use the wave of home invasions to cover up the crime; he'd taken the collection of watches to make it look like a burglary and then tossed them into the sea to get rid of the evidence in case there was a search.

I shot Maxime a look and both of us turned back to the girls. I felt a cold shiver course through me. Whoever was tracking us was a cunning, determined enemy, not—as I had assumed—a blackmailer or someone trying to frighten us.

We were dealing with a murderer.

A killer prepared to stop at nothing in his quest for revenge.

DIFFERENT
FROM OTHER BOYS

I put the top down on my mother's convertible, and, surrounded by the azure sky and the lush scrubland, I drove inland. The view was pastoral, the weather was calm—the complete opposite of how I felt.

I was terrified, yes, but excited too, almost elated. Though I dared not admit it even to myself, for the first time in twenty-five years I had a flicker of hope: I was utterly convinced that Vinca was alive, that I would track her down, and that, once I did so, my life would again have meaning and gaiety, and the guilt I had been dragging around for years would finally fade away.

Not only would I discover the truth about the Vinca Rockwell affair; I would emerge from my investigation revitalized, maybe even happy. I really believed that I would free Vinca from the mysterious prison where she languished, and she in turn would free me from the pain and suffering of my lost decades.

In the early days, I had searched tirelessly for Vinca. Then, as the years passed, I waited for her to find me. But I never gave up, because I had an ace up my sleeve that only I knew about. Another memory. Not concrete evidence, perhaps, but a firm conviction. One that, in a court of law, can destroy a life or give it new impetus.

* * *

It had happened some years earlier. In 2010, between Christmas and New Year's, New York was brought to a shuddering halt by a blizzard, one of the worst the city had ever seen. The airports were closed, all flights canceled, and for three days, Manhattan was buried under a mantle of snow and ice. On December 28, when the storm passed, the sun emerged and the whole city shimmered. At about midday, I left my apartment and strolled toward Washington Square. On the west side of the park, where the chess players gathered, I agreed to a game with Sergei, an elderly Russian who'd beaten me twice before, winning twenty bucks each time. I sat down at the stone table determined to take my revenge.

I remembered the moment perfectly. I was just about to take his bishop, and as I picked up my knight, I looked up and it was as though I had been stabbed through the heart.

There was Vinca, sitting on a bench not more than fifteen meters away.

She was reading a book, her legs crossed, holding a Starbucks cup. She looked radiant. More fulfilled, more gentle than she had ever been at school. She was wearing stonewashed jeans, a suede jacket, a thick scarf, and a woolen cap. Despite the cap, I could tell that her hair was shorter and no longer had red highlights. I rubbed my eyes. The book she was reading was one of mine. As I was about to call out, she looked up. For a second, our eyes met, and—

"Shit, man! You gonna play or what?" Sergei said.

I lost sight of Vinca as a gaggle of Chinese tourists traipsed into the park. I got to my feet and pushed my way through them, but when I reached the bench, she had disappeared.

★ ★ ★

How much should I trust that memory? It had been only a fleeting glimpse, I admit. Fearing that I might forget it, I had played it over and over in my mind to engrave it in my brain forever. Because I found the memory calming, I clung to it, knowing that it was fragile. All memories are reconstructions and contain some element of fiction, and this one seemed too good to be true.

As the years passed, I began to doubt its authenticity. But now, the incident acquired new meaning. I thought about what Claude Angevin had said: *Everyone—the cops, the press, the families—missed something in the investigation. Actually, to be honest, I think the whole investigation was flawed. From the start, we missed out on something crucial.*

Angevin was right. But things were changing now. Truth was on the march. Maybe there was a killer tracking me, but I was not afraid, because through him, I would be able to find Vinca. The killer was my only chance.

But I could not beat him alone. To uncover the secret of Vinca's disappearance, I needed to go back to the past, to revisit the boy who was not like other boys, the boy I had been in my last years at Saint-Ex. The young man who had been positive, courageous, pure of heart, touched by a sort of grace. I knew that I could not bring him back to life, but he had never completely disappeared. Even in my darkest moments, I carried him within me. Sometimes a smile, a word, a flash of wisdom reminded me of who I used to be.

In my search for Vinca, I was also—perhaps especially— investigating myself.

11

BEHIND HER SMILE

1.

Yves Dalanegra lived in a huge house in the hills above Biot. Rather than show up unannounced, I called the number Claude Angevin had given me. First stroke of luck: although Dalanegra spent half the year living in Los Angeles, he was currently on the Côte d'Azur. Second stroke of luck: he knew who I was—Florence and Olivia, the lanky daughters I had known at school and only vaguely remembered, liked me and read my novels. He immediately suggested I pop by and see him at his villa cum studio on the chemin des Vignasses.

Prepare yourself for a surprise, Angevin had said. From Dalanegra's website, his Wikipedia page, and a number of online articles, I quickly realized that, these days, the man was considered one of the great living photographers, having taken a career path as surprising as it was unusual. Until his forties, Dalanegra had been a respectable family man, an auditor with a small accounting firm in Nice; he had been married to his wife, Catherine, for more than twenty years, and they had two daughters. Then, in 1995, his mother died, and this triggered a sudden and complete change. Dalanegra got divorced, quit his job, and moved to New York to follow his dream: photography.

Two years later, in an interview with *Libération,* he explained that it was at this point that he'd decided to come out as gay. He'd shot to fame with photographic nudes whose aesthetic owed something to the work of Irving Penn and Helmut Newton. Then, over the years, his work became more individual, and he photographed only bodies that fell outside the traditional canon of beauty—women who were heavily overweight or particularly small; models who had suffered severe burns; amputees; patients undergoing chemotherapy—singular bodies that Dalanegra managed to transform into something pure and flawless.

Although initially dubious, I found that I was dazzled by the raw power of his work, which was neither tasteless nor voyeuristic. The aesthetic was closer to that of the great Flemish artists than to a politically correct advertising campaign celebrating the diversity of the human form. Sophisticated, imaginatively composed, with studied lighting, his photographs were like the paintings of the old masters, taking the viewer into a world where beauty flirted with pleasure, sensual delight, and rapture.

I drove slowly along the little road flanked by olive groves and drystone walls that wound steeply uphill. From each patch of flat terrain, a narrower road branched off toward a group of houses— renovated farmhouses, contemporary residences, small developments built in the 1970s. I rounded a hairpin bend and was startled to see that the gnarled olive trees with their rustling leaves had disappeared; in their place was a glorious palm grove, as though a Moroccan oasis had been relocated to Provence. Yves Dalanegra had given me the access code. I parked in front of the wrought-iron gate and walked up the palm-lined pathway toward the house.

Unexpectedly, something bounded toward me, growling—a huge Anatolian sheepdog. I had been terrified of dogs ever since I was attacked by a Beauceron at a friend's birthday party when I was six. I had almost lost an eye, and the incident had left me with a scar on the bridge of my nose and a visceral fear of dogs.

"Ulysses! Down, boy!"

Someone I assumed was the groundskeeper, a short man whose brawny arms were disproportionate to his frame, appeared behind the huge hound, wearing a sailor's shirt and a cap that made him look like Popeye.

"Settle down!" he said, raising his voice. "Good dog!"

The dog stood its ground, refusing to let me pass. It could clearly sense my fear.

"I'm here to see Monsieur Dalanegra," I called. "He gave me the code to the gate."

The man was more than happy to believe me, but Ulysses had already sunk his teeth into my trouser cuff. I tried and failed to choke back a scream, which forced the groundskeeper to intervene. He pulled the dog away with his bare hands.

"Get off, Ulysses!" A little vexed, Popeye apologized profusely. "I don't know what's gotten into him. Usually, he's like a big teddy bear. Must be something he can smell on you."

The smell of fear, I thought as I walked on.

Yves Dalanegra had had an architect design the house, an L-shaped mansion in the Californian style built from blocks of translucent concrete. A vast infinity pool offered a stunning view of the hills and the village of Biot. An operatic aria drifted from the half-open windows, the famous act-two duet from Strauss's *Rosenkavalier.* Curiously, there was no bell by the front door. I knocked, but there was no answer, probably because the music was so loud. In true Provençal manner, I went around to the garden, heading toward the source of the music.

Dalanegra spotted me and gestured for me to come through one of the French doors.

He was just finishing a shoot. The whole house was one vast loft space that served as a photographer's studio. Dalanegra's model, now getting dressed, was a voluptuous beauty whom—I could tell from the staging and the props—the artist had just immortalized in the pose of one of Goya's masterpieces, *La Maja desnuda*. I had read somewhere that this was Dalanegra's latest obsession, reproducing old masters using plus-size models. The staging was kitsch but not tacky—a green velvet chaise longue, soft cushions, lace fringes, and gossamer sheets foaming like waves.

Dalanegra greeted me in English.

"Hey, Thomas. How are you? Come on in, come on in, we're just finished!"

Physically, he looked like Christ, or—to continue with more artistic comparisons—like a self-portrait by Albrecht Dürer: curly, shoulder-length hair; a gaunt, symmetrical face; a neatly trimmed beard; deep-set, piercing eyes. His clothes, however, were a very different matter: embroidered jeans, a fringed buckskin jacket, and leather ankle boots.

"I couldn't work out what you were trying to explain over the phone. I just flew in from LA last night and I'm extremely jet-lagged."

He gestured for me to sit at one end of a long wooden table while he showed his model out. Looking at the photos plastered everywhere, I realized that men did not exist in Dalanegra's work. They were banished, wiped off the map, leaving women to blossom in a world delivered from (male) evil.

When he reappeared, Dalanegra chatted animatedly about his daughters, then about an actress he had photographed who'd starred in a film based on one of my books. When he had finally exhausted these subjects, he said, "So, what can I do for you?"

2.

"Oh yes, of course I took that photo," Dalanegra said.

I had gotten straight to the point and showed him the cover of Pianelli's book. He almost snatched it from my hands to examine it, acting as though he hadn't seen it in years. "It was at the prom, wasn't it?"

"More likely the winter dance, mid-December 1992."

He nodded. "I was running the school photography club at the time. I popped in only to take a few snaps of Florence and Olivia, but once there, I got carried away and took photos of anything and everything. It was only weeks later, when people started talking about the girl who had run away with her teacher, that it occurred to me to develop the shots. This was part of the first contact sheet. I offered it to *Nice-Matin,* and they bought it immediately."

"But it's been cropped, hasn't it?"

He peered at the picture. "You're right—you've got a good eye. I obviously cropped it to focus on the two dancers, make it more dramatic."

"Have you still got the original?"

"I've had all my photographs since 1974 converted to digital."

I assumed that meant I was in luck, but then he frowned.

"They're all stored on a server somewhere—*in the cloud,* as they say these days."

Seeing my reaction, he offered to Skype his assistant in LA. A young Japanese woman appeared on his computer screen. She was not quite awake.

With her long turquoise pigtails, her immaculate white shirt, and her school tie, she looked like a cosplayer heading to a manga convention.

"Hey, Yuko, could you do me a favor?" Dalanegra explained exactly what he was looking for and Yuko promised to get back to us as quickly as possible. When he ended the call, he went around the granite kitchen counter, grabbed a blender, filled it with a handful of spinach, some slices of banana, and some coconut milk, and whizzed it into a greenish smoothie that he poured into two tall glasses.

"Taste that," he said, coming back to join me. "Very good for your stomach lining."

"I don't suppose you've got a whiskey?"

"Sorry, I quit drinking about twenty years ago." He took a long swig of the smoothie and then returned to the subject of Vinca. "The thing about that girl was you didn't have to be a pro to take a decent photo of her," he said, setting his glass down. "You just pushed the button and when you developed the shot, she looked even better than she had in real life. I've rarely seen someone with such extraordinary grace."

I raised an eyebrow. Dalanegra was talking as though he had photographed Vinca on numerous occasions.

"Sure I did," he said when I posed the question.

Seeing that I was confused, he related an incident I'd known nothing about.

"Two or three months before she disappeared, Vinca asked me to take some photos of her. I thought she wanted to be a model and was trying to put together a portfolio like a couple of my daughters' friends, but she told me that the photos were for her boyfriend."

He reached over, grabbed the mouse, and opened up a browser.

"We did two really good sessions. Soft-core—what they used to call glamour shots."

"Did you keep copies?"

"No. That was part of the deal, and I didn't insist. But the strange thing is that they showed up online a couple of weeks ago."

He turned the monitor toward me. It was the Instagram page for the Heterodites, the feminist club at Saint-Ex obsessed with Vinca. The girls had uploaded about twenty photographs from the sessions Dalanegra had been discussing.

"How did they get hold of the pictures?"

Dalanegra turned up his palms in a helpless gesture.

"My agent got in touch because there were copyright issues. The girls claim they were sent to them anonymously."

I studied the previously unpublished pictures, feeling a swell of emotion. It was a hymn to beauty. Everything that made Vinca so attractive was there. Nothing about Vinca was perfect. Her singular beauty was made up of a collection of tiny imperfections that, together, created a poised, graceful unity, proving the old maxim that the whole is more than the sum of its parts.

Behind her smile, behind her faintly arrogant mask, I could make out an anguish I had not noticed at the time, an insecurity that confirmed something I had later experienced with other women: beauty was not simply physical, it was an intellectual experience, a nebulous power—it was sometimes unclear whether you were using it or it was using you.

"Later, Vinca asked me to take more photos," Dalanegra went on, "trashy photos, almost porn. I refused because I got the impression that her boyfriend wanted her to do it, but she wasn't really happy about it."

"By her boyfriend, you mean Alexis Clément?"

"I assume. These days, stuff like that is banal, but back then it was pretty shady. I didn't want to get involved. Especially since..." He trailed off, groping for words.

"Especially since what?"

"It's not easy to explain. One day, Vinca would be radiant, and the next, she'd look exhausted or wasted. I thought she was pretty unstable. And then she asked me to do something that made my blood run cold—she asked me to follow her and take photos she could use to blackmail an older guy. It was sleazy and—"

Dalanegra was interrupted by a *ping* announcing the arrival of an e-mail.

"Ah, it's from Yuko," he said, glancing at the computer screen.

He double-clicked the e-mail, which contained about fifty photographs taken at the winter dance. He put on his half-moon glasses and quickly spotted the picture of Vinca and Alexis Clément dancing.

Rafa was right; the photograph had been cropped. Seen in its original size, the snapshot looked very different. Vinca and Clément were not dancing together—she was dancing by herself and staring at someone else, a man with his back to the camera, a blurred figure in the foreground.

"Shit!"

"What?"

"Your photo is a lie."

"As are all photos," he said coolly.

I grabbed a pencil and pointed to the blurred figure.

"I want to know who this guy here is. He might have had something to do with Vinca's disappearance."

"Let's look through the rest of the photos."

I pulled my chair closer to the computer, right beside Dalanegra, so we could go through the pictures together. Most of the shots were of his daughters, but in some of them, you could make out other people. Maxime's face in the background, Fanny's, some of the alumni I had met this morning, like Éric Lafitte, Hervé Lesage (Nigel from *This Is Spinal Tap*), and the brilliant Kathy Laneau. There was even a shot of me, although I had no memory of that night. I looked uncomfortable, wearing the same old blue shirt and blazer I usually wore. The teachers were always grouped in the same configuration: N'Dong, the sadistic math teacher who took a twisted pleasure in humiliating students at the blackboard; Lehmann, the manic-depressive physics teacher; and the most twisted of them all, Madame Fontana, who was utterly incapable of keeping order in class but relished settling scores in the cruelest way imaginable during staff meetings. On the other side, the more humane teachers: Miss

DeVille, the pretty English teacher known for her wit—with a quote from Shakespeare or Epictetus, she could shut up any disruptive student—and Monsieur Graff, my former tutor, the brilliant French teacher who had taught me in my last two years at the lycée.

"Shit! All the shots are from the same angle," I fumed as we reached the last of the images. I knew that I had come within inches of a revelation.

"It is pretty annoying," Dalanegra said, finishing his smoothie.

I hadn't even touched mine, I simply couldn't face it. The light in the room had waned. Designed to heighten the play of light, the translucent concrete transformed the house into a chamber where the slightest shift in daylight created flickering shadows that glided like ghosts.

I thanked Dalanegra for his help and before I left asked if he could e-mail me the complete set of pictures, which he did there and then.

"Do you know whether anyone else was taking photos that night?" I said as I reached the door.

"A couple of the students, maybe," he said. "But this was before digital cameras came along, and people were careful about wasting film in those days."

In those days . . . these last words echoed in the vast, vaulted room and suddenly I felt terribly old.

3.

I climbed back into my mother's Mercedes and drove for a while, not quite knowing where I was heading. The visit to Dalanegra had left me disappointed. Perhaps this was a wild-goose chase, but I had to follow the lead to the bitter end. I had to find out the identity of the blurred figure in the photograph.

As I approached Biot, I turned onto the route des Colles, which led to the Sophia Antipolis technology park. Some force was drawing

me back to Saint-Ex, where only this morning I had not had the
courage to face the ghosts whose existence I had so long denied.

As I drove, I mentally flicked through the photographs I had seen
at Dalanegra's place. One of them had been particularly unsettling,
a picture of a genuine ghost: Jean-Christophe Graff, my old French
teacher. I blinked, and the memories came flooding back, trailing
grief in their wake. Monsieur Graff was the teacher who had guided
my reading, fostered my desire to write from the very first. He was
kind, astute, and generous. A tall, gangly man with delicate, almost
feminine features, he always wore a scarf, even at the height of
summer. A teacher capable of extraordinary insight when it came
to literature, yet a man who seemed a little lost when it came
to reality.

Jean-Christophe Graff had committed suicide in 2002. Fifteen
years ago now. To me, he was another victim of the curse of the nice
guys—that cruel destiny that crushes people who are a little fragile
and whose only mistake is to treat others with kindness. I couldn't
remember who it was who'd claimed that fate metes out to a man
only what he can bear, but it's not true; more often than not, fate is
a cruel, twisted fucker that gets off on ruining the lives of the weak
and leaves arrogant assholes to lead long and happy lives.

I had been devastated by the news of Graff's suicide. Before jumping to his death from the balcony of his apartment, he had written to
me; the letter arrived in New York a week later. I had never talked
about it with anyone. He told me that he felt ill-equipped to deal
with life's cruelties and confessed that loneliness was killing him. He
wrote of his distress on discovering that books, which had so often
helped him survive the darkest times, no longer seemed enough to
keep his head above water. He discreetly mentioned an unrequited
love that had broken his heart. In the closing lines, he wished me
good luck with my life and told me that he felt sure that I would
succeed where he had failed: I would find a soul mate with whom to

confront life's sea of troubles. But he was wrong about me, and often now, in my darkest moments, I thought that it was not inconceivable that I might end my days as he had.

I shook off these depressing thoughts as I entered the pine forest. This time, I did not stop off at Dino's but drove on to the main gate of the lycée. From the look of him, the young guard was Pavel Fabianski's son. He was watching an episode of *Seinfeld* on his cell phone. I didn't have a pass, but I pretended I was here to help with preparations for the Alumni Prom, and he raised the barrier and then went back to staring at his screen. I drove onto the campus and, since I was flouting the rules, decided to park in the plaza right outside the Agora.

I walked into the library, hopped over the turnstile, and made my way to the main reading room. Good news: Zélie was nowhere to be seen. A notice pinned to a corkboard by the desk announced that the drama club—of which she was the high priestess—met every Wednesday and Saturday afternoon.

In her place behind the reception desk, a young woman with glasses was sitting cross-legged on the office chair reading Bukowski's *On Writing* in English. She had soft features and was wearing a sailor's top, tweed shorts, embroidered tights, and two-tone lace-up oxfords.

"Hello. Do you work with Eline Bookmans?"

She looked up from her book and smiled.

I instantly took a liking to her. I liked the way her severe chignon contrasted with her diamond nose piercing; I liked the tattoo that swirled down from behind her ear and disappeared under the collar of her top; I liked the READING IS SEXY mug from which she was drinking tea. It was something that rarely happened to me. It was nothing like love at first sight, simply an immediate sense that the person I was dealing with was *on my side* rather than in the enemy camp or in the vast no-man's-land of people with whom I had nothing in common.

"I'm Pauline Delatour," she said. "Are you one of the new teachers?"

"Not really, I'm—"

"Just kidding; I know who you are, Thomas Degalais. Everyone saw you on the place des Marronniers this morning."

"I used to go to school here, a long time ago," I said. "Probably before you were born."

"I think that's a bit of an exaggeration, and if you're attempting to pay me a compliment, you'll have to try harder." Pauline Delatour laughed, pushed a stray lock of hair behind her ear, uncrossed her legs, and stood up. I realized what it was about her that I found attractive—she was confident in her sexuality without being in the least conceited; she had a real joie de vivre and a sort of natural grace.

"You're not from around here, are you?" I asked.

"Around here?"

"The south, the Côte d'Azur."

"No, I'm from Paris. I came here six months ago when the position was created."

"Maybe you can help me, Pauline. Back when I was here, there was a school paper called *Courrier Sud*."

"There still is."

"I'd like to consult some old issues."

"I'll get them for you. What year are you interested in?"

"Let's say 1992 to '93. And if you could bring me the yearbook too, that would be great."

"Are you looking for anything in particular?"

"I'm looking for information about a former student, Vinca Rockwell."

"Of course, the famous Vinca Rockwell. Everyone here has heard about her."

"Is that because of Stéphane Pianelli's book, the one Zélie is trying to ban?"

"It's because of the spoiled rich girls who claim to be feminists be-cause they've read the first three chapters of *The Handmaid's Tale*."

"The Heterodites..."

"They're appropriating the memory of this girl and trying to turn her into some sort of symbolic figure she never was."

Pauline Delatour tapped at her computer and copied out the reference numbers for the issues I had asked for on a Post-it.

"Take a seat. I'll bring you the issues as soon as I find them."

4.

I sat where I always used to sit, at the far end of the room in a little alcove next to the window that looked out onto a completely anachronistic courtyard. With its flagstones, its ivy-covered fountain, and a colonnade in pink limestone, it had always reminded me of a cloister. All that was missing were the Gregorian chants.

I placed the blue Eastpak backpack I'd retrieved from my parents' basement on the desk and took out my pens and books as though I were about to write an essay. I felt content. Whenever I was surrounded with books or in an academic environment, I would feel a calmness flow through me, feel my worries physically ebb—it was as effective as Valium, but not as portable.

Suffused with the smell of wax and melted candles, this area of the library—pompously named the Literary Chamber—had retained its charm. I felt as though I were in a sanctuary. Old Lagarde et Michard grammar manuals were gathering dust on the shelves. On the wall behind me, a Vidal Lablache school map—hopelessly outdated even when I was a student—showed the world as it had been in the 1950s, with countries that had long since disappeared: the USSR, the GDR, Yugoslavia, Czechoslovakia...

Like Proust with his madeleine, I felt memories flooding back. This was the desk where I had done my homework and my studying. This was where I had written my first short story. I remembered something my father had said: *You live in this romantic, literary world, but real life is nothing like that. Real life is brutal... "All existence is a battle."* And my mother's comment: *You didn't have any friends, Thomas. The only friends you had were your books.*

It was true, and I was proud of it. I had always been convinced that books had saved me, but could they really keep doing that for the rest of my life? Probably not. Reading between the lines, I thought that surely this was what Jean-Christophe Graff was trying to say in his letter: there had come a point when books had let him down and he had jumped to his death. To solve the Vinca Rockwell case, perhaps I had to abandon the sheltered world of books and grapple with the dark, brutal world my father talked about.

Go into battle, whispered a voice inside me.

"These are the issues you wanted, and the yearbook."

The confident voice of Pauline Delatour brought me back to reality.

"Can I ask you a question?" she said, setting down several issues of the *Courrier Sud.*

"You don't seem to be someone who waits for permission."

"Why did you never write anything about the Vinca Rockwell affair?"

Whatever I did, whatever I said, there was always someone to steer me back to books.

"I'm a novelist, not a journalist."

"You know what I mean," she insisted. "Why did you never tell Vinca's story?"

"Because it's a tragic story and I've had enough of tragedy."

It would take more than this to put off Pauline Delatour.

"But surely that's the gift of the novelist, isn't it? To write fiction in order to confront reality. Not simply to put it right, but to fight it on its own ground. To analyze it, the better to refute it. To understand it so that, in good conscience, you can present a different world."

"Did you come up with that little speech?"

"No, of course not—*you* did. You come out with it in interviews all the time. But I suppose it's more difficult to apply it in real life, isn't it?"

And with these words, she turned and left, satisfied with the effect they had had.

12

THE GIRLS WITH
FLAME-RED HAIR

1.

I spread the copies of *Courrier Sud* out in front of me and immediately picked up the January 1993 issue, the one that had an article about the winter dance. I hoped there would be a lot of photographs, but unfortunately there were only a couple of official school pictures of the dance, and the blurred figure I was looking for was not in either of them.

Disappointed, I leafed through other issues to immerse myself in the atmosphere of the time. *Courrier Sud* was a perfect window onto school life in the early 1990s. Every possible activity was covered in detail. I flicked through the pages at random, dipping into the events that punctuated the monotony of school life: the sports results, the fifth-year class trip to San Francisco, the listings for the film club (Hitchcock, Cassavetes, Pollack), behind the scenes of the school radio station, poems and prose by students taking the writers' workshop. Jean-Christophe Graff had published my first short story in the spring of 1992. In September, the drama club announced its program for the coming year. Among the plays was a loose adaptation—probably by my mother, who was running the club at the time—of scenes from Patrick Süskind's *Perfume,* with Vinca as "the girl from the rue des Marais" and Fanny as Laure Richis. Two redheads with pale blue eyes, pure, seductive, and—if my memory of the novel serves—both murdered by Jean-Baptiste Grenouille. I had no memory of seeing the play or of what the response to it was. I opened Pianelli's book to see whether the play had cropped up during his investigation, but he made no mention of it. But as I scanned the book, I came across copies of the letters Alexis Clément had sent to Vinca.

As I reread the letters for the hundredth time, a shiver ran through me. I felt that same frustration I had experienced at Dalanegra's house, of being within a hairbreadth of the truth only to have it slip through my fingers. There was some connection between the contents of these letters and Clément's personality, but, try as I might, I came up against a mental block, as though my conscious mind feared these "repressed memories." The problem was me—my guilt, my long-standing belief that I was to blame for the tragedy, that, consumed by my own pain, my own destructive passion, I had been too blind to realize that Vinca was going off the rails.

On a hunch, I picked up my cell phone and called my father.

"Could you do me a favor, Dad?"

"What is it?" he grumbled.

"I left some papers on the table in the kitchen."

"I noticed. It's a mess."

"Among them are some of my old philosophy essays. Do you see them?"

"No."

"Oh, come on, Dad, make an effort. Or put Mom on."

"She's not back yet. Okay, hang on, I'll need my glasses."

I explained that I needed him to use his phone to take photos of the notes Alexis Clément had scribbled in the margins of my essays and text the pictures to me. It was a two-minute job for most people, but it took my father at least fifteen, punctuated by caustic comments. He was so furious by the time he finished that he ended the conversation by saying, "You're forty-two years old, for God's sake. Don't you have anything better to do than trawl through memories of your school days? Is that the sum total of your life? Stirring up the past and annoying the shit out of the rest of us?"

"Thanks, Dad. See you later."

I opened up the pictures of Alexis Clément's notes. Like many pretentious writers, he liked nothing more than his own words, but it was not his philosophical musings I was interested in; it was his handwriting. I zoomed in. It was sloppy—not a spidery scrawl, more like a doctor's writing on a prescription. You had to pause every now and then over a word or phrase.

As I studied the pictures, my heart began to race. I compared them with the letters Vinca had received and the dedication in the book of poems by Marina Tsvetaeva. Before long, there was no doubt in my mind. While the letters and the dedication were written by the same hand, they were absolutely *nothing* like Alexis Clément's notes on my philosophy essays.

2.

I could feel my whole body trembling. Vinca's lover had not been Alexis *Clément*. There was another man, another Alexis. Probably the blurred figure with his back to the camera in the photographs; that was the man she ran away with that Sunday morning in December. *Alexis forced me. I didn't want to sleep with him!* Vinca's words were right, but my interpretation had been wrong. Because of a cropped photograph and some rumors spread by classmates, everyone had assumed that Vinca had had an affair with a man who had never been her lover.

My ears were thrumming. The discovery had so many implications that I was having trouble getting my head around them. The first was also the most tragic: Maxime and I had killed an innocent man. I could still hear Alexis Clément's screams as I shattered his ribs and his knee. The whole scene came back to me in flashes that were crystal clear. His vacant expression as I lashed out with the crowbar. *How dare you touch her, you fucking creep?* His face had been a mask of surprise and incomprehension. He had not defended himself simply because he didn't know what he was being accused of. Seeing his bewilderment at the time, I had heard a small voice inside my head, felt a force that made me drop my weapon. And it was at this point that Maxime arrived on the scene.

Tears in my eyes, I buried my face in my hands. It was my fault that Alexis Clément was dead. There was nothing I could do to bring him back. I spent ten minutes utterly distraught before I could even begin to think about what came next. I thought about my misunderstanding. Vinca had clearly had a lover named Alexis, but it had not been my philosophy teacher. It was scarcely believable. Too bizarre to be true. And yet it was the only possible explanation.

So who was he? After racking my brain, I dimly remembered a student named Alexis Stephanopoulos or something like that. A caricature of a rich Greek kid; the son of a shipowner who, during summer vacations, invited his friends on cruises around the Cyclades. Needless to say, I was never invited.

I picked up the 1992–1993 yearbook. It was very American in style, with photographs of all the students and teachers at Saint-Ex that year. Feverishly, I thumbed the pages. People were listed in alphabetical order, so I quickly came across the Greek boy: Antonopoulos, Alexis, born April 26, 1974, in Thessaloniki. In the photo, he was just as I remembered him; he had curly, shoulder-length hair and was wearing a white shirt and a polo sweater with an embroidered crest. The picture kindled other memories.

I remembered that he was one of the few boys studying humanities. He was an athlete of some sort, a champion rower or fencer. Not terribly intelligent but capable of reciting passages by Sappho or Theocritus. Beneath the veneer of sophistication, however, Alexis Antonopoulos was a dumb wannabe Latin lover. I had trouble imagining Vinca falling head over heels for such a moron. Of course, I was hardly the best person to hold forth on that subject.

But what if, for some reason I couldn't begin to image, Antonopoulos did have it in for Maxime and me? I rummaged through my bag for my iPad then remembered I had left it in the rental car my mother had borrowed. I had to make do with my phone. I Googled the name, and the first mention of Alexis Antonopoulos I found was in a *Point de Vue* article about the marriage of Prince Carl Philip of Sweden in 2015. Antonopoulos, accompanied by his third wife, was among the happy few invited to the ceremony. As I continued clicking, I developed a sense of the man. Part-time businessman, part-time philanthropist, he lived a jet-setting life, dividing his time between California and the Cyclades. *Vanity Fair* mentioned that he regularly attended the annual amfAR Gala at Cannes, held during the Cannes Film Festival at the celebrated Eden-Roc hotel, which raised money for AIDS research. So Antonopoulos still had ties to the Côte d'Azur, but I could find nothing to link him directly to us.

Since I was making little headway, I decided to change tack. The fundamental cause of our fears was the forthcoming demolition of the old gym. This in turn was only a small part of the pharaonic project to completely remodel the campus, a mission that included the construction of a glass-and-steel tower, a state-of-the-art sports facility with an Olympic-size pool, and a landscaped garden.

This vast project was a recurring topic—people had been talking about it for the past twenty-five years—but before this, work had not begun because the lycée simply could not raise the necessary funds. From what I knew, the funding for the school had changed radically over its history. When it was founded, Saint-Exupéry had been a private institution, but later it had been brought into France's national education system and was awarded regional grants. However, in recent years, the winds of revolution had swept through Saint-Ex, accompanied by the administrators' firm desire to free the lycée from red tape and bureaucracy. Things accelerated after the election of François Hollande, and the battle between the lycée and the government had ended in a sort of secession. Saint-Ex had regained its autonomy, but in the process it had lost any right to public funds. The school fees rose sharply, but by my calculations, this new influx of cash would be a drop in the ocean compared to the money needed for the project. In order to break ground, the lycée's administrators must have received a substantial private donation. I remembered what the headmistress had said this morning at the laying of the foundation stone. She had thanked the generous donors who had made it possible to embark on "the most ambitious building project in the history of this institution," but she had been careful not to name names. It was a lead worth investigating.

I could find nothing online—or at least, nothing that was publicly accessible. Financing for the project was shrouded in mystery. If I wanted to get anywhere, I had no choice but to get Stéphane Pianelli involved. I sent him a text message summarizing what I'd found out, and to add weight to the story, I sent him the samples of Alexis Clément's handwriting and those of the mystery man who had written the letters to Vinca.

He called back within a nanosecond. I was a little apprehensive when I answered. Pianelli was a talented sparring partner. He had a quick mind, but given my situation, I would have to feed him information while making sure that nothing I said could later be used against me, Maxime, or Fanny.

3.

"Shit, this is fucking insane!" Pianelli said with a slight Marseillaise twang. "How could we have missed it?"

He was forced to shout to be heard over the roar of the crowds in the stands watching the race in Monaco.

"All the witness statements and the rumors backed up the hypothesis," I said. "Your friend Angevin was right—we were all brainwashed from the start."

I told him about my visit to Dalanegra, the cropped photograph, and the other man in the shot.

"Hang on. Are you saying there was another guy called Alexis?"

"You got it."

There was a long silence during which Pianelli was, I knew, thinking hard. I could almost hear the cogs of his brain turning on the other end of the line. In less than a minute, he came to the same conclusion I had.

"There was another Alexis at Saint-Ex," he said. "A Greek guy. We used to tease him and call him Rastapopoulous, remember?"

"Alexis Antonopoulos."

"That's him!"

"I thought about that, but I'm pretty sure he's not the guy we're looking for."

"Why not?"

"He was an idiot. I can't imagine Vinca hooking up with him."

"That's a bit simplistic, don't you think? The guy was rich, good-looking…and if teenage girls only dated smart guys, I think you and I would have heard. Do you remember the shit we had to put up with?"

I changed the subject.

"I don't suppose you've got the lowdown on who's financing the construction at the school?"

The background noise had faded, as though Pianelli had found refuge in a soundproof room.

"In recent years, Saint-Ex has adopted the American model, tuition that costs an arm and a leg, donations by rich parents who want to see their names on a building, and a handful of scholarships awarded to poor, deserving disadvantaged kids to salve their consciences."

"But this project must run into the millions. How the hell could the school come up with that kind of cash?"

"I'm guessing they borrowed some of it. Interest rates are pretty low at the moment."

"There's no way they could get a loan to cover the full cost, Stéphane. Maybe you could look into it?"

"I don't see how it's connected to Vinca's disappearance."

"Just do it, please. There's something I want to know."

"Unless you tell me what you're looking for, I'd just be wasting my time."

"I'm trying to find out whether an individual or a single company has made a significant donation toward the construction of the new buildings, the pool, and the gardens."

"Okay, I'll get one of my interns on it."

"No, not an intern! This is serious, and it could be tricky. Ask a seasoned pro."

"Trust me, the guy I've got in mind is like a bloodhound. And he's not exactly fond of the class of people trying to take over Saint-Ex."

"A bit like you, then."

Pianelli gave a little laugh, then said, "Whose name are you expecting to come up?"

"I have no idea, Stéphane. And while we're at it, there's something else I wanted to ask you. What do you think about the murder of Francis Biancardini?"

4.

"Broadly, I think it's a good thing. It means one less evil fucker on this planet."

The joke did not make me laugh. "Seriously, though."

"I thought this was about Vinca. What the hell are you playing at?"

"I'll give you all the information I have, I promise. Do you believe the theory that it was a home invasion that went wrong?"

"Not since his collection of watches has washed up on the beach, no."

Pianelli was well informed. Chief Debruyne had probably been in touch.

"So what was it, then?"

"I think it was a revenge killing. Biancardini was the living embodiment of the cancer eating away at the Côte d'Azur—racketeering, political corruption, possible connections to the Mafia."

I leaped to the defense of Francis.

"You're way off there. The whole thing about Biancardini's links to the Calabrian Mafia is bullshit. Even when Debruyne senior was public prosecutor, he couldn't make it stick."

"As it happens, I knew Yvan Debruyne pretty well, and he let me look through some of the files."

"That's what I love about the justice system, prosecutors leaking information to journalists—"

"That's a different matter," he interrupted, "but what I *can* tell you is that Francis was in it up to his neck. You know what the guys in the Calabrian Mafia called him? Whirlpool! Because he was the one who supervised the money laundering."

"If Debruyne had had any evidence, Francis would have been charged."

"If only it were that simple." He sighed. "But I've seen the sketchy bank statements, the cash being transferred to the States, where the Calabrians have been trying to set themselves up for years."

I shunted the conversation onto a different track.

"Maxime says you've been hassling him ever since he announced that he was going into politics. Why have you been dragging up all the old files about his father? You know as well as I do that Maxime is clean, and he can't be held responsible for his father's actions."

"Where do you think the money for Maxime to set up his eco-construction company and his start-up incubator came from? Where did he get the money to finance his campaign? With the dirty money that Francis made back in the eighties. The rot set in right from the start, my friend."

"So, because of who his father was, Maxime has no right to do anything?"

"Don't pretend you don't understand."

"What I've always hated about guys like you, Stéphane, is your intransigence, the moralistic, Grand Inquisitor pose. The Committee of Public Safety as run by Robespierre."

"What I've always hated about guys like you, Thomas, is your ability to dismiss anything you find unsettling, your gift of never blaming yourself for anything."

Pianelli's tone was increasingly disparaging. I could have told him to go fuck himself, but I needed his help. I beat a tactical retreat.

"We can talk about that some other time."

"I can't understand why you'd want to defend Francis."

"Because I knew him better than you did. In the meantime, if you want to know more about his death, I can give you a tip."

"You're really good at changing the subject."

"Do you know a reporter at the *Nouvel Observateur* named Angélique Guibal?"

"Doesn't ring a bell."

"Apparently, she had access to the police file. From what I've read, Francis dragged himself through a pool of blood and tried to write the name of his killer on the window."

"Oh yeah, I read that article—bullshit Paris journalism."

"That's right—I'm so glad that, in the era of fake news, we've still got *Nice-Matin* to uphold the honor of the profession."

"You can laugh, but there's some truth in that."

"Couldn't you call up Angélique Guibal and pump her for information?"

"You really think journalists go around sharing stories with each other? I suppose you're friends with every writer in Paris?"

"If you're so much better than all the Parisian journalists, then prove it, Stéphane. Get your hands on that police file."

He paused for a second and then allowed my trap to spring shut.

"Of course we're better than the Parisians," he fumed. "Fine, I'll get your fucking police file for you."

5.

I got up to get a coffee from the vending machine on the far side of the room. Next to the machine was a door that allowed people to go out and stretch their legs in the courtyard. I wandered out and walked as far as the school's "historic" red-brick Gothic buildings.

By special dispensation, the drama club had always been allowed to use one wing of the most prestigious building. As I came to the side door, chattering students were coming down the steps. It was six o'clock; the sun was beginning to set and classes had just finished. I took the stairs that led to the little lecture hall that smelled of cedar and sandalwood. The room was empty. The walls were hung with framed photographs, the same ones that had been there for twenty-five years (Madeleine Renaud, Jean-Louis Barrault, Maria Casarès...), and posters of previous productions (*A Midsummer Night's Dream*, *L'Échange*, *Six Characters in Search of an Author*...). The Saint-Exupéry drama club had always been elitist and I had never really felt comfortable here. According to its regulations, the club accepted only twenty students. I had never wanted to join, not even when my mother was running it with Zélie. To her credit, my mother had done her best to open the club up to more students and take a less rigid approach to the repertoire, but old habits die hard and no one really wanted this bastion of old-world elitism to become an open-mic event.

Suddenly, a door at the back of the auditorium opened and Zélie appeared on the stage.

"What are you doing hanging around here, Thomas?"

I leaped up onto the stage next to her.

"Your hospitality is truly heartwarming."

She stared at me without blinking. "This isn't your home any-more. Those days are over."

"I never really felt at home anywhere, so..."

"Stop or you'll have me in tears."

Since I had only the vaguest idea of how to reel her in, I cast my first line at random.

"You're still on the board of governors, aren't you?"

"What has that got to do with you?" she said, packing her things into a leather satchel.

"Only that, if you are, you'll know who is financing all this construction work. I assume that the governors were briefed and put it to a vote."

She looked at me with renewed interest.

"The first stage of the work is being financed by a loan," she said. "That much was voted on at a meeting of the governors."

"And the rest?"

She shrugged as she closed her satchel.

"The rest will be voted on in due course, though I have to say, I have no idea how the management is planning to come up with the money."

One point to me. On the spur of the moment, I asked an unrelated question. "Do you remember Jean-Christophe Graff?"

"Of course," she said. "An excellent teacher. A fragile creature, but a decent man."

Not everything Zélie said was bullshit. "Do you know why he took his own life?"

She put me firmly in my place. "Do you really think that there is a single, logical reason to explain why people commit suicide?"

"Before he died, Jean-Christophe wrote to me. He told me that he had been in love with a woman, but that it wasn't reciprocated."

"To love and not be loved in return is the fate of many."

"Be serious, please."

"Sadly, I'm being completely serious."

"Did you know about it?"

"Jean-Christophe talked to me about it, yes."

For some unknown reason, Graff, my mentor, the most tactful and generous person I had ever known, had been fond of Zélie Bookmans.

"Do you know who the woman was?"

"Yes."

"Who?"

"You're starting to get on my nerves."

"That's the second time someone has said that to me today."

"And I fear it won't be the last."

"So who was this woman?"

"If Jean-Christophe chose not to tell you, I hardly think it is my place to do so." She sighed.

She was right, and it saddened me. But I knew why he hadn't told me.

"He was being discreet."

"Well, then, respect his discretion."

"I'll give you three names and you can tell me if they're all wrong, okay?"

"Let's not play games. Don't sully the memory of the dead."

But I knew Zélie would not be able to resist my game; for a few short minutes, it would give her power over me.

True to form, as she slipped on her jacket, she changed her mind about answering me. "If you were to suggest a name, who would be first on your list?"

The first name was obvious. "It wasn't my mother, was it?"

"No! Where do you get such ideas?" She started down the steps from the stage.

"Was it you?"

She laughed nervously. "I would have been flattered, but no."

As she reached the door, she turned. "Close the door on your way out." A malicious smile played on her lips. I had one last chance.

"Was it Vinca?"

"Game, set, and match to me. Bye-bye, Thomas!" she said and stalked out of the lecture hall.

6.

I stood on the stage before an invisible audience. The door next to the blackboard was still ajar. I vaguely remembered that it led to a room we called the sacristy. I pushed open the door and saw that little had changed. It was a large, low-ceilinged space that served a variety of functions—rehearsal area, prop room, records office.

At the far end of the room was a set of metal shelves groaning with boxes and files. Each box was labeled with a school year. I went back to the year 1992–1993. Inside, there were flyers and posters and a large Moleskine notebook detailing ticket sales for the various shows and listing sets, props, and costumes.

Everything was methodically laid out, not in my mother's small, neat handwriting, but in the sweeping, cursive strokes of Zélie Bookmans. I took the notebook over to the only window. At first glance, nothing jumped out at me, but on closer inspection I noticed something. In an inventory on March 27, 1993, Zélie noted this:

One red wig missing.

This detail did not prove anything—props were regularly mislaid, and it was not unknown for a costume to disappear. Even so, I felt that this was another step toward the truth. But toward a dark and bitter truth I did not want to uncover.

I left the lecture hall and headed back to the library. I packed my things and went over to the lending desk.

Her head thrown back, her eyes smoldering, Pauline Delatour gave a slightly affected laugh as she flirted with two of the senior students, tall, muscular, blond guys who, judging from their clothes, their comments, and their copious sweating, had just come from playing a heated tennis match.

"Thank you," I said, handing her the copies of *Courrier Sud.*

"Glad I could help, Thomas."

"Can I hang on to the yearbook for a while?"

"Sure, I'll square things with Zélie. But don't forget to send it back."

"One last thing. There was an issue missing, October 1992."

"I noticed that. It wasn't on the shelf, and I checked to see whether it had fallen down the back, but I couldn't find it."

The tennis players were giving me the evil eye. They were eager for me to leave so they could have Pauline's coquettish attentions all to themselves.

"Don't worry," I said.

I was already turning to leave when she grabbed my sleeve.

"Wait a minute. The school digitized the archives of *Courrier Sud* in 2012."

"So could you find the missing issue?"

"I can do better than that," she said as she dragged me toward her office. The two jocks, frustrated at being ignored, walked off. "I can print it out for you."

"Thanks."

It took less than a minute to print. Then she carefully stapled the pages together and proffered the document to me. But as I reached out to take it, she snatched it away.

"Surely it's worth a dinner invitation, at least?"

"I'm guessing you don't need me to get an invitation to dinner."

"Why don't I give you my cell phone number?"

"No, honestly, just give me the pages you've been kind enough to print out."

Still smiling, she scribbled her number on the top page.

"What do you expect me to do with that, Pauline?"

"I like you; you like me. It's a start, isn't it?" she said as though it were obvious.

"That's not how things work."

"That's exactly how things have worked for centuries."

I simply held out my hand, and eventually, she handed over the pages.

I waited until I was back in my car before leafing through them. The article that caught my attention was a review of the play adapted from *Perfume*. Written by one of the students, it described the piece as "profoundly moving, with two intensely powerful performances by the leading actresses." But I was more interested in the photographs. In the largest of the pictures, Vinca and Fanny were standing face-to-face. They looked almost like twins. I thought of Hitchcock's *Vertigo* and of Madeleine Elster and Judy Barton, two faces of the same woman.

Vinca was herself onstage, but Fanny was completely transformed. I thought about the conversation I had had with her earlier that afternoon. A detail suddenly came back to me, and I knew that she had not told me everything.

DEATH AND THE
MAIDEN

13

LA PLACE DE LA CATASTROPHE

1.

7:00 p.m.

I left the lycée and headed back to La Fontonne Hospital. This time, I avoided the reception desk and went straight up to the cardiology unit. I had barely stepped out of the elevator when a nurse in pink scrubs called to me:

"Hey! You're Annabelle Degalais's son!"

Dark-skinned, with dreadlocks streaked with blond highlights and a thousand-watt smile, the young woman radiated joy in the bleak hospital corridor. She looked a little like Lauryn Hill when she was with the Fugees.

"I'm Sophia," she said. "I know your mom well. Every time she comes to see us, she talks about you!"

"You must be confusing me with my brother Jérôme. He works for Doctors Without Borders."

I was used to my mother's panegyrics about my older brother and did not doubt that Jérôme deserved them. Besides, it's impossible to compete with someone who spends every day saving lives in war-torn countries and disaster zones.

"No, no, you're the one she talks about, the writer. She even got you to sign one of your books for me."

"I'd be very surprised."

But Sophia would not budge an inch.

"I've got the book in the call room. Come have a look. It's right over there."

Since she had piqued my curiosity, I followed her to the end of the corridor and into a long, narrow room. She showed me a copy of my most recent novel, *A Few Days with You,* and it was indeed inscribed *For Sophia, hoping that this story will give you pleasure and make you think. Warm regards, Thomas Degalais.* Except it was not my handwriting but my mother's! A surreal image popped into my head of my mother trying to fake my signature to respond to readers' requests.

"Have I signed many books for people here?"

"A dozen or so. A lot of people in the hospital read your books."

I was intrigued by this discovery. I was clearly missing something.

"How long has my mother been coming here for treatment?"

"Since Christmas last year, I'd say. The first time, I was the one looking after her—it was one of the holiday shifts. She'd had a heart attack in the middle of the night."

I made a mental note of this.

"I'm here to see Fanny Brahimi."

"The doctor's just left for the day," Sophia said. "Did you want to talk to her about your mother?"

"Not exactly. Fanny is an old friend. We've known each other since elementary school."

Sophia nodded. "Yes, she told me when I started taking care of your mother. It's too bad you just missed her."

"I really need to see her. It's important. I don't suppose you'd have her cell phone number?"

Sophia hesitated for a moment and then gave a regretful smile.

"I'm really sorry, but I'm not allowed to give out staff numbers. But if I were you, I'd go take a walk around Biot."

"Why?"

"It's Saturday night. She usually has dinner with Dr. Sénéca on the place des Arcades."

"Thierry Sénéca, the biologist?"

"That's right."

I remembered him. He had been a year or two ahead of us at Saint-Ex. Later he had set up a medical laboratory in Biot 3000, the technology park just outside the village. I knew it because my parents had their blood tests done there.

"So Sénéca and Fanny are an item?"

"I suppose you could say that." Sophia nodded, a little concerned that she had said too much.

"Okay, thanks."

I was already at the far end of the corridor when Sophia called after me.

"When is your next novel out?"

I pretended not to hear and stepped into the elevator. Generally, I found the question flattering; it was a mark of affection from readers. But as the doors closed, I realized that there would not be a next novel. On Monday, the body of Alexis Clément would be found and I would spend the next fifteen to twenty years behind bars. And, more than my freedom, I would lose the only thing that made me feel alive.

To dispel this gloomy thought, I checked my phone. I had a missed call from my father—who never called me—and a text message from Pauline Delatour, who had somehow managed to get hold of my number. Sorry about earlier, I don't know what got into me. I do dumb stuff sometimes. PS: I've come up with a title for the book you will one day write about Vinca: "Night and the Maiden."

2.

Back in the car, I headed toward the village of Biot. I found it difficult to concentrate on the road. My mind was still buzzing about the photograph I had seen in the school paper. In her red wig, Fanny—who was a blonde—looked unsettlingly like Vinca. It was not just her hair color; it was her manner, her facial expression, the way she held her head. This twinship made me think of the improv exercises my mother used to have students in the drama club do, lively scenarios that the kids loved to perform. The basic idea was for them to play real characters they had met in the street, at a bus stop, in a gallery. They called it the Chameleon Game, and Fanny was a natural.

A theory began to form in my mind. What if Fanny and Vinca had switched places? What if, on that famous Sunday morning, it was Fanny who caught the train to Paris? It seemed far-fetched, but it was not impossible. I could still remember the statements gathered during the various investigations. What exactly had they said, the school caretaker, the garbage collectors, the passengers on the TGV, the porter at the hotel? That they had seen a *young red-haired girl, a pretty redhead, a girl with pale blue eyes and rust-colored hair.* Descriptions that were vague enough to fit my theory. Perhaps I had finally found the lead I'd been searching for all these years. It meant there was a real possibility that Vinca was still alive. All the way to Biot, I mentally played out this scenario in order to make it real. For some reason I did not know, Fanny had faked Vinca and her lover's elopement. Everyone was looking for Vinca in Paris, but she had probably never even caught that train.

As I arrived in Biot, the sun was dipping below the horizon. The public parking lot was full, and a stream of cars, hazard lights blinking, were double-parked, all of them waiting for someone to leave.

Having driven around the village twice without finding a spot, I gave up and coasted down the chemin des Vachettes toward the valley of Combes. I finally found a parking place some eight hundred meters downhill, next to the tennis courts. I had to trudge back up the steep gradient, which was agony on the legs and brutal on the lungs. I had almost reached the summit when my father phoned again.

"I'm worried, Thomas. Your mother still isn't home. I don't understand. She only popped out to do some shopping."

"I assume you've tried calling her."

"That's the thing—she left her cell phone here. What am I supposed to do?"

"I don't know, Dad. Are you sure you're not getting worked up over nothing?"

I was more surprised by my father's reaction than by the notion that my mother was off gallivanting somewhere. In the early 2000s, she had been involved with an NGO that was teaching young girls in Africa and she was often away from home, something that had never seemed to bother her husband.

"No," Richard said. "We have guests coming over for dinner. She'd never leave me in the lurch like this."

"If you're really worried, you could start by calling the hospitals."

"All right," he grumbled.

By the time I hung up, I had finally reached the pedestrian area. The village of Biot was even more picturesque than I remembered. Although there were still vestiges of the Knights Templar here, the architecture owed more to people who had come from northern Italy. At this time of day, the ocher glow of the façades warmed the cobbled streets, giving the casual visitor the impression that he was strolling through an alleyway in Savona or Genoa.

The main street was lined with shops selling the usual wares of Provence (soaps, perfumes, handicrafts made from olive wood), but there were also galleries exhibiting the work of local glassblowers, painters, and sculptors. Outside a wine bar, a girl with a guitar was murdering the Cranberries' back catalog, but she was surrounded by people clapping along, adding to the easy atmosphere of early evening.

And yet, in my mind, Biot was linked to a very specific memory. In sixth grade, when I was about twelve, I had done my very first presentation on a piece of local history that had always fascinated me. In the late nineteenth century, a huge building in the village had suddenly collapsed. The tragedy had occurred one evening when all the inhabitants were gathered there for a meal to celebrate a child's First Communion. Within seconds, they were all crushed and buried. Rescuers had pulled almost thirty corpses from the rubble. It was an incident that had left a lasting impression on the town and that, even a century later, was still evident, since no one had ever built over the ruins. Obdurately desolate, the site was now known as la place de la Catastrophe.

When I reached the place des Arcades, I was stunned to find that it was exactly as I had last seen it, twenty-five years earlier. The long, narrow plaza extended as far as the church of Sainte-Marie-Madeleine and was flanked by twin arcades of colorful two- and three-story buildings.

It did not take long to find Thierry Sénéca. Sitting on the terrace of the Café Les Arcades, he beckoned me over, as though it was me rather than Fanny he was waiting for. Sénéca had not changed much. He had dark, close-cropped hair, an aquiline nose, and a well-trimmed goatee. His clothes could best be described as "cool"—linen pants, short-sleeved shirt, sweater draped around his shoulders. He looked as though he had just stepped off a yacht and reminded me of the old advertisements for Sebago or the election posters of my youth featuring conservative RPR candidates desperately trying to pass themselves off as hip, cool guys. The result was usually the opposite of what was intended.

"Hi, Thierry," I said, stepping under the arch.

"Evening, Thomas, it's been ages."

"I was looking for Fanny. I heard she's having dinner with you."

He gestured for me to take the chair opposite.

"She should be here any minute. She mentioned that she'd seen you this morning."

The rose-tinted sky cast a honeyed glow over the ancient stones. The air was fragrant with *soupe au pistou* and simmering ragouts.

"Don't worry, I won't spoil your evening," I said. "There's something I wanted to check. It won't take more than two minutes."

"No problem."

Les Arcades was a veritable institution in Biot. Picasso, Fernand Léger, and Chagall had all been regulars here once. The tables, covered with checkered cloths, spilled out into the square.

"Is the food as good as it used to be? My parents used to bring us here all the time," I said.

"Well, you're not in for any surprises. The menu hasn't changed in forty years."

We talked for a while about roasted peppers and stuffed zucchini, about braised rabbit with herbes de Provence, and about the wonderful ceiling with its exposed beams. There followed an awkward silence and I did my best to keep the conversation going.

"How are things with the lab?"

"Don't waste your time trying to make conversation, Thomas," he said, a sudden shift in his tone.

Like Pianelli this morning, Thierry took out an e-cigarette and started sucking on something that smelled like crème caramel. I wondered what men like Francis Biancardini and my father thought when they saw guys getting their kicks smoking things that smelled like sweets and drinking spinach detox smoothies instead of a glass of Scotch.

"You know that pathetic old theory about soul mates?" Thierry

Sénéca said, glaring at me. "The one that says we're all looking for the perfect other half, the one and only person capable of forever easing our loneliness?"

"In *The Symposium,* Plato has Aristophanes present the idea, and I don't think it's pathetic. I think it's poetic. I like the symbolism."

"Oh yeah, I forgot that you always were the on-call romantic," he said mockingly.

I let him continue.

"Well, Fanny also believes in that stuff. And it's all well and good when you're fourteen or fifteen, but when you're in your forties, it becomes a bit of an issue."

"What exactly are you trying to say, Thierry?"

"There are people who get stuck in time. People for whom the past is never really in the rearview mirror."

I had the impression that Sénéca was sketching a portrait of me, but it turned out that I was not the subject of his rant.

"Do you know what Fanny believes, deep down? That, one day, you'll come back for her. She genuinely thinks that sooner or later you'll realize that she's the love of your life and you'll show up on your white horse and take her away to a better life. In psychiatry, they call it—"

"I think you're exaggerating," I said, interrupting him.

"I wish."

"How long have you two been together?"

"Five or six years. We've had some great times and some tough times. But the thing is, even when we're happy, even when we're having fun together, it's you she's thinking about. Fanny can't help but imagine that whatever this is, it would be more intense, more *fulfilling* with you."

Eyes fixed on the ground, a lump in his throat, Thierry Sénéca spoke in a hollow voice. His pain was all too real.

"It's tough, trying to compete with you, you know, the one

who's *different from other boys.* But what exactly is different about you, Thomas Degalais, aside from the fact that you're a homewrecker and a dream merchant?"

He stared at me with a mixture of hostility and anguish, as though I were both the cause of his pain and, potentially, his savior. What he was saying seemed so preposterous that I did not even try to explain myself.

He stroked his beard, then took his phone from his pocket and showed me the picture he used as his wallpaper: a boy of about eight or nine playing tennis.

"Is that your son?"

"Yeah, that's Marco. His mother got sole custody and took him to Argentina, where she lives with her new guy. It kills me that I don't see more of him."

It was a touching story, but this sudden unburdening by someone to whom I had never been close made me uncomfortable.

"I want to have another kid," Séneca said. "I'd like it to be with Fanny, but there's a problem standing in our way. And that problem is you, Thomas."

I wanted to say that I wasn't his shrink and that if Fanny did not want to have a child, the problem was probably *him,* not me, but the guy was so miserable that I could not bring myself to stick the knife in.

"I'm not going to wait around forever," he warned.

"That's your problem—"

I did not get to finish the sentence. Fanny had just appeared at the far end of the arcade, and, seeing us together, she froze. She waved to me—*Come with me*—then crossed the square and went into the church.

"I'm glad you came, Thomas," Thierry Sénéca said as I got to my feet. "There has always been some unfinished business from back then. I hope maybe you'll deal with it tonight."

I left without saying goodbye, walked across the cobbled square, and stepped into the church.

3.

The moment I stepped inside, the smell of incense and wood smoke made me feel reflective. The church was beautiful in its simplicity, with stairs running from the main door down to the nave. Fanny was waiting for me, sitting at the bottom of the steps next to a massive brass votive holder on which dozens of candles were burning.

She was wearing the same jeans, the same shoes, the same blouse I had seen her in that morning. She had buttoned up her trench coat and was hugging her knees as though freezing cold.

"Hi, Fanny."

Her face was ashen, her eyes puffy, her face crumpled.

"We need to talk, don't we?"

My tone was harsher than I had intended. She nodded. I was about to question her about the theory I had come up with while driving here, but she looked up at me, and the pain I could see in her eyes was so terrifying that, for the first time, I was not sure I wanted to know the truth.

"I lied to you, Thomas."

"When?"

"Today, yesterday, the day before yesterday, twenty-five years ago . . . I've always lied to you."

"You lied when you said you knew there was a body walled up in the gym?"

"No, that part was true."

The candles flickered above her head and the panels of a fifteenth-century altarpiece shimmered in the quivering light. In a gilt frame, Our Lady of the Rosary cradled the Christ Child; in one out-stretched hand, she held a bloodred rosary.

"I've known for twenty-five years that there was a body walled up in the gym," Fanny said.

I wished that time would stand still. Wished there were some way to stop her from speaking.

"But until you told me today, I didn't know Alexis Clément was there too."

"I don't understand."

"There are two bodies in that fucking wall," she spluttered, struggling to her feet. "I didn't know about Clément. I lied; Ahmed never said anything to me. But I knew about the other body."

"What other body?"

I knew what she was about to say, and my mind was already creating barriers to shield me from the truth.

"Vinca," she said at length.

"No, you're wrong."

"This time, I'm telling you the truth, Thomas. Vinca is dead."

"When did she die?"

"The same day Alexis Clément died. Saturday, December nineteenth, 1992, the day of the snowstorm."

"How can you be so sure?"

Now it was Fanny's turn to look up at Our Lady of the Rosary. Behind Mary, two angels were holding open her mantle so that the meek might find shelter there. In that moment, I wished that I could join them. But Fanny raised her head, looked into my eyes, and, with her next words, destroyed everything I cared about.

"Because I'm the one who killed her, Thomas."

FANNY

Utterly exhausted, I stifle yawn after yawn. Pages and pages of my notes on molecular biology dance before my eyes, but my brain refuses to take them in. I'm fighting sleep. The cold is the worst, cutting me to the bone. The battered heater is about to give up the ghost, and right now it's barely breathing dusty lukewarm air. I've put music on to keep myself awake. "Disintegration," "Plainsong," "Last Dance"...the speakers pour out the exquisite melancholy of the Cure. A perfect mirror of my forlorn soul.

I wipe condensation from the dorm-room window with my sleeve. Outside, the landscape looks surreal. The campus is silent and deserted, frozen beneath an opalescent carapace. For a moment, I gaze into the distance, beyond the pearl-gray sky from which snow is still falling.

My stomach is rumbling and beginning to cramp. I haven't eaten a thing since yesterday. The cupboards and the fridge are empty. I know I should face the fact that I need to sleep a little, stop setting my alarm clock for four thirty a.m., but I feel so guilty that I can't. I think about the crazy study schedule I drew up for this two-week vacation. I think about the brutal first year of pre-med that will chew up and spit out two-thirds of the students in my class. And I wonder whether there is any point. Or, rather, I wonder whether there is any point for me. Do I really want to be a doctor? What will my life be like if I don't get into medical school? Every time I imagine my future, all I see is a bleak, dreary landscape. Not a wintry plain, but a boundless expanse of gray, the gray of concrete and tower blocks, of highways and getting up at five a.m. The gray of hospital rooms, of the metallic taste in your mouth when you wake up, sweating, next to the wrong person. I know that this is what awaits me, because I have never had that lightness, that carefree spirit, that optimism so many students at the lycée wear like a badge of honor. Every time I imagine my future, I see fear, weariness, emptiness, pain.

And then suddenly I see you, Thomas! Looking out my window, I see your silhouette hunched against the wind, framed against the milky whiteness of the winter afternoon. And as it always does, my heart leaps in my chest and I feel calmer. Suddenly I no longer feel tired. Suddenly, I want to live, to forge ahead. Because only with you could my life ever be carefree, filled with possibilities and plans, with journeys, sunshine, and laughing children. I can sense that there exists a narrow path to happiness, but I can take it only with you by my side. I don't know by what magic the pain, the grime, the blackness that I have carried with me since childhood seems to vanish when we're together. But I know that, without you, I will always be alone.

But the illusion vanishes almost as quickly as it appeared, and I realize that you are not coming to see *me*. I hear your footsteps on the stairs, hear you go into *her* room. You never come to see me anymore. You come for *her*. Always for *her*.

I know Vinca better than you do. I know she has that way about her, that look in her eyes, the way she moves or pushes a lock of hair behind her ear or parts her lips in that smile that is not a smile. And I know that it is not simply toxic—it is lethal. My mother had it too, that sort of maleficent aura that drives men wild. I never told you, but when she walked out on us, my father tried to commit suicide. He impaled himself on a rusty bar. Because of the insurance, we had to pretend it was an accident, but he was trying to kill himself. After everything that my mother had put him through, he thought he couldn't live without her and was prepared to leave behind three young children.

You're different, Thomas, but you have to shake off this hold she has on you before it destroys you. Before it makes you do something you'll regret for the rest of your life.

★ ★ ★

You knock on my door and I open it.

"Hey, Thomas," I say, taking off my glasses.

"Hey, Fanny, I need a hand."

You explain that Vinca is not feeling well, that she needs someone to talk to, and she needs some paracetamol. You ask me to look in my medicine cabinet and make Vinca some tea. Like an idiot, all I can think to say is *I'm on it*. And because I don't have any tea left, I have to fish a teabag out of the trash.

Obviously, that's all I'm good for, taking care of Vinca, the poor little wounded bird. Who do you think I am? We were happy before she came along and ruined our lives. Look what she makes us do. Look what *you* make me do in order to get your attention, to try to make you jealous. It's because of *you* that I throw myself at every guy I meet. It's because of *you* that I hurt myself.

I wipe away the tears before stepping out into the corridor. As you race past, you bump into me, and then, without a word, without an apology, you hurtle down the stairs.

★ ★ ★

So here I am in Vinca's room and I feel stupid, standing there with my cup of tea. I didn't hear what she said to you, but I assume she played the same old charade. She is an expert by now, pulling the strings in her little puppet show, with her in the role of hapless victim.

I set the mug of tea on the nightstand and stare at Vinca, who has already fallen asleep. A part of me understands the passion she inspires. A part of me wants to lie down beside her, stroke her delicate skin, taste her red lips and her delicately rimmed ears, kiss her long, curved lashes. But another part of me despises her. For a split second, I see my mother's face superimposed over Vinca's and I recoil.

★ ★ ★

I should get back to work, but something holds me here in this room. There is a half-full vodka bottle on the windowsill. I pick it up and swig straight from it. Then I rummage around, leaf through the papers on Vinca's desk, flick through her diary. I open the wardrobes, try on some of her clothes. I discover the contents of her bathroom cabinet. I am not really surprised to find it stuffed with sleeping pills and tranquilizers.

She has everything for the discerning junkie: Rohypnol, Xanax, lorazepam. Although the last two boxes are almost empty, the bottle of Rohypnol is full. I wonder how she managed to get hold of these drugs. Under the boxes, I find a prescription signed by a Dr. Frédéric Rubens in Cannes. He obviously doles these things out like sweets.

I'm familiar with the properties of Rohypnol, the brand name for the drug flunitrazepam. It's used to treat severe insomnia, but since it's habit-forming and has a long half-life, it is prescribed for only short periods. It's not a drug to be taken lightly or for prolonged periods. I know that some people take it with booze or even morphine to get high. I've never done it, but I've heard that the effects can be devastating: loss of control, erratic behavior, amnesia. One of our teachers, a specialist in emergency medicine, told us that there has been an increasing number of overdose cases and that rapists have been known to use the drug to break down a victim's defenses and ensure she has no memory of the attack. There is even an urban legend making the rounds, something about a rave somewhere near Grasse and a girl who took too much and set herself on fire before jumping off a cliff.

I'm so exhausted that I can't think straight. Suddenly, without knowing where the idea came from, I'm toying with the notion of dissolving the tablets in her tea. I don't want to *kill* Vinca; I just want her out of my life and yours. I often dream about her being hit by a car, about her committing suicide. I don't want to kill her, but still I tip some tablets out into my hand and then from my hand into the mug of hot tea. It takes only a few seconds, during which it's as though I am in two places at once, as though I am on the outside watching someone else.

I close the door and go back to my own room. I can hardly stand. Exhaustion overwhelms me, and I lie down on the bed, taking my folders and my notes. I have to study, I have to concentrate, but already my eyes are closing and I am being dragged down into sleep.

★ ★ ★

When I wake up again, it's pitch-dark. I'm soaked with sweat, as though I'm running a fever. The clock radio reads half past midnight.

I can't believe that I've slept for eight hours straight. I have no idea whether you've been back in the meantime, Thomas. And I've no idea how Vinca is.

Panicked and terrified, I go and knock on her door. When there's no answer, I let myself into the room. The mug on the nightstand is empty. Vinca is still asleep, still in the same position as when I left. At least, that's what I try to tell myself, but when I bend down, I realize her body is cold and she's not breathing. My heart stops; I feel a shock wave blast through me. I collapse onto the floor.

Perhaps this is how it was written. Perhaps, from the beginning, things were fated to end this way, in fear and death. And I already know the next step: End it all. Put an end once and for all to the insidious pain that for too long has been like a second skin. I throw open the window of Vinca's room. The bitter cold pulls at me, claws at me, devours me. I climb onto the window ledge to jump, but I cannot see it through. As though night, having scented me, has decided it does not want me. As though death itself did not have time to waste on someone as insignificant as me.

★ ★ ★

Completely distraught, I stumble across the campus like a zombie, past the lake, the place des Marronniers, the administration buildings. Everything is dark, drab, lifeless. Everything except your mother's office, and she is the person I'm looking for. I see her through the window, and as I come closer, I realize she is talking to Francis Biancardini. The moment she spots me, she can tell that something terrible has happened. She and Francis run toward me. My legs are barely holding me up. I collapse into their arms and blurt out the whole story in garbled sentences punctuated by sobs. Before calling the emergency services, they hurry over to Vinca's room. It is Francis who goes over to inspect the body. When they come back, with a shake of his head, Francis confirms that it is too late to call an ambulance.

It is at this point that I pass out.

★ ★ ★

When I come to, I am lying on the couch in your mother's office with a blanket draped over me.

Annabelle is sitting next to me. I'm surprised but reassured by how calm she is. I like your mother. She has always been kind and generous to me. She has always helped me when I needed it. It was thanks to her that I got a room on campus. She was the one who gave me the confidence to study medicine, and she was the one who consoled me when you became distant.

She asks whether I'm feeling better, then insists that I tell her exactly what happened. "Don't leave out a single detail."

As I tell her, I am forced to relive the terrible sequence of events that led to Vinca's death. My jealousy, the moment of madness, the Rohypnol. When I try to justify what I did, she presses a finger to my lips.

"All the regrets in the world won't bring her back. Has anyone other than you seen Vinca's body?"

"Maybe Thomas, but I don't think so. Vinca and I were the only students in the building who didn't go home for Christmas."

She lays a hand on my arm, looks me in the eye, and says gravely, "This is the most important moment of your life, Fanny. Not only will you have to make a difficult decision, but you will have to make it quickly.

"There are two possibilities. The first is that we call the police and tell them everything. By tonight, you'll be sleeping in a cell. When the trial comes, the prosecutor and the court of public opinion will rip your life to shreds. The media will be gripped by the case. You'll be painted as the evil, jealous bitch, the monster who cold-bloodedly killed her best friend, a girl everyone in school adored. Since you are over eighteen, you will be given a long sentence."

I am already overwhelmed, but Annabelle drives home the final nail.

"By the time you get out of prison you will be thirty-five, and for the rest of your days you will be branded a murderer. In other words, your life is over before it has really begun. Tonight, you stepped into a hell from which you can never escape."

I feel as though I am drowning, as though I've been knocked on the head and am underwater and cannot catch my breath. For a full minute, I am speechless, then finally I manage to stammer, "Wh-what's the other possibility?"

"That you fight your way out of this hell. And I'm prepared to help you do that."

"I don't see how."

Your mother gets up from her chair. "That's something you don't have to deal with directly. The first problem is to make Vinca's body disappear. As for the rest, the less you know, the better."

"It's impossible to just make a body disappear," I say.

Just then, Francis comes into the office and lays a passport and a credit card on the coffee table. He picks up the phone, dials a number, and puts the call on speaker.

"Hôtel Sainte-Clotilde, good evening."

"Good evening. I was wondering if you might have a room for two people for tomorrow night."

"We do, but it's the last available room," the receptionist says and informs him of the room rates.

Francis says that he'll take it and makes the reservation in the name of Alexis Clément.

Your mother looks at me as if to say that the wheels are already turning and she is waiting only for my signal to continue.

"I'll leave you to think for ten minutes," she says.

"I don't need time to choose between my life and that hell."

In her eyes, I can see this is the answer she's hoping for. She sits down next to me and takes me by the shoulders.

"You have to understand one thing. This will work only if you do exactly what I tell you. No questions, no looking for reasons or explanations. That's my only condition, but it is nonnegotiable."

I have no idea how such a plan could possibly work, but—unbelievably—I feel as though Annabelle and Francis have every-thing under control, that they'll be able to repair the irreparable.

"The slightest mistake, and this is over," Annabelle warns me. "Not only will you go to jail, but you'll send Francis and me to jail too."

I silently nod and ask what the plan is.

"Right now, the plan is for you to get a good night's sleep so you'll be fit and ready in the morning," Annabelle says.

★ ★ ★

You know the craziest thing? That night, I slept like a baby. When your mother woke me the next morning, she was wearing jeans and a man's jacket. She'd pinned her hair into a bun and hidden it under a cap—a German soccer cap. When she handed me the red wig and Vinca's pink polka-dot sweater, I understood her plan. It was like the improv exercises we did in drama club when she'd tell us to slip into someone else's skin. This was often how she set about casting a play. The difference was that, this time, the improvisation wouldn't last five minutes, it would last a whole day, and I wouldn't be playing for a role, I would be playing for my life.

I still remember how I felt as I put on Vinca's clothes and the red wig. It was a feeling of fulfilment, of excitement, of consummation. I *was* Vinca. I had her lightness, her easy grace, her quick wit, that elegant indifference that was hers alone.

Your mother got behind the wheel of the Renault Alpine and we set off. I rolled down my window and waved to the caretaker as he raised the barrier; I waved to the two guys collecting garbage by the traffic circle. When we got to the Antibes train station, we discovered that, in order to make up for trains canceled the day before, the SNCF had added another fast train to Paris. Your mother bought the tickets. The journey to Paris passed like a breath. I wandered through every carriage so that I would be seen, so that passengers would remember me, but I never stayed in one place for long. When we arrived, your mother told me she'd chosen that hotel on the rue de Saint-Simon because she'd stayed there six months earlier and because the elderly night watchman was a little senile and would be easy to dupe. We got there at about ten o'clock and asked if we could pay for the room in advance, saying we needed to leave very early in the morning. We left just enough clues to make it seem as though Vinca had really been there. I was the one who came up with the idea of ordering Cherry Coke. Your mother had the idea of "forgetting" the toiletry bag with the hairbrush that had Vinca's DNA on it.

And do you want to know what was *really* insane? That day—I had to drink two beers and take a Rohypnol to get to sleep—was probably the most exhilarating of my whole life.

★ ★ ★

The comedown was as brutal as the excitement had been thrilling. By the following morning, everything was once again bleak and terrifying. The moment I woke up, I nearly had a breakdown. I couldn't imagine myself getting through another day dragging around this terrible weight of guilt and self-loathing. But I had promised your mother I would see it through. I'd already ruined my own life; I wasn't going to bring her down with me.

We left the hotel at dawn and took the Métro, line 12 from rue du Bac to Concorde, then line 1 to the Gare de Lyon. Annabelle handed me my ticket back to Nice and told me she was heading to Montparnasse to take a later train to her sister's in the Landes.

In a café outside the station, she warned me that there would be worse days ahead while I learned to live with what I had done and immediately added that she knew that I could do it because, like her, I was a fighter, and fighters were the only people she respected.

She told me that for women like us, women who came from nothing, life was one long battle and that we would always have to fight for everything. "The strong and the weak are not always who you think they are," she said. "There are lots of people who wage private, painful wars." The real task was learning to lie over the long term. And to lie to other people, you first have to learn to lie to yourself.

There's only one way to lie, Fanny, and that is to repudiate the truth, to obliterate the truth with your lie until, eventually, your lie becomes the truth.

Annabelle walked me along the platform to my carriage and kissed me goodbye. It is possible to live with a blood memory, she said. She told me she knew this from personal experience. And she left me to think about this quote: "Civilization is like a thin layer of ice upon a deep ocean of chaos and darkness."

14

THE PROM

1.

Fanny concluded her story in a fever close to frenzy. She was no longer sitting on the carved stone steps but standing in the middle of the church, teetering as though on the verge of collapse. As she took a few steps and staggered between the pews, she reminded me of the last passenger on a sinking ship.

I was scarcely in better shape. I could hardly breathe. My mind was racing; I was unable to put these events in any sort of perspective. *Vinca had been murdered by Fanny, and my mother had helped to dispose of the body.* I couldn't reject the truth, but it seemed utterly at odds with everything I knew about the characters of both my mother and my friend.

"Fanny, wait!"

She had just raced out of the church. A second earlier, she had looked as though she might faint, but now she was running as though her life depended on it.

By the time I stumbled out of the church and onto the square, Fanny was long gone. I tried to run after her, but I had twisted my ankle and she had a head start and was faster than me. I limped through the village and down the chemin des Vachettes as quickly as I could. There was a parking ticket on my car. I crumpled it up, slid in behind the steering wheel, and tried to decide what to do next.

My mother. I needed to talk to my mother. She was the only one who could confirm what Fanny had told me, the only one who could help me disentangle the lies from the truth. Having turned off my phone in the church, I now turned it on again. No word from my father, but a text message from Maxime asking me to call him back. I put the key in the ignition as I hit Redial.

"We need to talk, Thomas. I've found out something—something really fucking serious that..."

I could hear the tremor in his voice.

"Tell me."

"Not over the phone. Let's meet up later at the Eagle's Nest. I've just arrived at the Alumni Prom, so I need to press the flesh a little."

In the quiet of the Mercedes, I tried to organize my thoughts as I drove. On Saturday, December 19, 1992, two people had been murdered only hours apart in Saint-Ex. First Alexis Clément, then Vinca. It had been that coincidence that had made it possible for Francis and my mother to create an unshakable alibi to protect Maxime, Fanny, and me, first by making the bodies disappear and then—and this was the real stroke of genius—by shifting the scene of the crime from Saint-Ex to Paris.

Thinking back over what Fanny had said, I decided I needed a second opinion on something that had puzzled me. I tried calling my own doctor in New York, but I only had his office number and the practice was not open on weekends. Having no alternative, I called my brother.

It would be an understatement to say we didn't talk much. Being the brother of a hero was daunting. Whenever I phoned him, I felt like I was taking up time he could be spending treating disadvantaged children, which made our conversations somewhat awkward.

"Hey, bro!" he said when he answered.

As always, his enthusiasm, far from being contagious, actually drained the energy from me.

"Hey, Jérôme, how's life?"

"Why don't we skip the small talk, Thomas. What do you need?"

Today, for once, he made the conversation easier.

"I saw Mom today. Did you know about her heart attack?"

"Of course."

"Why didn't you tell me?"

"She asked me not to. She didn't want you to worry."

Yeah, right.

"You're familiar with Rohypnol, yeah?"

"Of course. It's a vicious drug, but it is not really prescribed these days."

"Have you ever taken it?"

"No. Why on earth do you want to know about Rohypnol?"

"I'm writing a novel set in the 1990s...how many pills would someone have to take for it to be fatal?"

"Impossible to say. It depends on the dosage. Most tablets contain one milligram of flunitrazepam."

"Meaning?"

"Meaning it still depends on the person who's taking them."

"You're a great help!"

"Kurt Cobain tried to kill himself using Rohypnol."

"I thought he shot himself in the head."

"I'm talking about a failed suicide attempt a few months before he died. They found fifty pills in his stomach."

Fanny said she'd given Vinca a handful of pills. That was a far cry from fifty. "What if you took fifteen?"

"You'd be pretty fucked up, and you could end up in a coma, especially if you took them with alcohol. But, like I said, it all depends on the dose. Back in the nineties, the lab producing it also made a two-milligram tablet—fifteen of those and some Jim Beam might finish you off."

Back to square one.

Another question popped into my head.

"I don't suppose you've heard of a doctor in Cannes called Frédéric Rubens?"

"Ha! You mean Dr. Mabuse? Everyone knew him, and not for the right reasons."

"Mabuse was his nickname?"

"One of many." Jérôme sniggered. "Freddy the freak, Freddy Krueger, Candy Man...he didn't just supply; he was a junkie himself. He was involved in all sorts of illegal stuff—dealing, practicing medicine without a license, selling prescriptions..."

"I assume he lost his license?"

"Oh yes, but not soon enough, in my opinion."

"Do you know if he still lives around here?"

"With all the shit he was taking, he was never likely to make it to old age. No, Rubens died back when I was a med student. So this next novel, is it a medical thriller?"

2.

It was getting dark as I pulled up outside the school. The security guard had left the barrier open and was simply checking names against a guest list. I wasn't on any list, but having seen me a couple of hours earlier, he waved me through and told me to park my car down by the lake.

In the gathering darkness, the campus looked magnificent, more unified and cohesive than it did in daylight. Swept clean by the mistral, the sky was cloudless and stippled with stars. Seen from the parking lot, tea lights, flaming torches, and strings of Christmas lights created a magical atmosphere as they led guests to the celebrations. There were a number of different events for different classes. The prom in the gym welcomed those students who had graduated between 1990 and 1995.

Stepping into the vast hall, I felt a sudden queasiness. It looked dangerously close to a Worst Outfits of the 1990s costume party. Forty-somethings had raided their wardrobes for their old Converse high-tops, ripped 501s, Schott bomber jackets, and lumberjack shirts. Most of the athletes were wearing baggy pants, Tacchini tracksuits, and Chevignon jackets.

I spotted Maxime, wearing a Chicago Bulls jersey. People were flocking around him as though he'd already been elected. The name Macron was on everyone's lips.

When Maxime saw me, he made a little gesture: *Ten minutes?* I nodded and, while I waited, melted into the crowd. I made my way across the gym to the bar. The whole place was festooned with paper chains and vintage posters. I felt no more uncomfortable than I had this morning. No bad vibes. Of course, I knew that my brain was doing everything in its power to reject Vinca's death.

"What can I get you, monsieur?"

Thankfully, there was alcohol. There was even a bartender making cocktails to order.

"Could you make me a caipirinha?"

"With pleasure."

"Make that two!" I heard a voice from behind me and, turning, saw that it was Maxime's partner, Olivier Mons, who ran the multi-media library in Antibes. I congratulated him on their two beautiful little daughters and we swapped stories about the "good old days" that had never really been *that* good. While I remembered him as a bit of a poser, he was actually charming and very funny. We chatted for a couple of minutes, and then he confided that he had been a little worried about Maxime over the past few days. He was convinced there was something Maxime was not telling him and equally convinced that I knew something about it.

I opted for a half-truth and told him that, with the upcoming elections, some of Maxime's rivals were trying to find skeletons in his closet to stop him from running. I was ambiguous, saying vaguely that this was the price of being involved in politics. I promised to do whatever I could to help Maxime and said that the whole thing would quickly blow over anyway.

And Olivier believed me. It was one of the weirdest things about my life. Though a worrier by nature, I had the strange ability to reassure other people that everything was going to be okay.

The bartender brought our cocktails and we clinked glasses and stood laughing at the hideous outfits of the other guests. Like me, Olivier was fairly conservative in his style. The same could not be said about our former classmates. Some of the women seemed nostalgic for the days of crop tops and exposed belly buttons. Others were wearing denim shorts, black camisoles over white T-shirts, choker necklaces, or bandannas tied around the handles of their handbags. Thankfully, no one had dared to wear Buffalo platform wedges. What was it all for? Were they just having fun, or were they trying to recapture their lost youth?

We ordered two more cocktails.

"And this time, don't be so stingy with the cachaça!" I said.

The barman took me at my word and made stiff caipirinhas. I took my leave of Olivier and, cocktail in hand, went out onto the terrace where the smokers were gathered.

3.

The night was still young, but already some guy in a dark corner was openly dealing coke and dope. Everything I had always loathed. Dressed in a battered leather jacket and a Depeche Mode T-shirt,

Stéphane Pianelli was leaning on the fence, vaping and sipping alcohol-free beer.

"So you didn't go to the concert in the end?"

He nodded to a five-year-old playing under the tables. "My parents were supposed to be babysitting Ernesto, but something came up at the last minute," he said, exhaling a plume of vapor that smelled like gingerbread.

"Ernesto? After Ernesto 'Che' Guevara?"

"Why? Have you got a problem with it?" Pianelli raised a warning eyebrow.

"No, no," I said, eager not to offend him.

"His mother thought it was a bit clichéd."

"Who's his mother?"

He looked at me, poker-faced. "No one you know."

I had to laugh. As a journalist, Pianelli thought everyone's private life was fair game except his own.

"It's Céline Feulpin, isn't it?"

"Yes, that's her."

I remembered her well from my last year in school. She had always been very passionate about injustice and had been on the front lines of every student protest; she was a female version of Stéphane, and, like him, she had gone on to study literature. As left-wing activists, they had fought together for the rights of students and minorities. I had bumped into Céline two or three years earlier, on a flight from New York to Geneva. She was a completely different person. She was dressed in Lady Dior and was draped over a Swiss doctor she seemed enamored with. We had chatted a little and I thought she seemed happy and fulfilled, something I was careful not to mention to Pianelli.

"I've got some info for you," he said, changing the subject.

He stepped to one side, and for a moment, his face was lit up by the Christmas lights. His eyes were bloodshot, and there were dark circles under them, as though he hadn't slept in days.

"Did you manage to get information on the financing of the school construction work?"

"Not really. I put my intern on the case, but it's all pretty hush-hush. He'll get in touch with you when he has something."

He caught his son's eye and gave him a little wave.

"However, I did manage to get a look at the final plans. It's massive. There are some really expensive features that serve no purpose I can think of."

"Like what?"

"Part of the project involves a huge rose garden—the Garden of Angels. Have you heard about this?"

"No."

"It's completely insane. The plan is to create a contemplative space that would extend from where the lavender fields are now right down to the lake."

"What do you mean, a contemplative space?"

He shrugged.

"It's something my intern mentioned over the phone. To be honest, I don't get it either. But I've got something else for you."

He gave me a mysterious look, dipped into his pocket, and brought out a piece of paper scrawled with handwritten notes.

"I managed to get hold of the police report about Francis Biancardini's death. Whoever it was really did a number on the poor bastard."

"So he was tortured?"

I saw an evil glint in his eyes.

"Oh yes, seriously. As far as I'm concerned, this backs up my theory that it was someone settling old scores."

I heaved a sigh. "What old scores, Stéphane? Are we back to your conspiracy theory about money laundering and the Mafia? Just think about it, for fuck's sake. Even if Francis was working for the Mafia—and I don't believe it for a minute—why would they bump him off?"

"Maybe he tried to double-cross the guys in Calabria."

"Why? Francis was seventy-four and he was rich as Croesus."

"For guys like that, you can never be too rich."

"The whole idea is ridiculous. It just doesn't make sense. So, did he try to write the killer's name in blood?"

"No, the journalist from the *Nouvel Obs* admitted she made that bit up to give the story some drama. But he did phone someone just before he died."

"Do we know who?"

"Yes—your mother."

I looked at him, deadpan, mentally trying to defuse the bomb he had just set. "I suppose it's logical. After all, they were neighbors and our families have always been close."

He nodded, but I could see what he was thinking: *You keep telling yourself that, my friend, but don't think I'm going to fall for it.*

"Do we know whether she picked up?"

"Why don't you ask her?" he said and drained his drink. "Come on, Ernesto," he called, going over to fetch his son. "Let's go home. You've got soccer practice tomorrow."

4.

I glanced around the room. Maxime was still surrounded by his admirers. At the far end of the terrace there was another bar, decorated to look like it belonged in a sleazy dive, that was serving shots of vodka.

I ordered a vodka shot (mint) and then another (lemon). It was irresponsible, but after all, I didn't have a son to take home or to soccer practice in the morning, and besides, I have always hated alcohol-free beer and I was probably just a couple of days away from a life in prison.

I had to track down my mother. Why had she run off? Was she afraid that I'd discover the truth? Or was she afraid she might suffer the same fate as Francis?

I ordered a third shot (cherry), convinced that I might think more clearly while intoxicated. There was often a moment of lucidity along the path to drunkenness, a moment when ideas collided and when, before chaos set in, there might be a glimmer of understanding. My mother had taken my rental car, which was equipped with GPS. Maybe I could call the rental company and claim someone had stolen the car and ask for the location? It sounded plausible, but it was Saturday night, so it would be tricky.

One last shot (orange) for the road. My brain was now running at full speed. It was exhilarating, though I knew it wouldn't last. Then I had a brilliant idea. Why not just try to locate the iPad I'd left in the car? Modern surveillance made this only too easy. I took out my phone and launched the app, which was pretty efficient and worked most of the time. I logged in and held my breath. A blue dot began to flash on the map. I zoomed in. If my tablet was still in the car, the car was now at the southern tip of Cap d'Antibes in a spot I knew only too well: the parking lot next to Keller Beach, the lot used by tourists who wanted to walk along the coastal path.

I immediately called my father.

"I've tracked down Mom's car!"

"How did you manage that?"

"We can talk about that later. She's parked down by Keller Beach."

"What the bloody hell would Annabelle be doing there, for God's sake?"

Once again, I felt that he sounded unduly worried and realized that he was hiding something from me. He vehemently denied this, and I flew into a rage.

"You really piss me off, Richard! You're happy to call me when there's a problem, but then you don't trust me. What the hell is going on?"

"All right, all right," he said. "When your mother left this afternoon, she took something with her."

"What?"

"One of my hunting rifles."

My head was spinning. I could not imagine my mother with a gun. I closed my eyes for a second and tried to picture her.

That's when I suddenly realized I had been wrong; I could *easily* imagine Annabelle with a rifle.

"Does she know how to use it?" I asked my father.

"I'm heading down to Cap d'Antibes" was all he said in response.

I was not convinced that was a good idea, but I didn't see what else we could do.

"I'll just finish up here and then meet you there. Okay, Dad?"

"Okay. Make it quick."

I hung up and went back into the gym. The mood had changed somewhat. Fueled by alcohol and drugs, people had begun to let their hair down. The music was deafening. I looked around for Maxime but couldn't see him. Then I thought maybe he had gone outside to wait for me.

Of course—the Eagle's Nest.

I ducked out of the gym and headed up the steep path leading to the ledge. There were candles and paper lanterns at intervals to guide my steps.

Reaching the foot of the rocky outcropping, I looked up and saw the glowing tip of a cigarette in the darkness. Leaning over the railing, Maxime gave me a wave.

"Careful as you climb up!" he called. "It's really dangerous in the dark."

I turned on the flashlight in my phone. The ankle I had twisted in the church was still throbbing. Every step was painful. As I scrambled over the boulders, I noticed that the wind that had been blowing since morning had finally abated. The sky was overcast now, the stars gone. I had made it about halfway when a terrible cry made me look up. I saw two figures silhouetted against a gray wash. One was Maxime; the other was a stranger trying to push him over the railing. I let out a roar and climbed faster so I could reach him, but I arrived too late. Maxime had fallen almost ten meters.

I set off in pursuit of his attacker but did not get far on my ankle. As I turned back, I saw that a small group of partygoers had gathered around Maxime and one of them was calling an ambulance.

I blinked back tears. For a split second, I thought I saw the ghostly figure of Vinca moving among the alums. Translucent and bewitching, the apparition, in a black leather jacket thrown over a slip dress, fishnet stockings, and ankle boots, cleaved the darkness.

Beyond all reach, the specter seemed more alive than all the people gathered around my oldest friend.

ANNABELLE

Saturday, December 19, 1992

My name is Annabelle Degalais. I was born in Italy, in a little village in Piedmont, in the mid-1940s. At school, the other children called me the Austrian. These days, to the students and teachers at the lycée, I am the dean of the faculty. My name is Annabelle Degalais, and before the night is over, I will be a murderer.

And yet nothing in this late afternoon gives any inkling of the tragedy that is about to occur on this, the first day of the Christmas vacation. My husband, Richard, has taken two of our three children on vacation to Tahiti, leaving me at the helm of the school. I have been on duty since first light, but I love being in the thick of the action. I love making decisions. The blizzard has caused chaos in the area. It is six p.m., and this is the first moment I have had to finally draw breath. My thermos is empty, so I decide to go get some tea from the machine in the staff room. I've just gotten up from my chair when the door to my office opens and a young woman strides in uninvited.

"Hello, Vinca."

"Hello."

Looking at Vinca Rockwell, I have a flicker of apprehension. Despite the bitter cold, she is wearing a short plaid skirt, a leather jacket, and high-heeled ankle boots. I can immediately tell that she is stoned out of her mind.

"What can I do for you?"

"You can give me another seventy-five thousand francs."

I know Vinca pretty well and I kind of like her, even though my son is in love with her and it's breaking his heart. She is in the drama club and she's one of my most gifted students, simultaneously cerebral and sensual with a crazy streak that makes her more endearing. She is sophisticated, artistic, accomplished. She's played me some of the songs she has been writing, graceful melodies that have the mystical beauty of P. J. Harvey and Leonard Cohen.

"Seventy-five thousand francs?"

She hands me a plain brown envelope and, without waiting to be asked, slumps into the chair opposite. I open the envelope and look at the pictures. I am surprised without being surprised. I am certainly not hurt, because every decision I make has been influenced by a single precept: Never allow yourself to be vulnerable. And that is my strength.

"You don't look too good, Vinca," I say, handing back the envelope.

"You're the one who won't look too good when the parents' committee sees these photos of your sleazy husband."

I can see that she is shivering. She looks feverish, agitated, and exhausted.

"Why did you say *another* seventy-five thousand francs? Has Richard already given you money?"

"He gave me a hundred thousand francs, but it's not enough."

Richard's family has never had a penny. All the money in our family is mine, inherited from my adoptive father, Roberto Orsini, who earned it working with his bare hands, building houses and villas along the Mediterranean coast.

"I don't have that kind of money on me, Vinca."

I'm playing for time, but she is not about to be browbeaten.

"I don't care what you have to do. I want the cash by Sunday night."

I can tell that she's both disoriented and out of control. Probably under the influence of a mixture of alcohol and medication.

"You won't get money out of me," I snap. "I can't stand black-mailers. Richard was an idiot to pay you."

"Fine—you asked for it!" Vinca says, then stalks out and slams the door.

★ ★ ★

I sit behind my desk for a moment. I think about my son, so madly in love with this girl that he's about to fuck up his education. I think about Richard, who thinks only with his prick. I think about the family I have to protect. And I think about Vinca.

I spend a long time thinking, then I go out into the darkness and trudge through the snow to the Nicolas de Staël building. I have to try to reason with her. When she opens the door, she assumes I've come to give her the money.

"Listen, Vinca. You're not well. I'd like to try and help you. Why don't you tell me what's wrong. Why do you need all this money?"

She suddenly explodes and starts to threaten me. I offer to call a doctor or take her to the hospital.

"There's something not right with you, Vinca. But together we can find a solution to whatever the problem is."

I try to calm her. I use all my powers of persuasion, but I have no hold over her. She is like a woman possessed, capable of anything. Between racking sobs, she lets out a bitter laugh. Then, out of the blue, she takes a pregnancy test from her pocket.

"Your darling husband did this!"

For the first time since I can remember, I am shaken. I feel a fault line opening up inside me, a terrifying private earthquake I don't know how to stop. I see my whole life going up in flames. My life, and my family's. I cannot simply stand here and do nothing. I cannot let our lives be reduced to ashes by some nineteen-year-old pyromaniac. As Vinca continues to taunt me, I look around and see the replica of a Brancusi statue I bought at the Louvre for Thomas and that he immediately gave to her. A red mist descends, blotting out everything. I grab the statue and bring it down hard on Vinca's skull. She crumples like a rag doll under the force of the blow.

★ ★ ★

The blackout lasts for a long moment. Time stops. Nothing exists anymore. My mind is frozen, just like the snow outside. When, finally, I come to my senses, I realize that Vinca is dead. The only thing I can do is to play for time. I drag Vinca over to her bed, lay her on her side to hide the wound, and pull a blanket over her.

I trudge back through a landscape as mournful as a ghostly heath to the safe cocoon of my office. Sitting in my chair, I call Francis again and again, but he doesn't answer. This time, it's over.

I close my eyes and, despite my agitation, try to think. Life has taught me that most problems can be overcome by the power of thought. The first thing that occurs to me—the most obvious—is that I simply need to get rid of Vinca's body before she is found. It would be tricky, but possible. I consider a number of scenarios, but each time I come to the same conclusion: If the Rockwell heiress suddenly disappears from the lycée, it will trigger a shock wave. Every possible means will be used to find her. The police will search the school from top to bottom, bring in forensics teams, question students, investigate anyone Vinca has been seeing. There might be witnesses of her affair with Richard. Whoever has taken the photos Vinca showed me will probably try to blackmail us or turn us in to the police. There is no escape.

For the first time in my life, I feel completely besieged. Forced to surrender. By ten p.m., I have decided to call the police. I am just about to pick up the phone when I see Francis walking around the Agora with Ahmed and heading toward my office. I run out to meet him. The look on his face is unlike anything I have ever seen.

"Annabelle!" he calls, instinctively realizing that something is very wrong.

"I've done something terrible," I say, and I fall into his arms.

★ ★ ★

And I tell him about my confrontation with Vinca Rockwell.

"I need you to be brave," he whispers when I have finally finished, "because there's something I have to tell you."

I thought I had already stared into the abyss but, as Francis tells me about the death of Alexis Clément, about how Thomas and Maxime are involved, I start to gasp for breath. I am completely at a loss. He explains that, since they were already at work on the new gym, he and Ahmed have walled up the body in the new building.

He takes me into his arms and tells me that he will find some way out of this, reminds me of the ordeals that we have already faced together.

★ ★ ★

He is the one who comes up with the idea.

He is the one who points out that, ironically, two people disappearing will seem less suspicious than one. That Vinca's murder might make it easier to disguise the murder of Alexis and vice versa, if only we can find some way to link them.

For two hours, we try to come up with a plausible scenario. I tell him about the rumors of the affair and the letters Thomas found that give credence to the story. Suddenly, Francis feels hopeful, but I don't share his optimism. Even if we can make the bodies disappear, any investigation will still focus on the lycée, and the pressure on us will be unbearable. He agrees, weighs the pros and cons, even suggests confessing to the murders himself. This is the first time in our lives that we are prepared to surrender. Not for want of strength or courage but simply because there are some battles that cannot be won.

Suddenly, in the silence of the night, we are startled by a loud hammering. We turn toward the window. Outside, banging on the glass, is a girl whose face is haggard and distraught. It is not the ghost of Vinca Rockwell come back to haunt us. It is Fanny Brahimi, who is staying in the dorms over Christmas vacation.

"Dean Degalais!"

I shoot Francis a worried look. Fanny lives in the same building as Vinca. I am convinced she is about to tell me that she has just found Vinca's body.

"It's over, Francis," I say. "We'll have to call the police."

But the door to my office flies opens and Fanny falls into my arms, sobbing hysterically. In that moment, I do not yet know that God has just sent the solution to all our problems. The God of the Italians. The one we prayed to as children in the little church of Montaldicio.

"I killed Vinca!" she wails. "I killed Vinca!"

15

THE PRETTIEST GIRL IN
THE SCHOOL

1.

By the time I left the emergency department at La Fontonne Hospital it was two a.m. What does death smell like? To me, it is that smell of medication, bleach, and cleaning products that pervades the corridors of every hospital.

Maxime had fallen at least ten meters and landed on the paved path below. Shrubs and branches on the slope had broken his fall, but that had not been enough to prevent multiple fractures to his vertebrae, pelvis, legs, and ribs.

Taking Olivier with me in the car, I followed the ambulance to the hospital and caught a brief glimpse of Maxime as he was being admitted. His body was covered in bruises, immobilized by a rigid brace and a cervical collar. His face, pale and expressionless, half hidden by IV tubes, was a painful reminder that I had not been able to protect him.

The doctors that Olivier managed to talk to had been pessimistic. Maxime was in a coma. His blood pressure was very low despite an infusion of norepinephrine. He had suffered a skull fracture and bruising to the brain, possibly even a subdural hematoma. We sat for a long time in the waiting room until the hospital staff made it clear that there was little point in our hanging around. The prognosis was not good, although they were taking Maxime for a CT scan to get a clearer picture of the extent of his injuries. The next seventy-two hours would prove crucial. I knew from what they did not say that Maxime's life was hanging by a thread. Olivier refused to leave, but he insisted that I go and get some sleep.

"You look terrible, and anyway, I'd rather wait on my own—you understand."

I nodded. In fact, I had no real desire to be there when the police came to take statements. Stepping out into the parking lot, I was met by driving rain. In only a few hours, the weather had changed drastically; the wind had dropped to make way for a lowering gray sky streaked with flashes of lightning.

I climbed into my mother's Mercedes with some difficulty and checked my phone. No messages from Fanny or from my father. I tried calling but neither of them picked up. This was typical of Richard. He had probably found his wife, and now that he was reassured, everyone else could go to hell.

I turned the key in the ignition but stayed there in the parking lot with the engine idling. I felt cold. My eyes were heavy, my throat was dry, and my mind was still hazy with alcohol. I had rarely felt so exhausted. I hadn't slept on the red-eye the night before and not much on the night before that. I was suffering from crippling jet lag, too much vodka, and too much stress. I could no longer control my thoughts, which were careening off in all directions. As rain hammered on the hood, I slumped against the steering wheel.

We need to talk, Thomas. I've found out something—something really fucking serious that... Maxime's last words rang in my ears. What was it that he needed to tell me so urgently? What could he have discovered that was so serious? The future seemed grim. Though I had not yet reached the end of my investigation, I was forced to accept that I would never see Vinca again.

Alexis, Vinca, Francis, Maxime... the list of victims was growing. It was up to me to end this, but how? The smell inside my mother's car took me back to my childhood. It was the perfume she had always worn—Jicky by Guerlain. An intoxicating, mysterious perfume that combined the scents of Provence—lavender, citrus, rosemary—with lingering notes of old leather and civet musk. For a moment, I soaked in the smell. Everything led back to my mother...

I turned on the overhead light. A frivolous question occurred to me: How much did a car like this cost? Somewhere in the neighborhood of a hundred and fifty thousand euros, probably. Where had my mother gotten the money to pay for it? My parents both had decent pensions, and they had a beautiful house they had bought back in the 1970s, when the middle class could still afford to buy on the Côte d'Azur. But this car did not fit with my image of my mother. Suddenly, it occurred to me that Annabelle had not left me with the convertible by accident. It had been a deliberate ploy. I thought about the scene this afternoon. Annabelle had presented me with a fait accompli. She had given me no choice but to borrow her car. Why?

I looked down at the key ring. I recognized the keys to the villa and the mailbox, but there was another one, a large impressive key with a black head. The expensive oval key ring of calfskin leather was monogrammed in chrome with the twined initials *A* and *P*. I assumed that the *A* stood for Annabelle, but what did the *P* stand for?

I fired up the GPS system and scrolled through the preset addresses but found nothing suspicious. I pressed the first item—HOME—but

GUILLAUME MUSSO

though the hospital was barely two kilometers from my parents' villa in La Constance, the GPS showed a winding route running for twenty kilometers along the coast toward Nice.

Confused, I released the hand brake and drove out of the parking lot, wondering what this place was that my mother considered home.

2.

Despite the pitch-dark and the driving rain, traffic was moving smoothly. In less than twenty minutes, the GPS told me I had arrived at my destination, a gated community midway between Cagnes-sur-Mer and Saint-Paul de Vence. This was Aurelia Park, the place where Francis had had his bachelor pad and where he had been murdered. I pulled over about thirty meters from the imposing wrought-iron gates. Since the wave of home invasions, security had been drastically ramped up. A night watchman who looked like he was ex-army was on duty.

A Maserati drove past and pulled up to the gates. There were two lanes; the left was for visitors, who had to report to the security guard, and the right was for residents, who drove past a sensor that scanned their license plates and automatically opened the gate. Letting the engine idle, I took some time to think. The initials *AP* referred to Aurelia Park, the development Francis had had a stake in building. Abruptly, I remembered that Aurelia was my mother's middle name—one she much preferred to Annabelle. Instantly, I had another realization: Francis had given my mother the Mercedes convertible.

Had my mother and Francis been lovers? The thought had never occurred to me until then, but it didn't seem entirely far-fetched. I put on my signal and turned into the lane reserved for residents. It was raining so hard that the guard would not be able to see my face. A sensor scanned the license plate of the Mercedes, and the gate swung open. If the plate was in the system, it meant my mother was a regular visitor here.

I drove slowly along the path that wound through a forest of pine and olive trees. Built in the late 1990s, Aurelia Park was famous for its landscaped Mediterranean grounds with its rare and exotic plant species. The development's pièce de résistance, much praised by *Architectural Digest,* was an artificial river running through the vast gardens.

There were only thirty houses in the community, each secluded from the others. From the article in the *Nouvel Observateur,* I knew that Francis's villa was number 27. It was at the top of a hill, surrounded by lush vegetation. In the darkness, I could make out palm trees and magnolias. I parked in front of another wrought-iron gate, this one flanked by thick rows of cypresses.

I got out of the car, and when I'd taken a few steps, I heard a click and the gate swung open. The unfamiliar key on the ring was obviously an electronic smart key. As I walked up the flagstone driveway, I heard rushing water. It was not a distant murmur; it sounded as though the river was flowing beneath my feet. I flicked the outdoor switch, and the garden and terraces were instantly flooded with light. Walking around the house, I realized that, like Frank Lloyd Wright's masterpiece Fallingwater, the villa was built over a river.

A slick, contemporary building with no trace of Provence or the Mediterranean, it reminded me of mid-century American architecture. Two cantilevered stories of glass, pale limestone, and reinforced concrete, it was perfectly in harmony with the vegetation and the rocky outcropping on which it was built.

The digital lock opened as I came to the door. I was worried about setting off the alarm system—there was a sign on the wall outside—but nothing happened. As in the garden, there was a single button to activate all the lights. I pushed it and discovered an interior as elegant as it was spectacular.

The ground floor comprised a living room, a dining room, and a kitchen. The style was Japanese, everything open plan, with various living areas separated only by lattice screens that allowed light to stream through.

I stepped into the space and gazed around. I had never imagined Francis's bachelor pad would look like this. Everything was warm and sophisticated—the vast limestone hearth, the pale oak beams, the smooth curves of the walnut furniture. A half-finished bottle of Corona stood on the cocktail bar, indicating that someone had been here recently. Next to the beer lay a pack of cigarettes and a lighter with a carved lacquer case.

Maxime's Zippo.

Of course. He had come straight here after our conversation at my mother's house, and what he had discovered had been so upsetting that he had rushed out, leaving his cigarettes and his lighter.

Standing next to the large sliding glass doors, I realized that it was the spot where Francis had been murdered. He had been tortured next to the fireplace and left for dead but had managed to drag himself across the parquet floor to the wall of glass overlooking the river. It was from here that he had phoned my mother. But I didn't know whether she had answered that call.

3.

My mother...

I could feel her presence everywhere in this house. I sensed her guiding hand behind every piece of furniture, every element of the design. This was her home too. Startled by a creaking floorboard, I spun around and found myself face-to-face with my mother.

Or rather, her portrait, which was hanging on the far wall of the room. Slowly, I wandered over toward the living-room area lined with bookshelves. There were other photographs. The closer I came, the more I understood what, until now, had been a mystery.

Fifteen photographs sketched out a retrospective of the parallel life that Francis and Annabelle had shared for years. They had been all around the world together. I recognized iconic places: the Sahara Desert, Vienna shrouded in snow, a tram in Lisbon, the roaring Gullfoss waterfall in Iceland, the cypresses of the Tuscan countryside, Eilean Donan Castle in Scotland, New York before the fall of the Twin Towers.

More than the places, it was the smiles, the serenity on their faces, that gave me goose bumps. My mother and Francis had been in love. For decades, they had shared an idyllic, illicit love affair, a long-term relationship that no one suspected.

But why? Why had they not simply made their relationship official?

Deep down, I knew the answer. It was complicated and owed much to their remarkable personalities. Both Annabelle and Francis were tough, no-nonsense individuals who would have found it comforting to build a world that was theirs alone. They had always carved out their lives *against the world,* against the mediocrity, against the hell that was other people and from which they longed to be free. Beauty and the Beast. Two extraordinary people who scorned respectability, propriety, marriage.

I became aware that I was crying. Probably because in the photographs, my mother was smiling, and because I had rediscovered the person I had known as a child, the woman whose gentleness would sometimes appear from beneath the icy mask of the Austrian. I wasn't crazy. I hadn't dreamed it. This other woman existed—the proof was right there before my eyes.

I wiped away my tears, but still they flowed. I found this double life, this unique love story, profoundly moving. Surely, at heart, true love paid no heed to convention. Francis and my mother had experienced that purity, that chemistry, while I had merely dreamed it or experienced it vicariously in novels.

One last picture caught my eye. It was a small sepia print, a class photo taken on a village square. It was inscribed in pen: *Montaldicio, October 12, 1954.* In it were three rows of children, about ten years old, all of them with raven-black hair except for one little girl standing off to the side who had blond hair and pale eyes. All the children were looking straight at the lens except for one little boy with a chubby, expressionless face. As the photographer clicked the shutter, Francis only had eyes for the Austrian. The prettiest girl in the school. Their story was foretold in this photo. Everything had started here, when they were children, in the little Italian village where they had grown up.

4.

A floating hardwood staircase led to the upper floor. At a glance, I took in the layout: a huge master suite with an adjoining study, a dressing room, and a built-in sauna. Even more than on the ground floor, the glass walls blurred the boundaries between inside and out. The setting was exceptional. You could feel the surrounding forest, hear the babble of the river mingling with the patter of the rain. A covered terrace led to a swimming pool that opened onto the sky and a hanging garden planted with wisteria, mimosa, and Japanese cherry.

For a moment, I almost turned back for fear of what I was about to discover. But now was not the time for stalling. I pushed open the door to the other room and discovered something even more intimate. There were more photographs, but here they were all of me and spanned my life from earliest childhood. I remembered the impression that had struck me earlier, one that had grown more forceful as my investigation progressed: in my search for Vinca, I was also, perhaps especially, looking for myself.

The oldest of the photographs was a black-and-white snapshot: *Birth of T., Jeanne-d'Arc Maternity Ward, October 8, 1974.* An early example of a selfie. Francis is holding the camera and has his arm around my mother, who is cradling a newborn. And the baby is me.

It was both shocking and obvious. The truth was staring me in the face. I felt a wave of emotion crash over me, and as it ebbed, the catharsis left me dazed. Suddenly, everything was clear—all the pieces fit together—but the realization was tempered with grief. I kept staring at the photo. I looked at Francis and it was like looking in the mirror. How could I have been so blind? I finally understood everything, why I had never truly felt like Richard's son, why I had thought of Maxime as a brother, why some instinct prompted me to spring into action whenever Francis was attacked.

Not quite knowing what to feel, I sat on the edge of the bed and wiped away my tears. Knowing that I was Francis's son felt like a burden being lifted from me, but knowing that I would never be able to talk to him left me filled with regrets. One question nagged at me—did Richard know about the family secret, about his wife's double life? Probably, but I could not be sure. Maybe he had simply buried his head in the sand all these years, oblivious to the reason Annabelle tolerated his countless infidelities.

I got up to leave the room, then immediately turned back to take the maternity-ward photo. I needed it as proof of where I came from. As I picked up the frame, I noticed a small wall safe. The keypad required a six-digit code. *My date of birth?* I didn't believe it could be so simple, but it was worth a shot. Sometimes the simplest solution...

With a click, the safe door swung open. It was not very deep. I put my hand inside and took out a pistol. The famous gun Francis hadn't had time to use the night he was attacked. In a small burlap bag, I found a dozen .38-caliber cartridges. I'd never been fascinated by guns. As a rule, I found them repellent. But I'd had to do some research while writing my novels. I felt the weight of it. It was heavy and compact and looked like an old Smith and Wesson Model 36, the famous Chief's Special, with its rosewood grip and nickel-plated body.

I slipped five cartridges into the cylinder and tucked it into my belt. I wasn't sure that I knew how to use it, but I was sure that danger was everywhere. Someone had decided to eliminate all those involved in Vinca's death. And I was probably next on the list.

As I went back down the stairs, my phone rang. I hesitated. When you get a call at three in the morning and the screen says Private number, it's never a good thing. Eventually, I picked up.

It was the police. Chief Vincent Debruyne was calling me from the Antibes police station to say that my mother had been found dead and my father was claiming to have killed her.

ANNABELLE

My name is Annabelle Degalais. I was born in Italy, in a little village in Piedmont, in the mid-1940s. And the following minutes may well be my last.

On December 25 last year, when Francis called me in the dead of night shortly before he died, he had time to say only one thing: *Protect Thomas and Maxime.*

That night, I realized that the past had come back to haunt us, trailing threats of danger and death. Later, when I read the newspaper account of how Francis had suffered before he died, I knew that this story would end as it had begun—in blood and fear.

For twenty-five years, we had managed to keep the past at bay. To protect our children, we had double-locked every door, ensuring that we had left no trace. Vigilance became second nature, though, over time, the constant suspicion ceases to feel morbid. There were days when the fear that had been gnawing at me for years seemed to fade, and so I lowered my guard. This was a mistake.

Francis's death almost destroyed me. My heart exploded. I thought I was dying. As I rode in the back of the ambulance on the way to the hospital, part of me wanted to let go, to be with Francis, but some unknown force kept me clinging to life.

I had to fight to protect my son. I might have lost Francis, but I was determined not to lose Thomas.

I would have to finish the job, and I knew this meant I would have to kill whoever was threatening my son's future. And make that person pay for murdering the only man I had ever loved.

When I was discharged from the hospital, I combed through my memories. I carried out my own investigation, determined to find out who had come looking for revenge after all these years. A revenge that was brutal, ruthless, and terrifying. Although I'm not a young woman anymore, I still have my wits about me. But even though I devoted all my time to searching for answers, I could not find the slightest lead. All the people who might have wanted revenge were old or dead. Something was disrupting the peaceful running of our lives and threatening to derail them. It was clear that Vinca had taken a secret to her grave. And now a secret we did not even know existed had suddenly resurfaced, trailing death in its wake.

I conducted exhaustive searches but found nothing. Until, earlier today, when Thomas dragged all his old things up from the basement and spread them out on the kitchen table. Suddenly, it was staring me in the face. I felt like sobbing with rage. The truth had been right there in front of our eyes all the time, shrouded by a single detail that none of us had been able to understand.

A detail that changed everything.

★ ★ ★

It is still light as I arrive at Cap d'Antibes. I pull up in front of a house overlooking the boulevard de Bacon, a house whose whitewashed façade gives little sense of the sheer size of the residence. I leave the car double-parked and press the entry-phone button. A gardener trimming hedges tells me that the person I am looking for has taken the dogs for a walk along the sentier de Tire-Poil.

I drive a few kilometers farther, to the parking lot at Keller Beach. The place is utterly deserted. I open the trunk and take out the rifle I "borrowed" from Richard.

To steel myself, I think back to the Sunday-morning hunting trips I used to take with my adoptive father. I loved going with him, even though we didn't talk much; those shared moments meant much more than long conversations. I think fondly of Butch, our Irish setter, always snuffling for partridges, woodcocks, and hares. There was no hunting dog like him for flushing out game so that we could shoot.

I test the weight of the rifle, then stroke the oiled walnut stock, linger for a moment on the intricate tracery on the barrel. With a click, I open the break-action and load two cartridges. Then I set off down the narrow coastal path.

Some fifty meters along, I come to a barrier with a sign: DANGER—NO ENTRY. The heavy tide last Wednesday must have triggered a rockslide. I duck around the barrier and clamber over the boulders.

The sea air is exhilarating, and the dazzling view that stretches all the way to the Alps reminds me of where I came from. As I scale a steep escarpment, I see the tall, slender figure of Francis's killer, surrounded by three huge hounds that begin to pad toward me.

I raise the rifle, point the barrel toward my target, peer through the sight. I know I will not get a second chance.

I hear the shot, clear, short, and swift, and suddenly my entire life hits me in the face.

Montaldicio, the rolling hills of Italy, the little school, the village square, the insults, the brutality, the blood, the pride of standing firm, Thomas's winning grin when he was three years old, the lifetime spent loving someone who was different from other men.

Everything that ever mattered in my life . . .

16

THE NIGHT STILL WAITS
FOR YOU

1.

In the raging storm, the streets of Antibes looked as though they had been splattered by some thick, viscous substance a clumsy painter had poured onto his canvas.

It was four a.m. and still raining. I was pacing up and down outside the police station on the avenue des Frères-Olivier. My hair was soaked and rain was seeping under my shirt collar. Cell phone pressed to my ear, I was trying to persuade one of the most prominent lawyers in Nice to represent my father if he was kept in custody.

I felt as though I were drowning in a torrent of catastrophes. Barely an hour earlier, when I left Aurelia Park, I had been stopped by the police for speeding. Frantic and distraught, I had been doing a hundred and eighty kilometers an hour on the highway. The cops insisted that I take a Breathalyzer, and the cocktails and vodka shots I had drunk earlier that evening meant that they immediately suspended my license. If I was to get anywhere, I had no choice but to call Stéphane Pianelli. He had already heard the news about my mother's death and said he would drive right over. He picked me up in his Dacia SUV with little Ernesto fast asleep in the back seat. The car smelled of gingerbread and had never seen a car wash in its life. As we drove to the police station, he briefed me, filling me in on the details I had not yet heard from Chief Debruyne. My mother's body had been found in Cap d'Antibes, on a rocky coastal path. It had been the police, called to the scene by local residents worried that they had heard gunshots, who pronounced her dead.

"I'm really sorry to have to tell you, Thomas, but the circumstances of her death are truly horrible. I've never seen the likes of it around here."

The dome light of the Dacia was still on. I could see that Pianelli was shaking. After all, he knew my parents. I was completely numb. Beyond exhaustion, beyond grief, beyond pain.

"There was a rifle near the crime scene, but Annabelle did not die of a gunshot wound."

He was reluctant to tell me exactly what had happened. I'd had to insist in order to get the truth.

And this was what I was now trying to explain to the lawyer as I paced up and down outside the precinct: My mother's face had been beaten to a bloody pulp with a rifle butt. It was clear that my father had not done it. Richard had gone there only because I'd given him the address, and Annabelle had been dead when he arrived. He had broken down in tears on the rocky terrain; his mistake, as he stared at the dead body of his wife, was to sob: "This is my fault!" He had not meant it literally, I explained to the lawyer. It was simply a way of saying that he hadn't been able to protect her, that he felt responsible. The lawyer accepted this without question and agreed to help us.

It was still raining when I hung up. I huddled under a deserted bus shelter on the place du Général-de-Gaulle while I made two agonizing phone calls, first to my brother and then to my sister, to tell them that our mother was dead. True to form, Jérôme remained stoic, though was clearly deeply upset. The conversation with my sister, however, was surreal. While I had assumed she was in bed with her husband in Paris, she was actually on a weekend trip to Stockholm with her new boyfriend. I didn't know it, but she had gotten divorced more than a year ago. She told me a little about the divorce and then I told her about the tragedy, though I was vague about the circumstances.

She burst into hysterical sobs and there was nothing that I or the guy in bed next to her could do to calm her.

Afterward, I spent a long time wandering aimlessly around the square while the storm raged. The square was flooded. A pipe had burst and water was gushing up through a hole in the pavement. The floodlit fountains sprayed long golden jets into the darkness, where they mingled with rain to form a mist.

I was soaked to the skin; my heart was broken, my brain fried, my body shattered. It felt as though the thick fog that drowned my footsteps and blotted out the square, the curbs, and the road markings had washed away my moral compass, my every point of reference. I no longer understood my role in this story that had haunted me for so many years. This never-ending fall. This film noir in which I was more victim than hero.

2.

Suddenly, twin headlights pierced the fog and came toward me; it was Stéphane Pianelli's Dacia.

"Get in, Thomas," he said, rolling down the window. "I thought maybe you'd have trouble getting home. I'll drive you."

Exhausted, I accepted. The passenger seat was still piled high with junk so, as I had earlier, I climbed into the back seat next to the sleeping Ernesto.

Pianelli explained that he was on his way back from the offices of *Nice-Matin*. Since the paper had been put to bed early in the evening, there would be no mention of my mother's death in the morning edition, but Stéphane had gone back to the office to write a piece for the online edition.

"I haven't mentioned anything about your father being suspected," he said.

As we drove along the coast toward La Fontonne, Pianelli finally admitted that he had run into Fanny earlier in the evening when he had stopped by the hospital to check on Maxime.

"She was a nervous wreck. I've never seen her like that."

Alarm bells started to ring in my frazzled brain. "What did she tell you?"

We had stopped at the intersection near Siesta. The longest traffic light in the world...

"Everything. She told me everything, Thomas. How she killed Vinca and how your mother and Francis helped her cover it up."

Suddenly I understood why Pianelli had seemed agitated when he drove me to the police station. He had not simply been upset by my mother's death; he was overwhelmed that he had stumbled onto a murder story.

"Did she tell you what happened to Alexis Clément?"

"No," he admitted. "That's the one piece of the puzzle I'm still missing."

The traffic light turned green and the Dacia turned onto the highway, heading toward La Constance. I felt completely crushed. I could barely think straight. I felt as though the day would never end, as though a wave would come and sweep everything away. There had been too many revelations, too many tragedies, too many deaths; there were too many threats still hanging over those dearest to me. So I did what no one should ever do. I let down my guard. I broke my twenty-five-year silence because I wanted to believe in people. I wanted to believe that Pianelli was a decent guy, that he would put our friendship before his job as a journalist.

I told him everything, about Clément's murder and what I had found out in the past few hours. When he reached my parents' house, Pianelli parked outside the gates and left the engine running. We sat talking in the battered SUV for half an hour, trying to figure things out. Stéphane patiently helped me piece together what had happened the previous afternoon. My mother had obviously over-heard my conversation with Maxime. Like me, she had probably spotted the difference between the handwriting in Vinca's book and the handwriting in the notes Alexis Clément had made on my essay. Unlike me, she had been able to use this to identify the person who had murdered Francis. Either she had arranged to meet the killer or she had tracked him to Cap d'Antibes, planning to kill him. In a nutshell, she had succeeded where we had failed; she had unmasked the monster whose murderous rage seemed boundless.

It was an insight that had cost her her life.

"Try to get some rest," Stéphane said, hugging me. "I'll call you later. We can go to the hospital and see how Maxime is doing."

Despite his affectionate words, I didn't have the strength to answer. I just slammed the car door. Since I did not have a key fob, I had to climb over the gates. I remembered that it was possible to get into the house through the garage, which my parents never locked. In the living room, I didn't even bother to turn on the light. I set my bag and Francis's pistol on the table. I pulled off my sodden clothes, stumbled across the living room like a sleepwalker, and collapsed on the sofa. I wrapped myself in a thick wool blanket and let sleep overcome me.

I had gambled and lost on every front. I had been crushed by fate. Utterly unprepared, I had just lived through the worst day of my life. Yesterday morning, as I landed on the Côte d'Azur, I'd known that an earthquake was looming, but I hadn't reckoned on its magnitude, its brutal, devastating consequences.

17

THE GARDEN OF ANGELS

Sunday, May 14, 2017

When I opened my eyes, the midday sun was streaming into the living room. It was one o'clock in the afternoon, and I had slept through half the day. A deep, dreamless sleep that allowed me to completely disconnect from the blackness of reality.

I had been woken by my cell phone ringing. I hadn't been quick enough to answer, so I listened to the message. Using his lawyer's phone, my father had called to tell me he had been released from custody and was on his way home. I tried calling him back, but my phone battery died. My charger was in the suitcase I had left in the rental car, so I vainly searched for a compatible charger for my phone, then gave up. Using the landline, I called the hospital, but there was no one who could update me on Maxime's condition.

I showered and pulled on some clothes I found in my father's wardrobe, a Charvet shirt and a vicuña jacket. I drank three straight espressos, gazing out the window as the sea unfurled its myriad shades of blue. In the kitchen, all my old things were exactly where I had left them. A large cardboard box was precariously balanced on a stool, and the hardwood counter was littered with old school essays, report cards, mixtapes, and the collection of Tsvetaeva's poetry. I opened it again and reread the beautiful dedication:

For Vinca,
I wish I were an incorporeal soul
that I might never leave you.
To love you is to live.
Alexis

I glanced through the book, distractedly at first and then with increasing attention. Published by Mercure de France, *Letter to an Amazon* was not, as I had thought, a collection of poems but an essay, and someone—either Vinca or the person who had given it to her— had annotated it extensively. I lingered over one of the sentences that had been underlined. *This is . . . the only tear in this perfect entity which is two women who love each other. The impossible thing is not resisting the temptation of a man but resisting the need for a child.*

Two women who love one another . . . Exquisitely written, the essay— penned in the early 1930s—was a poetic paean to lesbian love. Not a manifesto but a thoughtful reflection on the impossibility of two women having a child that was biologically both of theirs.

It was at this point that I finally understood what I had been missing all along. And it changed everything.

Vinca loved women. Or at least, Vinca had been in love with a woman. Alexis. The name was unisex. Although in France, it was almost exclusively a man's name, in English-speaking countries, it was more usually a woman's. I was blown away by what I had discovered, though I could not help but wonder whether I was on the wrong track again.

The buzzer for the front gate sounded. Assuming that it was my father, I pressed the button and went out to meet him. But rather than seeing Richard, I found myself face-to-face with a thin young man with delicate features and piercing eyes.

"I'm Corentin Meirieu, Monsieur Pianelli's assistant," he said as he took off his bicycle helmet and shook out his flame-red hair.

He leaned his contraption—a curious bamboo bicycle with a spring-mounted leather saddle—against the wall.

"Please accept my condolences," he said with a compassionate expression that was half hidden by a bushy red beard at odds with his youthful face.

I invited him in for a coffee.

"Thanks, as long as it's not Nespresso."

We went into the kitchen, and while he was studying a pack of arabica near the coffeemaker, he patted the messenger bag slung across his chest.

"I've got some info for you."

While I made the coffee, Corentin Meirieu sat on a stool and pulled out a sheaf of annotated documents. As I set down a cup in front of him, I caught a glimpse of the front page of the *Nice-Matin* late edition sticking out of his bag. There was a photograph of the coastal path with the headline "Fear Stalks the City."

"It wasn't exactly easy, but I managed to dig up some interesting information on who's financing the building project at Saint-Ex."

I took a seat opposite him and nodded for him to continue.

"You were right—funding for the project is completely dependent on a substantial donation recently made to the school."

"How recently?"

"Early this year."

Around the time Francis was murdered. "Who's behind the donation? Vinca Rockwell's family?" I had been considering the idea that

Vinca's grandfather, unable to cope with the loss of his grand-daughter, had somehow managed to organize a vendetta from beyond the grave.

"No," Meirieu said, adding sugar to his coffee.

"Who, then?"

The bearded hipster checked his notes. "The endowment was made by an American cultural association, the Hutchinson and DeVille Foundation."

The name did not immediately ring a bell. Meirieu drained his coffee in one gulp.

"As the name suggests, the foundation is funded by two families, the Hutchinsons and the DeVilles, who made their fortunes with a brokerage company they started in California after the war. They now have hundreds of branches all over America." He glanced down at his notes. "The foundation acts as a patron of the arts and most of its donations are to schools, universities, and museums—St. Jean Baptiste High School, Berkeley, UCLA, the SF MoMA, the Los Angeles County Museum of Art . . . " Meirieu tugged at the sleeves of a denim shirt that was so tight, it looked like a second skin. "At the last board meeting, the directors were called in to vote on an unusual proposal. For the first time, it was suggested that the foundation fund a project outside the United States."

"This was the project at the Lycée Saint-Exupéry?"

"Exactly. It was a very heated debate. The project in itself was not without merit, but it included a number of bizarre elements, like the creation of a garden by the lake to be called the Garden of Angels."

"Stéphane mentioned something about a huge rose garden."

"That's it. The intention was that it should be a contemplative space dedicated to the memory of Vinca Rockwell."

"But that's insane, isn't it? Why would the foundation rubber-stamp such a bizarre project?"

"That's the thing—a majority of the board voted against it. But one of the families is now represented by a single heir. Apparently, there is some history of mental illness, so the directors were wary of this person, but according to the statutes of the foundation, she holds a large number of votes and managed to get the necessary additional votes to win a narrow majority."

I rubbed my eyes. I had the strange impression that I was close to the truth and yet did not understand a thing. I got up to get my school backpack. I wanted to check something. I dug out the 1992–1993 school yearbook and as I flicked through the pages, Meirieu continued.

"The heiress in question is named Alexis Charlotte DeVille. I think you used to know her. She was a teacher at Saint-Ex when you were studying there."

Alexis DeVille . . . the charismatic English teacher.

Dumbfounded, I stared at the photograph of the woman everyone had called Miss DeVille. Even the yearbook did not give her first name, only the initials A.C. I had finally found Alexis, the woman who had murdered my mother, killed Francis, and tried to kill Maxime. The woman who, indirectly, had hastened Vinca's tragic fate.

"She now spends six months of the year on the Côte d'Azur," Meirieu reported. "She bought the old Fitzgerald villa down in Cap d'Antibes—you know the one I mean?"

I rushed out the door, only to realize that I didn't have a car. I considered stealing the bamboo bike but instead went down to the basement and pulled the plastic tarpaulin off my old moped. I sat on the saddle and, as I'd done so often when I was fifteen, tried to kick-start the Peugeot 103.

But the basement was cold and damp, and the engine stalled. I ferreted out a toolbox and came back, removed the suppressor cap, and took out the spark plug. It was black and caked with soot.

As I'd done a hundred times in the mornings before setting off for school, I wiped the spark plug with an old rag, rubbed it down with sandpaper, and put it back.

I wheeled the moped out into the driveway and tried to kick-start it again. There was a slight improvement, but I couldn't get the engine to idle. I flipped up the kickstand, jumped on the saddle, and let myself coast downhill. The engine sputtered, coughed, and then backfired and started. I swung onto the main road, praying that it would hold out for a few kilometers.

RICHARD

Images collide inside my head. Excruciating, unreal. More terrible than the worst nightmares. My wife's face, crushed, splintered, shattered. Annabelle's beautiful face reduced to a mask of bloody flesh.

My name is Richard Degalais and I am tired of living.

If life truly is war, I have not just faced an enemy assault, I am lying in the trenches, my belly sliced open by a bayonet. Forced to surrender unconditionally in the most painful of all battles.

I stand motionless in the living room amid the dust motes that glitter golden in the light. My house is empty now. It will forever be empty. I find it difficult to accept the reality of what has happened. I have lost Annabelle forever. But when did I really lose her? A few hours ago on the beach at Cap d'Antibes? A few years ago? A few decades ago? Or it might be better to say that I have not really lost Annabelle, since she was never mine to lose.

I stare, hypnotized, at the pistol on the table in front of me. I have no idea what it's doing there. It's the sort of Smith and Wesson with a wooden grip you sometimes see in old Westerns. The cylinder is full—five .38-caliber bullets. I pick up the gun, gauge its weight. The gun is calling to me. A swift and sure solution to all my problems. In the short term, I find the prospect of death comforting. Gone would be the nearly fifty years of a strange marriage spent living with an unknowable woman who claimed that she loved me in her own way, which in truth meant that she didn't love me.

The truth is that Annabelle tolerated me, and, all things considered, it was better than nothing. Living with her was painful, but living without her would have killed me. We had our little private arrangement whereby, in the eyes of the world, I was the philandering husband—which I was—and that shielded her from gossip. Nothing and no one had a hold over Annabelle. She defied all classification, all norms, all proprieties. It was her freedom that fascinated me. After all, surely what we love in another is the mystery? I loved her, but her heart was not to be won. I loved her, but I was unable to protect her.

I press the barrel of the Chief's Special to my temple and suddenly, I can breathe more easily. I would love to know who put this pistol here for me to find. Thomas, maybe? The son who is not my son. This child who, like his mother, never loved me. I shut my eyes and I see his face in a dozen precise memories from when he was little. Images tinged with wonder and with pain. Wonder at this boy who was intelligent, curious, and a little too wise; pain because I knew that I was not the father.

Squeeze the trigger if you're man enough.

In the end, it is not fear that makes me stop. It's Mozart. The three-note figure for harp and oboe that alerts me whenever Annabelle sends me a text message. I flinch. I put the gun down and dive for my phone. Richard, you have mail. A.

The message was sent just now from Annabelle's phone. Only

that's impossible because Annabelle is dead, and besides, she left her cell phone here. The only explanation is that she set a timer to send the message before she died.

Richard, you have mail. A.

Mail? What mail? I check my phone but find no new e-mail. I go out of the house and down to the mailbox outside the gate. Next to a flyer for a sushi-delivery place, I find a thick blue envelope that reminds me of the love letters she used to send a lifetime ago. There are no stamps. I tear open the envelope. Annabelle might have put it there herself yesterday afternoon, though more likely it was delivered by messenger. I read the first sentence: *Richard, if you are reading this letter, it means that Alexis DeVille has killed me.*

It takes me an inordinate length of time to read the three pages. The contents leave me shocked and upset. It is a postmortem confession. And, in her inimitable way, it is also a love letter. It ends: *Now you have the fate of our family in your hands. You are the only one left with the strength and the courage to protect it, to save our son.*

18

NIGHT AND THE MAIDEN

1.

The moped's engine had conked out. Looking over the handlebars, I was pedaling furiously, standing on the pedals as though I were competing in the Tour de France carrying a fifty-kilo weight.

From the street, Villa Fitzgerald looked like a bunker. Despite the name, F. Scott Fitzgerald had never lived there, but old myths die hard. Fifty meters before I reached the house, I abandoned the moped on the pavement and stepped over the railing that ran along the shore. In this part of Cap d'Antibes, the golden sandy beaches gave way to a rugged, inaccessible coastline—steep rocky bluffs sculpted by the mistral, cliffs that tumbled into the sea. I scrabbled over the rocks, risking life and limb, and climbed the steep ridge that backed up to the garden of the villa.

I stepped onto the polished-concrete deck that surrounded the long cobalt-blue swimming pool. It extended as far as the steep staircase carved into the rock face that led down to a small pier. Clinging to the cliff, the Villa Fitzgerald almost literally had its toes in the water; it was one of the modernist houses built during the Roaring Twenties, with art deco and Mediterranean touches. The lime-washed geometric façade was surmounted by a flat roof terrace that was sheltered by a pergola. At this hour of the day, sky and sea merged in a single, shimmering blue.

Beneath an arcade was a covered patio. I crept around the villa until I found a half-open patio door, then slipped into the house.

Except for the fact that the view was of the Mediterranean rather than the Hudson River, the living room looked much like my loft in Tribeca, a minimalist space where every detail was carefully curated. The kind of interior you might see in *Architectural Digest*. The library contained many of the same books that mine did, reflecting the same breadth of culture—classical, literary, international.

The place also had that strange perfection of houses where there are no children, the slightly melancholy coolness of homes that do not pulse with the very substance of life: kids' laughter, stuffed toys, pieces of Lego everywhere, food crumbs stuck all over the table...

"Clearly, people in your family have a habit of walking into the lion's den."

I spun around to find Alexis DeVille standing ten meters away. I had seen her the day before, at the fiftieth-anniversary ceremony for Saint-Ex. She was simply dressed—jeans, striped blouse, V-neck sweater, Converse sneakers—but she was the kind of person who had a naturally commanding presence whatever the circumstances. A presence emphasized here by the three large dogs behind her: a Doberman with cropped ears, a black and tan pit bull terrier, and a Rottweiler.

I regretted having come without any means to defend myself as soon as I spotted the dogs. I'd rushed out of my parents' house on impulse, driven by sheer rage. And I had always thought that my most effective weapon was my mind, a lesson I'd learned from my teacher Jean-Christophe Graff. But as I thought about what Alexis DeVille had done to my mother, to Francis, and to Maxime, I realized that I had been wrong to be so impulsive.

Now that I had traced the truth back to its source, I felt helpless. In the end, I did not expect Alexis DeVille to tell me anything new. I already understood. But I could well imagine the exhilaration these two intelligent, liberated, beautiful women must have felt at the time. The intellectual intimacy, the physical intoxication, the feverish feeling of transgression. Although the idea troubled me, I realized that Alexis DeVille and I were not so different. We had both fallen in love with the same girl twenty-five years ago, and neither of us had ever gotten over it.

Tall, slim, with smooth skin that made it impossible to guess her age, Alexis DeVille had pinned her hair into a chignon. She seemed convinced that she was in control of this situation. The dogs did not take their eyes off me, but Alexis nonchalantly turned her back to me and studied the countless photographs on the walls—the famous glamour shots of Vinca that Dalanegra had told me about. His work was equal to the beauty of his model. He had perfectly captured the troubling, enthralling beauty of Vinca. The ephemeral nature of her youth.

2.

I decided to go on the attack.

"You've convinced yourself that you still love Vinca, but you're wrong. We do not kill those we love."

DeVille tore herself away from the photographs and turned her icy gaze on me, looking me up and down contemptuously.

"I could easily counter that by telling you that sometimes, killing someone is the ultimate act of love. But that's not the issue. I didn't kill Vinca—you did."

"Me?"

"You, your mother, Fanny, Francis Biancardini, and Francis's son...on some level, you're all responsible. You're all guilty."

"I suppose Ahmed told you?"

She moved toward me, flanked by her hellhounds. I thought of Hecate, Greek goddess of the shades, always accompanied by a pack of dogs howling at the moon. Hecate, who reigned over nightmares and suppressed desires, those parts of the human spirit where men and women are the most impure and the most fragile.

"Despite the evidence, I never believed that Vinca ran away with that guy," Alexis said. "I've spent years uncovering the truth. And by a cruel twist of fate, when I least expected it, it was served up to me on a platter."

The dogs growled at me. Panic was beginning to set in. The very sight of the animals left me paralyzed. I tried not to look them in the eye, but they could sense my fear.

"It happened about seven months ago," Alexis explained, "in the fruit and vegetable aisle of a supermarket. I was doing my shopping, and Ahmed recognized me. He asked if he could talk to me. The night Vinca died, Francis had sent him to collect some of her things, clean up her room, and get rid of any evidence that might implicate you all. When he was going through her coat pockets, he came across a letter and a photograph. He was the only one who knew from the start that I was Alexis—a secret the dumb bastard kept for twenty-five years."

Beneath her apparent calm, I could sense her rage, her fury.

"Ahmed wanted money to get home to Tunisia, and I wanted information. I gave him five thousand euros and he told me everything: the bodies walled up in the gym, the horror of that blood-soaked December night in 1992, the fact that you had all gotten off scot-free."

"Saying something over and over doesn't make it true," I said.

"There's only one person to blame for Vinca's death, and that's you. The person responsible for a crime isn't always the one who held the gun, as you well know."

For the first time, Alexis DeVille's face glowered irritably. As though responding to some telepathic order from their goddess, the three hounds encircled me. I felt cold sweat trickle down the small of my back.

In spite of my rising panic, I continued.

"I remember you back then. Your charisma. All the students admired you. Me most of all. A bright, beautiful thirty-year-old teacher who respected her students and knew how to get the best out of them. All the girls longed to be like you. You represented a kind of freedom, an independence. To me, you represented the triumph of the intellect over the mediocrity of the world. A bit like a female version of Jean-Christophe Graff and—"

At the mention of my old teacher, Alexis gave a bitter laugh.

"Ah, poor old Graff! Another idiot, though admittedly a cultured idiot. He was another one who never guessed the truth. He wooed me for years, wrote me poems and passionate love letters. He idealized me just as you idealized Vinca. It's typical of men like you. You claim to love women, but you don't understand us and don't want to understand us. You don't listen to us and you refuse to hear us. As far as you're concerned, we're just extras in your romantic reveries."

She quoted Stendhal: "'From the moment you begin to be really interested in a woman, you no longer see her *as she really is,* but as it suits you to see her.'"

I was not about to let her get away with this pseudointellectual justification. In loving Vinca, Alexis DeVille had destroyed her, and I needed her to admit that.

"On the contrary, I knew Vinca as she really was. Or at least, I did before she met you. And I don't remember a girl who got drunk and popped pills. She was easy prey for you, a wild, uninhibited young girl just discovering life."

"So I perverted her, is that it?"

"No, I think you got her into booze and drugs because it clouded her judgment, made her more vulnerable."

Teeth bared, the dogs were now brushing up against me, sniffing my hands. The Doberman pressed its snout against my thigh, forcing me back against the sofa.

"I pushed her into your father's arms because it was the only way for us to have a baby."

"The truth is that you're the only one who wanted a baby."

"No, that's not true. Vinca wanted it too."

"With my father? I seriously doubt it."

"You have no right to judge us." Alexis DeVille flew into a rage. "These days, if two women want to have a child, it's accepted, even respected. People's attitudes have changed, the laws have changed. Science has moved on. But back in the 1990s, the very idea was rejected, dismissed."

"You had money; you could have gone about it a different way."

"I didn't have a red cent!" Alexis protested. "People aren't always as open-minded as they seem. The DeVilles might have been from California, but their broad-mindedness was all show. My family are hypocrites, cowards, and bullies. They disapproved of my 'lifestyle,' my sexual orientation. For years, they cut me off. In targeting your father, we were killing two birds with one stone—we could have a child *and* the money we needed."

The conversation was futile. Neither of us was prepared to give ground. Perhaps because it was pointless to try and assign blame; perhaps because both of us were simultaneously guilty and innocent, victim and executioner; perhaps because the only thing that could be said for certain was that in 1992 there had been a bewitching girl at the Lycée Saint-Exupéry who drove those she allowed into her

life insane. Because when you were with Vinca, you had the preposterous illusion that her very existence was the answer to a question
that we all ask ourselves: How can I make it through the night?

3.

The tension in the air was electric. The three dogs now had me
backed against the wall. I could feel the palpable danger—my heart
hammering in my chest, my shirt sticking to my skin—this inexo-
rable procession toward death. Alexis DeVille had the power to end
my life with a wave or a word. Now that I had finally come to the
end of my investigation, I realized that there were only two choices:
kill or be killed. Despite my fear, I kept talking.

"You could have adopted a child. You could have had one yourself."

Utterly in the grip of her dangerous delusion, Alexis DeVille
stepped closer and jabbed her finger at my face.

"No! Don't you understand, I wanted *Vinca's* baby. A baby with
her genes, her perfection, her grace, her beauty. A perpetuation of
our love."

"I know you supplied her with Rohypnol, thanks to the sketchy
prescriptions you got from Dr. Rubens. It's a pretty twisted kind
of love that can only blossom when you turn your lover into a
junkie."

"You disgusting little..."

Alexis DeVille was at a loss for words. She was finding it increasingly difficult to control the dogs. I felt my chest tighten, felt a
stabbing pain in my heart. I was on the brink of passing out. I tried
to ignore the panic and drove home the final nail.

"You know the last thing that Vinca said to me before she died?
She said, 'Alexis forced me. I didn't want to sleep with him!' For
twenty-five years, I completely misunderstood what she meant, and
it cost a man his life. But I know now. She meant: 'Alexis DeVille
forced me to sleep with your father, but I didn't want to.'"

My breathing was ragged. My whole body was shaking. I felt as though the only way out of this nightmare was to split myself in two.

"You see, Vinca died knowing what a vile human being you are. So you can build a thousand Gardens of Angels, but you'll never be able to rewrite history."

Overcome by rage, Alexis DeVille signaled to her dogs.

The pit bull was the first to attack. The sheer power of the dog knocked me off balance. As I fell, I hit my head on the wall and then on the sharp edge of a metal chair. I felt it sink its teeth into my throat, looking for the carotid artery. I tried in vain to push it off.

Three shots rang out. The first took out the dog about to rip out my throat and sent the other two scurrying away. The other two shots were fired while I was still sprawled on the ground. I came to my senses just in time to see the body of Alexis DeVille thrown back toward the stone fireplace in a spray of blood. I turned to the sliding door and saw my father framed against the sunlight.

"Everything's going to be fine, Thomas," he said in the same reassuring voice he had used when I was six years old and had nightmares. His hand, steady as a rock, gripped the rosewood handle of Francis Biancardini's Smith and Wesson.

My father helped me to my feet, keeping an eye out in case the hellhounds came back. For a moment, when he laid a hand on my shoulder, I was once again that six-year-old boy. And I thought about that endangered species, the dying generation of men like Francis and my father. Gruff, rugged men whose values belonged to a different age. Men I had been fortunate enough to encounter not once, but twice. Men who, in order to save my life, had not hesitated to get their hands dirty.

By plunging them into a bloodbath.

EPILOGUE(S)
BEYOND THE NIGHT

THE CURSE
OF THE NICE GUYS

The days that followed Alexis DeVille's death and my father's arrest were among the strangest of my life. Every morning, I woke up convinced that the ongoing police investigation would lead to the case of Vinca's and Clément's disappearances being reopened. But from his prison cell, my father skillfully managed to mitigate the danger.

He confessed that he had been having an affair with Alexis DeVille for months, that his wife had found out about the affair and gone to see his mistress armed with a rifle, that Alexis, feeling her life was threatened, had killed my mother, and that he, in turn, had killed her. It was a plausible scenario. It gave each of the central characters a clear and credible motive. Its chief advantage was in portraying the murders as crimes of passion. My father's lawyer was positively ecstatic at the prospect of a trial. The brutality of my mother's murder, Alexis DeVille's history of mental illness, to say nothing of her setting her vicious dogs on me, made my father's actions look like justifiable homicide, and while they would not lead to an acquittal, they made a lenient sentence more likely. Most of all, framing the murders as crimes of passion meant that there was no connection to the disappearances of Vinca and Clément.

But it all seemed too good to be true.

★ ★ ★

For a few weeks, I thought that fortune might continue to smile on us. Maxime had woken up from his coma and his condition quickly improved. In June, he was elected to Parliament, and his name was often mentioned in the press as a potential minister. The investigation into the attack on Maxime meant that the area surrounding the gym was a crime scene, so the demolition could not proceed according to schedule. Then at a board meeting of the Hutchinson and DeVille Foundation, it was decided, given the circumstances, to withdraw the proposed endowment to the Lycée Saint-Exupéry, and the project was shelved indefinitely. The school governors instantly put forward a rationale entirely at odds with their previous stance. Citing environmental and cultural reasons, the governors of Saint-Ex insisted that to build on a site of such natural beauty would threaten the very soul of the landscape they cherished.

★ ★ ★

Fanny called me when the news broke that my father had been arrested. We met up at the hospital and spent hours by the bedside of the still-unconscious Maxime, teasing out the truth of what had happened that night in 1992. The revelation that she had not been responsible for Vinca's death made it possible for Fanny to finally get on with her life. Not long afterward, she split up with Thierry Sénéca and got in touch with a fertility clinic in Barcelona to discuss

IVF. After Maxime regained consciousness, Fanny and I often met in his room at the hospital.

For a time, I truly believed that the three of us might escape the tragic fate to which the bodies walled up in the gym should have condemned us. For a time, I truly believed we had managed to overcome the curse of the nice guys.

But I had not reckoned on betrayal by the man I had mistakenly trusted: Stéphane Pianelli.

★ ★ ★

"You're not going to be happy about this, but I'm writing a book telling the truth about the death of Vinca Rockwell," Pianelli calmly announced one evening in late June as we were sitting at the bar in a pub in Antibes, where he'd invited me for a drink.

"What truth?"

"The only truth," Pianelli said coolly. "People have a right to know what happened to Vinca Rockwell and Alexis Clément. Parents of students at Saint-Ex have the right to know they're sending their kids to a school where two corpses have been walled up for twenty-five years."

"You realize that if you do that, you're as good as throwing me, Fanny, and Maxime in jail?"

"*Veritas omnia vincit!*" he declared, slapping the bar. "Truth conquers all!"

To muddy the waters, he launched into a long tirade about a cashier who'd lost her job because her till was a few bucks short and how this compared to the leniency of the judicial system when dealing with politicians or employers. He then segued into his predictable speech—the one he had been giving since high school—about class struggle and capitalism, *a system of slavery in the service of shareholders.*

"For God's sake, Stéphane, what the hell has all that got to do with us?"

He stared at me with a mixture of gravity and glee, as though, from the very first, he had been hoping to find himself in this position. And, for the first time, I realized the extent of Pianelli's visceral hatred for everything that we represented.

"You killed two people. You have to pay."

I sipped my beer and tried to seem offhand.

"I don't believe you. You'll never write that book."

He took an envelope from his pocket and handed it to me. Inside was a contract with a publisher in Paris for a nonfiction book titled *A Curious Affair: The Truth About the Vinca Rockwell Case*.

"You haven't got a shred of evidence for any of this, you idiot. All you're going to do is destroy your credibility as a journalist."

"The proof is the gym." Pianelli sniggered. "When the book is published, I'll rally the students' parents. There'll be so much pressure that the school will have no choice but to knock down the wall."

I knew the publishers who had offered him the contract. They weren't particularly prestigious or particularly rigorous, but they would make sure that the book got a lot of publicity. If Pianelli ever did publish this book, it would have dramatic repercussions.

"I don't understand why you'd betray us, Stéphane. For fifteen minutes of fame? That doesn't sound like you."

"I'm just doing my job."

"And your job is to betray your friends?"

"My job is being a journalist, and we were never friends."

I was reminded of the fable of the scorpion and the frog. "Why did you sting me?" the frog asks the scorpion that he is carrying across the river. "Now we're both going to die." And the scorpion says, "It's my nature."

As Pianelli ordered another beer, he twisted the knife in the wound.

"It's a fascinating story, like a modern version of the Borgias. How much do you want to bet that Netflix will make a series out of this?"

Watching him gloat over the ruin of my family, I wanted to kill him.

"I can see why Céline dumped you," I said. "You're a nasty little piece of shit."

Pianelli tried to throw his beer in my face, but I stepped smartly out of the way and lashed out with an uppercut to his chin and a punch in the belly that brought him to his knees.

As I left the bar, my enemy was down for the count, but I was the one who had lost. And this time, there was no one to protect me.

JEAN-CHRISTOPHE

Antibes, September 18, 2002

My dear Thomas,

After too long a silence, I am writing to you to say goodbye. Indeed, by the time this letter has crossed the Atlantic, I will have finished my earthly existence.

Before I die, I wanted to write to you one last time. I wanted to tell you again what a pleasure it was to teach you and that I have only fond memories of our long conversations and of the time we spent together. You were the most gifted student it has been my privilege to teach, Thomas. Not the most intelligent, nor the one who got the highest marks, but the most generous, the most sensitive, the most human, the most considerate in your dealings with others.

Please do not grieve for me. I have chosen my way out because I no longer have the strength to keep going. Rest assured that it is not for lack of courage but because life has visited upon me something that I cannot endure, and death now seems the only honorable way out of the hell into which I have foundered. Even books, my faithful companions, can no longer keep my head above water.

My tragedy is utterly banal, but that does not make it any less painful. For many years, I secretly loved a woman, never daring to confess my feelings lest she reject me. For a long time, the very air I breathed came from watching her live, smile, talk. Ours was a meeting of minds unlike any I have known, and the thought that my feelings might be reciprocated kept me strong in my darkest hours.

I confess that I have often reflected on your theory of the curse of the nice guys, and, naively, I hoped to disprove it, but life has not returned the favor.

Sadly, in recent weeks, it has become clear to me that my love will never be reciprocated and that the woman I love is perhaps not the person I thought she was. And I know I am not capable of changing the course of fate.

Take care, my dear Thomas, and above all, do not grieve for me. I can offer you no advice but this: Choose your battles well. Not all are worthy of being waged. Know that there are times when you should cling to your friends. Throw yourself heart and soul into this life, because solitude is fatal.

I wish you every happiness in the future. I do not doubt for a second that you will succeed where I have failed and find a soul mate with whom to confront life's sea of troubles.

Be demanding. Be different from other boys. And guard yourself against fools. In the tradition of the Stoics, remember: the best revenge is not to be like he who wronged you.

And although my fate might seem to attest to the contrary, I still believe that our weaknesses are our greatest strengths.

With much affection.
Yours,
Jean-Christophe Graff

THE MATERNITY WARD

Jeanne-d'Arc Clinic, Antibes, October 9, 1974

Francis Biancardini gently pushed open the door of the hospital room. The orange rays of the autumn sun streamed through the French doors that led to the balcony. In the late afternoon, the quiet of the maternity ward was broken only by the distant clamor of schoolchildren heading home.

Francis stepped into the room, his arms laden with presents: a teddy bear for his son Thomas, a bracelet for Annabelle, two packages of biscotti and a jar of Amarena cherries for the nurses who had taken such good care of them. He set the gifts down on the bedside table as quietly as possible so as not to wake Annabelle.

When he leaned over the crib, the newborn stared up at him with his new eyes.

"How are you, my little man?"

He took the baby in his arms and settled himself in a chair to enjoy the solemn yet magical moment that follows the birth of a child.

He felt a profound joy mingled with regret and helplessness. When Annabelle left the clinic, she would not be coming home with him. She would be going back to her husband, Richard, and he would be Thomas's legal father. It was a painful situation, but she was also a woman who defied all norms. A passionate lover who had a very personal concept of commitment but who valued love above all.

She had finally persuaded Francis not to say anything about their relationship. "It is precisely the secrecy of our love that makes it special," she said. "Flaunting your love to the world makes it vulgar. It loses something of its mystery." Francis saw another advantage to keeping their relationship secret: It would shelter those dearest to him from his enemies. To tell the world what truly matters to you is to make yourself vulnerable.

★ ★ ★

Francis sighed. The loutish character he was forced to play was simply a façade. But, other than Annabelle, no one truly knew him. They did not know the violence and the death wish he carried within him. The rage that had first erupted in 1959, when he was fifteen, in the little village of Montaldicio. It had happened on a summer evening by the fountain on the village square. Some young guys had been drinking heavily. One of them was propositioning Annabelle. She had pushed him away several times, but still he tried to paw at her. Francis had been staying on the sidelines. The boys were much older than he was. They were painters and glaziers from Turin who had come to refurbish the hothouses of someone in the village. When he realized that no one else was going to intercede, he had walked over to them and told the guy to clear off. At fifteen, Francis was not very tall, and he often gave the impression that he was somewhat clumsy. When they had laughed at him, Francis grabbed the boy by the throat and punched him in the face. Despite his build, he had the strength of an ox and was fueled by rage. After the first punch, he had continued battering the young laborer and no one had been able to pull him off.

A speech impediment he had had since he was a child meant that he had never dared talk to Annabelle. The words caught in his throat. So that night, he talked with his fists. By smashing the young man's face in, he was sending a message to Annabelle: *No one will ever hurt you while I'm around.*

By the time he finally stopped, the young man was unconscious, his face covered with blood, his mouth full of broken teeth.

The case caused a commotion in the area. Some days later, the carabinieri came to question Francis, but he had already left Italy for France.

When he met up with Annabelle again many years later, she thanked him for defending her but confessed that she was afraid of him. Nonetheless, they became close, and through her, Francis learned to control his violent temper.

As he cradled his son, Francis realized that the baby had fallen asleep. Gingerly, he kissed Thomas on the forehead, and the sweet, intoxicating smell of the baby was heart-wrenching, reminding him of milk bread and orange blossom. Thomas seemed so tiny in his arms and the serenity that radiated from the child's perfect face was filled with promise. And yet this tiny marvel seemed so delicate and utterly defenseless.

Francis became aware that he was crying. Not because he was sad, but because the thought of such fragility terrified him. He wiped a tear from his cheek and, with all the tenderness he could muster, laid Thomas back in the crib without waking him.

★ ★ ★

He opened the sliding door and stepped out onto the little balcony. He took a pack of Gauloises from his jacket pocket, lit one, and, on a whim, decided that this would be his last cigarette. Now that he had parental responsibilities, he needed to take care of himself. How long do children need their fathers? Fifteen years? Twenty? Their whole lives? As he inhaled the acrid smoke, he closed his eyes to soak up the last rays of sun that filtered through the branches of the linden tree.

Raising a child, protecting him, was a long-term struggle, one that would require constant vigilance. Terrible things could happen without warning. He could never allow his attention to falter. But Francis would not shirk his duty. He was thick-skinned.

Hearing the French door open, Francis was roused from his thoughts. He turned and saw Annabelle, smiling. As she melted in his arms, he felt all his fears fade. Enveloped by the warm breeze, Francis knew that for as long as Annabelle was by his side, he could face anything. Brute force is nothing without intelligence. Together, they would always be one step ahead of danger.

ONE STEP AHEAD OF DANGER

Despite the threat of Pianelli's book hanging over us, Maxime, Fanny, and I went on with our lives as though it didn't exist. We were resolved to no longer live in fear. We felt no need to explain or justify ourselves. We made one pledge: whatever happened from here on out, we would face it together.

Something in me had changed. I had a new confidence. The fear that had been gnawing away at me gradually disappeared. The new roots that I had discovered made a new man of me. Of course, I had my regrets—the fact that I had made peace with my mother only after her death; the fact that only now that Richard was in prison did I finally feel close to him; the fact that I had never been able to talk to Francis while knowing that he was my real father.

The fates of my three parents gave me pause, though.

Their lives had been extraordinary, marked by pain, passions, and contradictions. If sometimes they had lacked courage, they had also shown a selflessness that commanded respect. They had lived, they had loved, they had killed. At times, they had been carried away by their passions, but they had tried their best. Tried their best not to have humdrum lives, to reconcile their personal adventures with a sense of responsibility, to define the word *family* according to a grammar that was theirs alone.

Having come from such parents compelled me, not to imitate them, but to honor their heritage by learning certain lessons.

It is futile to deny the complexity of human emotions. Our lives are sometimes inscrutable, often disrupted by conflicting desires. Our lives are fragile, at once precious and insignificant, sometimes bathed in icy waters of loneliness, sometimes in the warm stream of a fountain of youth. Our lives, for the most part, are beyond our control. The slightest thing can turn them upside down. A whispered word, the twinkling of an eye, or a lingering smile can raise us up or cast us into oblivion. And yet, in spite of this uncertainty, we have no choice but to pretend we can control the chaos in the hope that the inclinations of our hearts will find a place in the secret plans of Providence.

★ ★ ★

On the evening of July 14, to celebrate Maxime's being discharged from the hospital, we all gathered at my parents' house: Olivier, Maxime, their two daughters, Fanny, even Pauline Delatour, who, now that I had made peace with her, proved to be smart and funny. I had barbecued steaks and some hot dogs for the children. We opened a bottle of Nuits-Saint-Georges and settled ourselves on the terrace to watch the Bastille Day fireworks over the bay of Antibes. The fireworks had just started when I heard the phone in the entryway buzz.

I left my guests, turned on the outdoor lights, and went down the driveway to the gates. On the other side stood Stéphane Pianelli. He was not looking his best; his hair was long, his beard unkempt, his eyes bloodshot.

"What do you want, Stéphane?"

"Hi, Thomas."

His breath stank of booze.

"Aren't you going to let me in?" he said, gripping the wrought-iron railings.

"Fuck off, Stéphane."

"I've got good news for you, Mr. Potboiler. I'm not going to publish my book."

From his pocket, he took a folded piece of paper and slipped it between the bars.

"Your mother and Francis were really two beautiful bastards!"

I unfolded it as pinwheels and rockets exploded in the sky. It was a photocopy of an old article from *Nice-Matin* dated December 28, 1997. Five years after the tragedy.

VANDALS CAUSE SIGNIFICANT DAMAGE AT THE LYCÉE SAINT-EXUPERY
by Claude Angevin

Sophia Antipolis technology park was targeted by vandals on Christmas Eve. Much of the more serious damage took place in the gym of the lycée.

The extent of the damage was discovered on the morning of December 25 by the dean of preparatory classes, Mme. Annabelle Degalais. Obscene graffiti had been sprayed on the walls of the gym. The culprit or culprits also shattered a number of windows, set off fire extinguishers, and broke into several lockers.

The dean—who reported the incident to the police—feels that there is no question that those responsible were not students at the school.

The police have carried out the usual searches and, pending further investigation, the school authorities have already begun an intensive cleanup and such construction work as will be necessary so that the gym is fit for use when classes resume on January 5.

Two photographs accompanied the article. The first showed the extent of the damage to the gym: the graffitied wall, fire extinguishers lying on the ground, broken windows.

"No one's going to find the bodies of Vinca and Clément now, are they?" Pianelli raged. "It's obvious, isn't it? Francis and your mother were too shrewd, too Machiavellian, to leave any evidence. Well, let me tell you something, Mr. Potboiler, you and your friends can thank your parents for digging you out of a whole heap of shit."

The second photograph showed my mother standing with her arms folded, wearing a smart pantsuit, her hair in a neat chignon, her expression deadpan. Behind her loomed the hulking figure of Francis Biancardini in his trusty leather jacket. He was posed with a trowel in one hand and a pen in the other.

What had happened was obvious. In 1997, five years after the murders and a few months before my mother resigned her post, she and her lover decided to move the bodies that had been buried in the wall of the gym. They were not prepared to live with such a potential threat hanging over their heads. They had faked the vandalism in order to give Francis free rein during the cleanup. The repair work had been carried out during the Christmas vacation, the one time of year when the lycée was almost deserted, making it easy for Francis—this time without Ahmed's help—to move the bodies so that they would never be found.

We had spent years terrified that the bodies might be discovered when, in fact, they had not been in the gym for more than two decades.

A little stunned, I looked again at the photograph of Francis. His

eyes seemed to be staring right through the photographer and anyone else who might one day stand in his way. A steely, swaggering
expression that seemed to say, *I'm not afraid of anyone, because I will be
one step ahead of danger.*

Pianelli left without further ado and I slowly wandered back to
join my friends. It took a long time for me to accept that we no
longer had anything to fear. When I reached the top of the driveway,
I glanced at the article again. Looking closely at my mother in the
photograph, I saw that she was holding a key ring. Probably the keys
to the fucking gym. The keys to the past, but also those that opened
the door to the future.

THE NOVELIST'S PRIVILEGE

In front of me is a Bic Cristal pen that cost thirty centimes and a ruled Seyes notebook. The only weapons I have ever owned.

I am sitting in the school library, in the same place where I always sat back then, a small alcove with a view of the courtyard and the ivy-covered fountain. The reading room is suffused with the smell of wax and melted candles. Old Lagarde et Michard grammar manuals are gathering dust on the shelves.

After Zélie retired, the school administration asked me if they could name the building where the drama club met in my honor. I declined and instead proposed that they name it after Jean-Christophe Graff, but I agreed to give a short inaugural speech to the students.

I take off the pen cap and I start to make notes. This is what I have done all my life. Write. It is a twofold, contradictory gesture: building walls and opening doors. Walls to hold back the devastating cruelty of the real world, doors to escape into a parallel world—into reality not as it is, but as it should be.

It does not always work, but sometimes, for a few hours, fiction is genuinely more powerful than life. This, perhaps, is the privilege of artists in general and novelists in particular—occasionally being able to win their battles against the real.

I write, I cross out, I rewrite. The ink-blackened pages accumulate. Gradually a story takes shape. An alternative story to explain what really happened on that night in December 1992.

Imagine...the snow, the cold, the darkness. Imagine that moment when Francis came back to Vinca's room, planning to wall her corpse into the gym. He went over to the body lying on the warm bed, picked her up, and, with the strength of an ox, carried her the way a knight carries a princess. But not to take her to a magical castle. He carried her to the dark, frozen building site that smelled of concrete and oozing damp. He was alone, accompanied only by his demons and his ghosts. He had already sent Ahmed home. He laid Vinca's body on a tarpaulin on the ground in the blaze of floodlights. He was mesmerized by the body of the girl and found it hard to believe that he was about to pour concrete over her. Some hours earlier, he had disposed of the body of Alexis Clément without asking any questions. But this was different. This was too hard. He gazed at her for a long time, then crept closer to drape her with a blanket, as though she might still catch cold. And, for a moment, as the tears rolled down his cheeks, he imagined that she was still alive. The illusion was so powerful, he could almost see her chest rise and fall.

Until he realized that Vinca *really was breathing*.

How was that possible? Annabelle had hit her on the head with a cast-iron statue. The girl had a bellyful of booze and pills. Obviously, tranquilizers slow the heart rate, but he had checked earlier and had felt no pulse. He put his ear to girl's chest and heard her heart pounding. And it was the most beautiful music he had ever heard.

Francis did not hesitate. He was not about to pick up his shovel and finish the job. He simply could not do that. He carried Vinca to his truck and laid her on the back seat. Then he drove toward Mercantour National Park, where he owned a hunting lodge, a small cottage where he sometimes spent the night when hunting chamois goats near Entraunes. Usually it was a two-hour drive, but traffic conditions then meant that it took him twice as long. By the time he reached the border of the Département Alpes-de-Haute-Provence, dawn was breaking. He laid Vinca on a sofa in the hunting lodge, lit a fire in the hearth, brought in firewood, and boiled some water.

He had been thinking long and hard while he drove, and he had come to a decision. If the girl woke up, he would help her disappear so she could start over. Another country, another identity, another life. Like a witness-protection program. Except that he was not about to ask the police for help. He would ask the Calabrian Mafia. They had been sniffing around him for some time, asking him to launder money. He would ask them to smuggle Vinca out of the country. By doing so, he knew he would be making a deal with the devil, but he liked the notion that life never metes out more than you can bear. *Good leads to evil and evil leads to good.* The story of his life.

Francis made himself a large pot of coffee, sat in an armchair, and waited. And Vinca woke up.

Then the days, the months, the years passed. Somewhere, a young woman who had left behind a blackened land was coming back into existence, as though reborn.

★ ★ ★

This meant that somewhere, Vinca was alive.

★ ★ ★

That is my version of the story. It is based on all the evidence, all the clues that I found during my investigation—the suspected

ties between Francis and the Calabrian Mafia, the money transferred to New York accounts, my accidental sighting of Vinca in
Manhattan.

I like to think that this story is true, even if the chances that it
happened this way are one in a thousand. Given the current state of
the investigation, no one could completely refute my version. It is
my contribution as a novelist to the Vinca Rockwell case.

I finished writing my speech, packed up my things, and left the
library. Outside, whipped up by the mistral, yellow leaves fluttered
in the autumn sun. I felt good. Life does not scare me as much now.
You can attack me, judge me, destroy me, but I will always have an
old chewed Bic and a crumpled notebook within reach. My only
weapons. As preposterous as they are powerful.

The only ones I have always been able to count on to get me
through the night.

CLASS OF
-1992-

25TH REUNION

Celebrate the good old days

MAY
13
SATURDAY

AUTHOR'S NOTE

For several years now, I have wanted to write a story set on the Côte d'Azur, where I spent my childhood, and in particular around the city of Antibes, of which I have so many memories.

But wanting to do something is not enough. Writing a novel is a fragile, complex, and uncertain process. When I began to write about the school campus buried beneath a mantle of snow, about adults paralyzed by the young people they had once been, I knew that the time had come. This is how *The Reunion* came to be set in the south of France. It was an enormous pleasure for me to describe these places as they were and as they are now.

Nevertheless, this is not a true story. The narrator is not the writer— the events that befall Thomas are his alone. Although the chemin de la Suquette, *Nice-Matin,* the Café Les Arcades, and La Fontonne Hospital exist, they are here transfigured by fiction. The school that Thomas attends, his teachers, his classmates, and his friends are inventions or very different from my own childhood memories. Last, I would like to make it clear that I have never yet walled up a body in a gym.

ABOUT THE AUTHOR

Emanuele Scorcelletti

Guillaume Musso is the number one bestselling author in France. He has written seventeen novels, including the thrillers *Afterwards...*, which was made into a feature film starring John Malkovich and Evangeline Lilly, and *Central Park*. He lives in Paris.